LAUGH
-O-
METER
UNCONTROLLABLE GUFFAW!!
ROFL-COPTER!
HA-HA!
LOL
ERM...

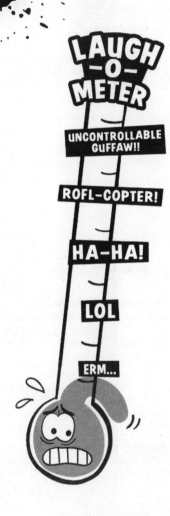

First published in Great Britain 2022 by Farshore
An imprint of HarperCollins*Publishers*
1 London Bridge Street, London, SE1 9GF
www.farshore.co.uk

HarperCollins*Publishers*
1st Floor, Watermarque Building, Ringsend Road
Dublin 4, Ireland

Written by Thomas McBrien

BEANO

BEANO.COM

A Beano Studios Product © DC Thomson Ltd (2022)

ISBN 978 0 0085 2999 4
Printed in Great Britain
001

All rights reserved. No part of this publication may be reproduced,
stored in a retrieval system, or transmitted, in any form or by any
means, electronic, mechanical, photocopying, recording or otherwise,
without the prior permission of the publisher and copyright owner.

Stay safe online. Any website addresses listed in this book are
correct at the time of going to print. However, Farshore is not
responsible for content hosted by third parties. Please be aware that
online content can be subject to change and websites can contain
content that is unsuitable for children. We advise that all children
are supervised when using the internet.

Experiments and activities are performed at your own risk,
follow the instructions and ALWAYS ask an adult for help.
HarperCollins is not responsible for the results of your experiments.

MIX
Paper from
responsible sources
FSC™ C007454

This book is produced from independently certified FSC™ paper
to ensure responsible forest management.

For more information visit: www.harpercollins.co.uk/green

BEANO®

JOKE BOOK

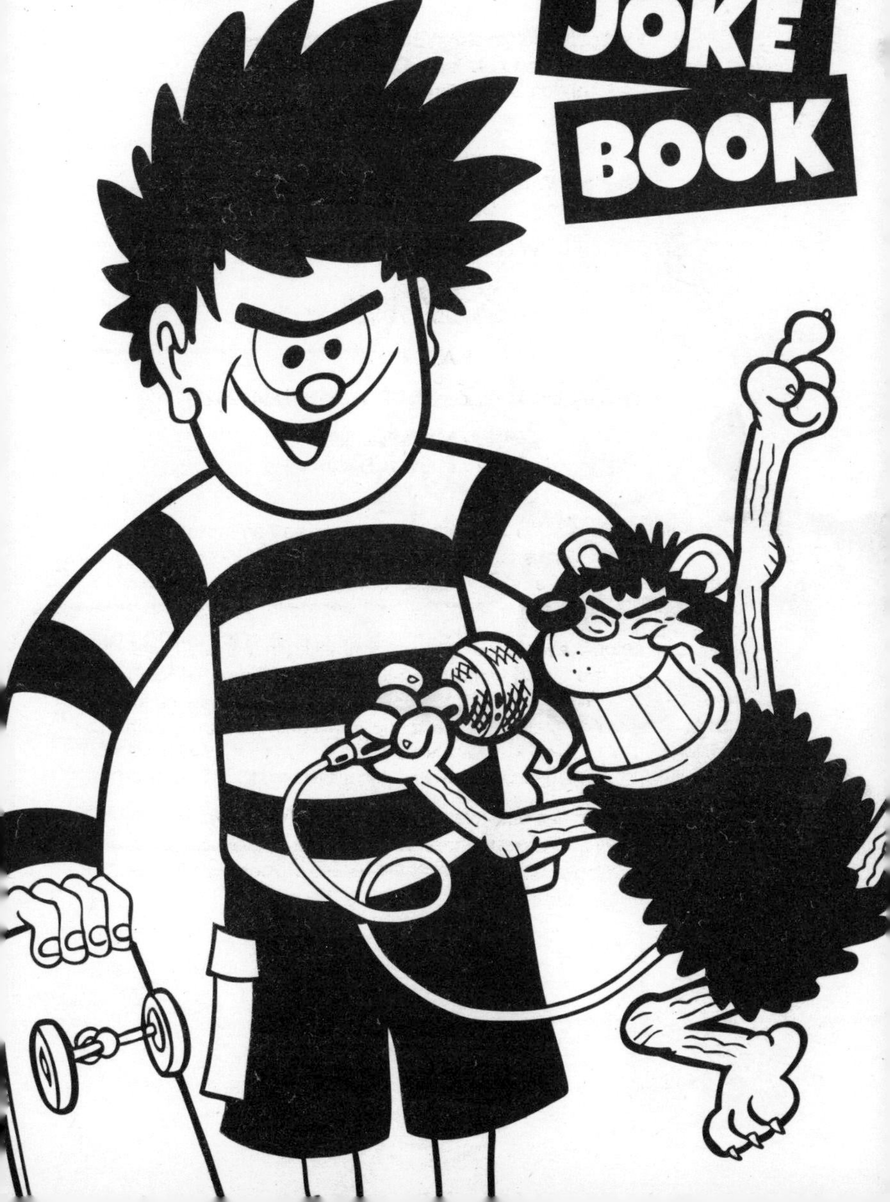

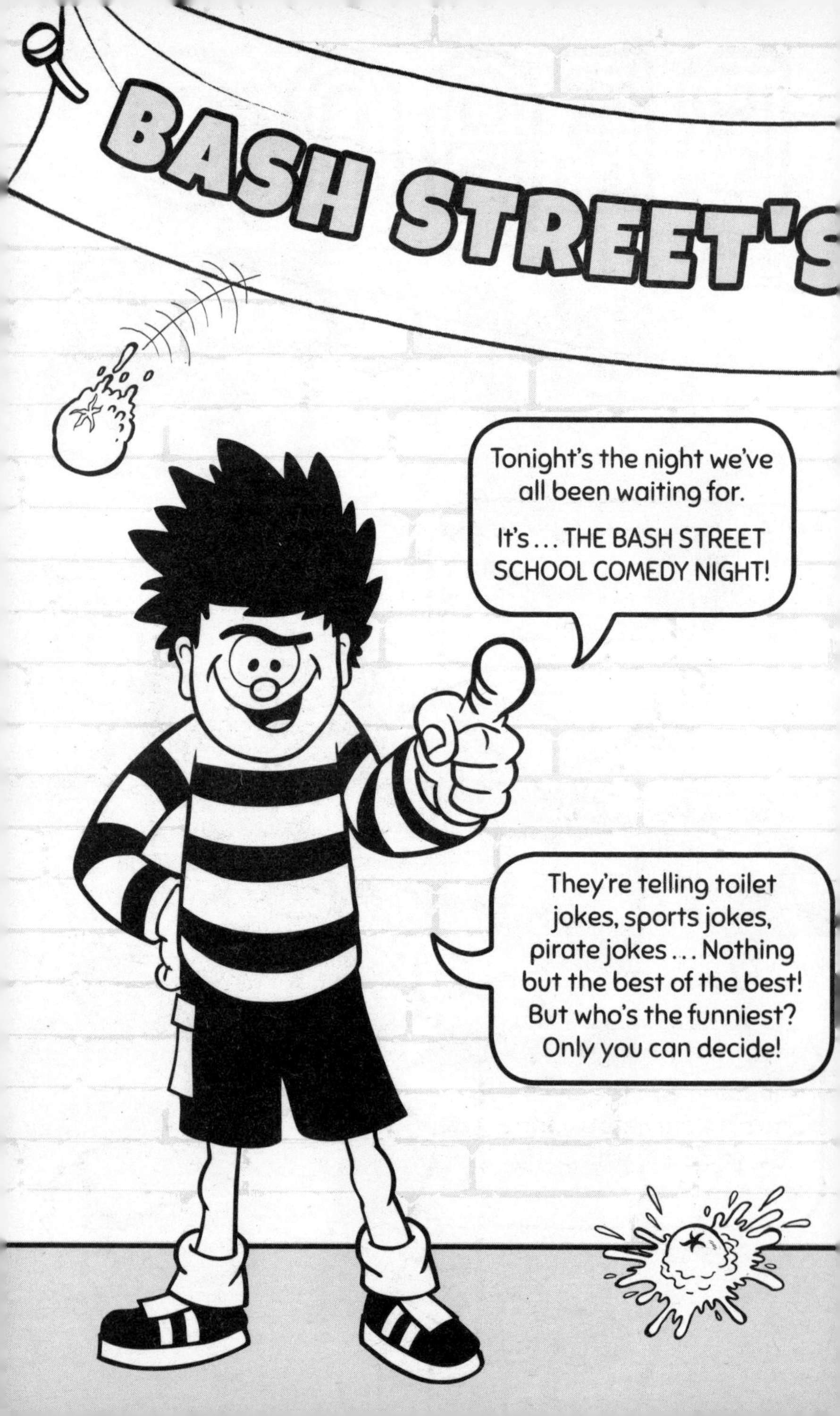
BASH STREET'S
Tonight's the night we've all been waiting for.
It's . . . THE BASH STREET SCHOOL COMEDY NIGHT!
They're telling toilet jokes, sports jokes, pirate jokes . . . Nothing but the best of the best! But who's the funniest? Only you can decide!

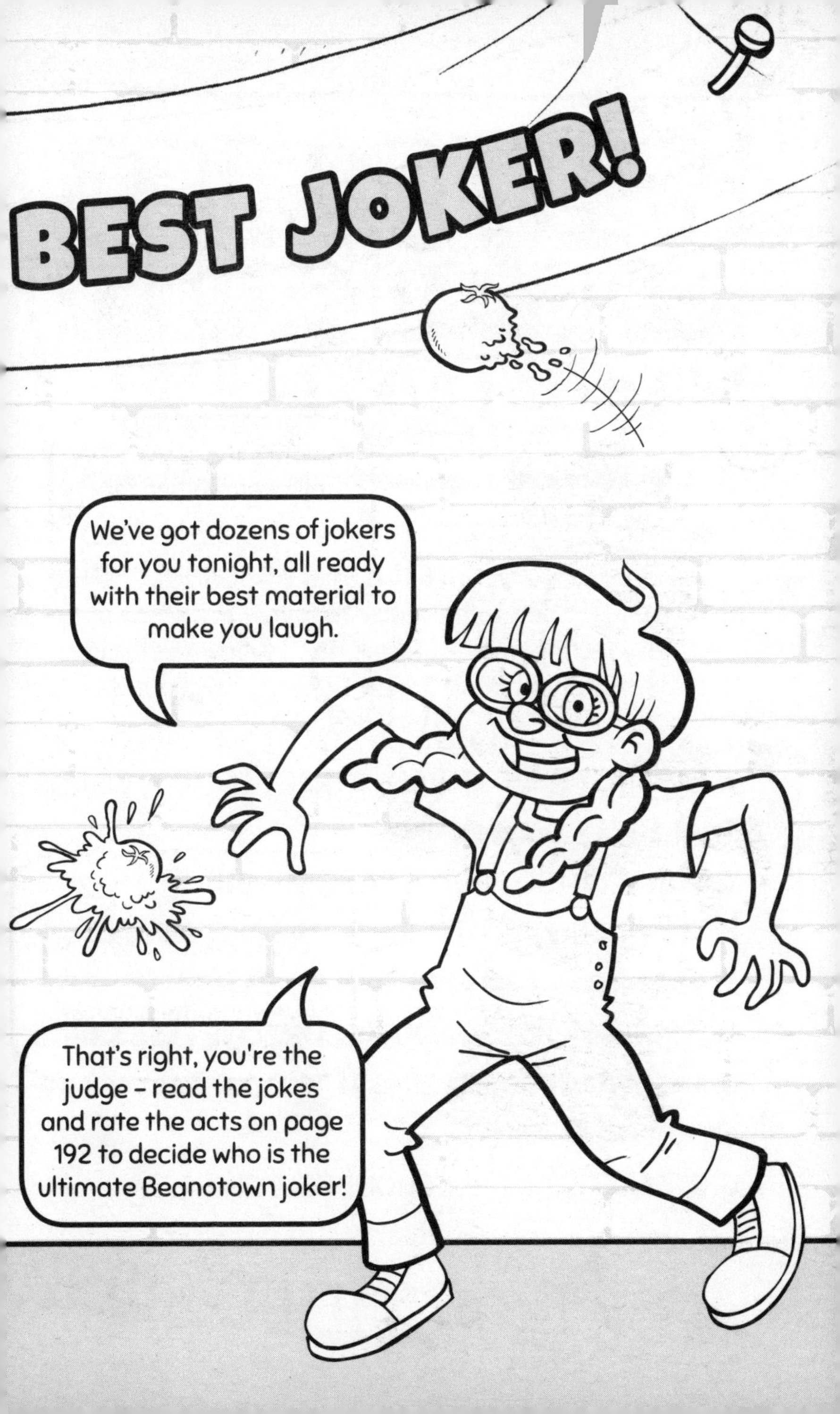
BEST JOKER!
We've got dozens of jokers for you tonight, all ready with their best material to make you laugh.
That's right, you're the judge – read the jokes and rate the acts on page 192 to decide who is the ultimate Beanotown joker!

THE RULES
OF BASH STREET
COMEDY CLUB

To create your very own BASH STREET SCHOOL COMEDY CLUB, you just need to be ready to follow the same simple rules that Dennis, Minnie, Rubi and JJ follow every day in Beanotown's Bash Street School playground:

1. THE FIRST RULE OF BASH STREET COMEDY CLUB IS THAT **EVERYONE IS FUNNY**.

2. STAND UP (SO PEOPLE CAN SEE YOU).

3. TELL A JOKE OR A FUNNY STORY (BUT **NEVER TEASE OR BE MEAN** ABOUT ANYONE ELSE).

4. (FINGERS CROSSED) MAKE SOMEONE ELSE **LAUGH**.

5. ENCOURAGE SOMEONE ELSE TO DO THE SAME AND ENJOY THEIR JOKE TOO.

6. REPEAT UNTIL THE SCHOOL BELL RINGS.

SIMPLE, HUH?

To join, you and your friends should take a simple test to check out your natural comedy skills.

THE 'YOU'VE GOTTA BE JOKING' TEST!

- [ ] DO YOU ENJOY LAUGHING AND HEARING JOKES?
- [ ] DO PEOPLE EVER LAUGH AT YOUR OWN JOKES?
- [ ] DO YOU NOTICE THE UNUSUAL THINGS IN LIFE?
- [ ] DO YOU LAUGH AT YOUR OWN BAD LUCK?
- [ ] DO YOU – SECRETLY – THINK YOU'RE THE FUNNIEST PERSON ALIVE?
- [ ] DO YOU SOMETIMES FIND SERIOUS SITUATIONS WEIRDLY FUNNY?
- [ ] DO YOU LIKE THE FEELING OF TELLING A JOKE?

If you ticked any of these, you've passed the test! **RESULT!** You likely have the natural ability to do comedy.

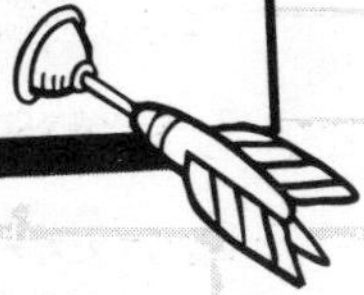

Laughter makes us feel less stressed and increases trust. Funny people are even smarter than average too! Everyone would feel better for laughing for a minimum of 15 minutes every single day, which makes school break time the perfect time for comedy.

Why not try stand-up comedy to make YOUR playground a better, funnier place?

JOKERS, GET READY!

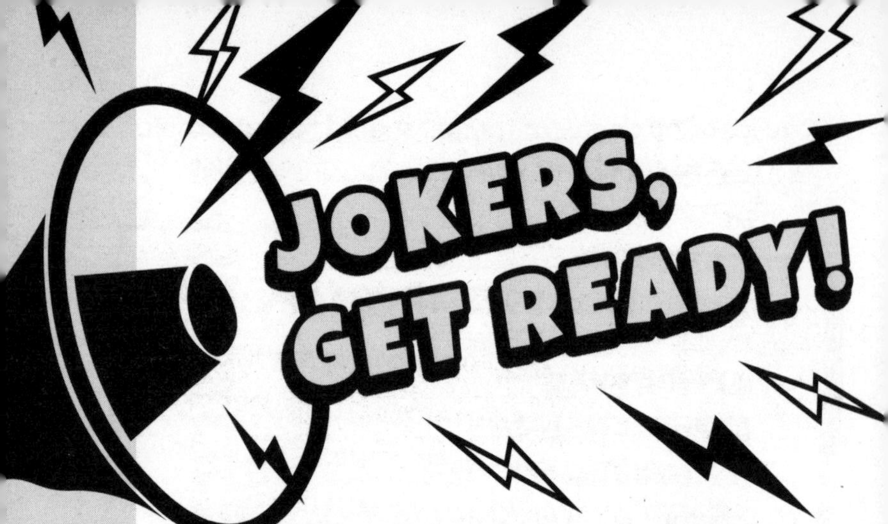

PAGE

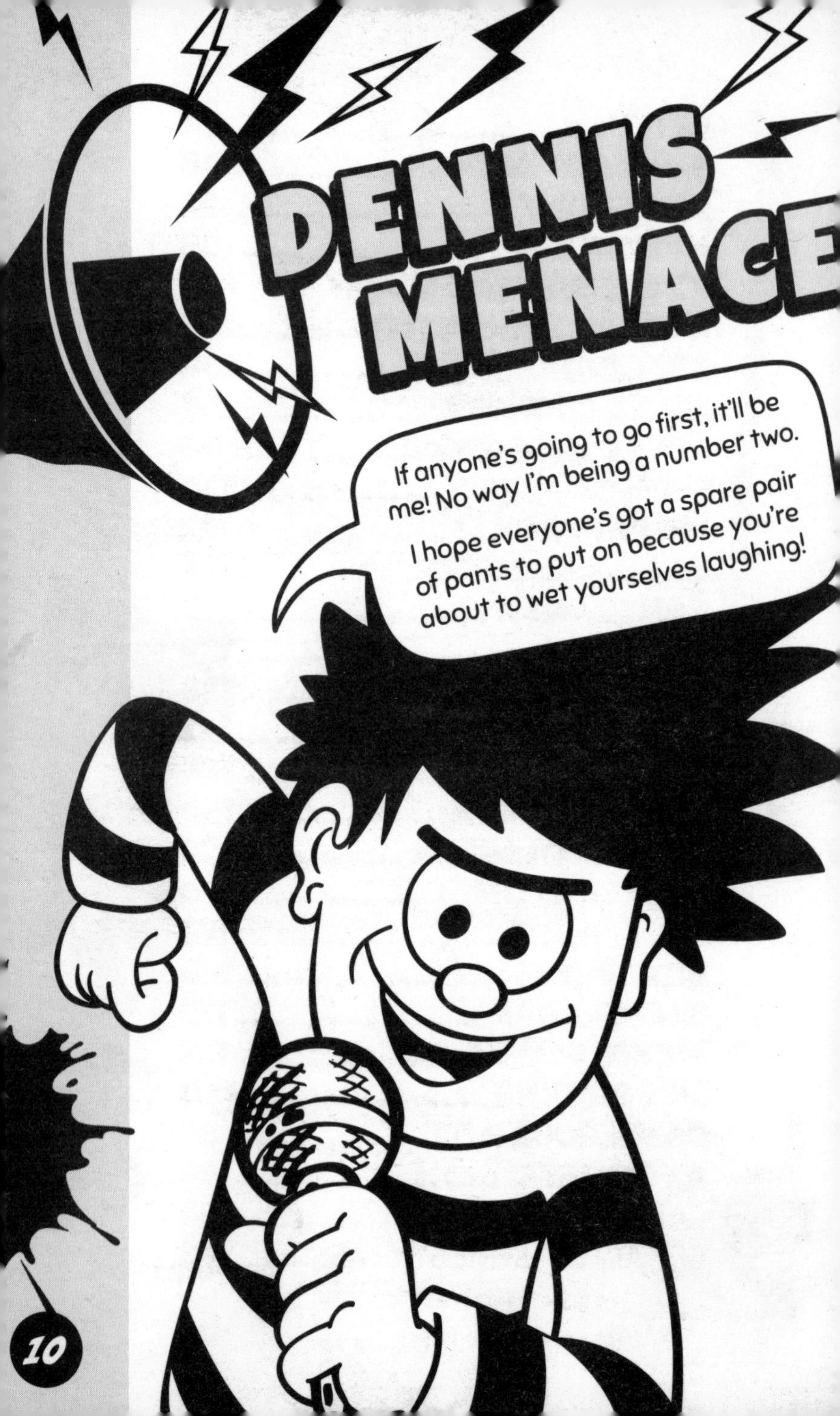
DENNIS MENACE
If anyone's going to go first, it'll be me! No way I'm being a number two.
I hope everyone's got a spare pair of pants to put on because you're about to wet yourselves laughing!

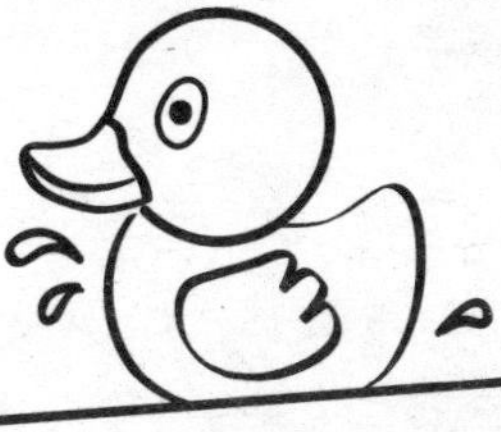

WHY DO DUCKS FLY SOUTH FOR THE WINTER?

BECAUSE IT'S TOO FAR TO WADDLE.

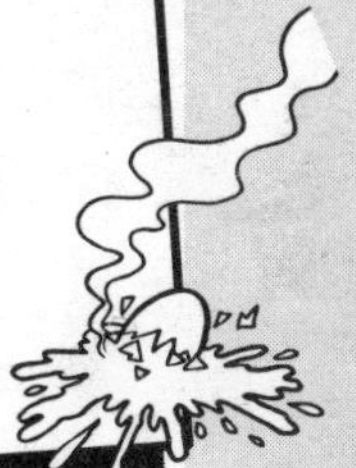

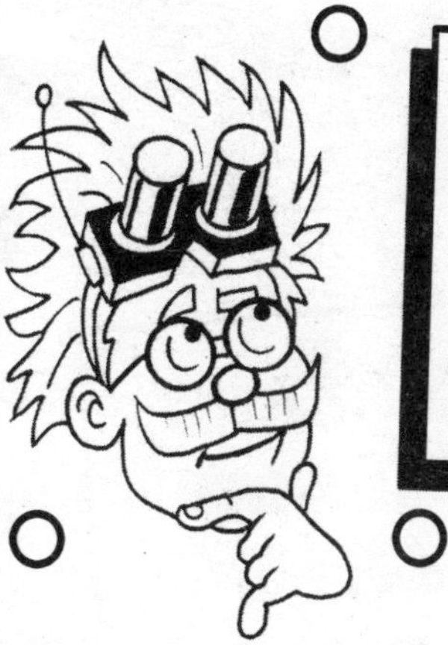

WHY CAN'T YOU TRUST ATOMS?

THEY MAKE UP EVERYTHING.

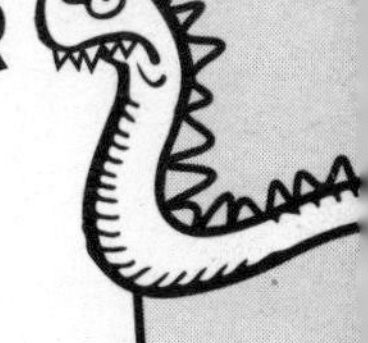

WHAT TYPE OF DINOSAUR PLAYS FORTNITE?

A FLOSSIRAPTOR.

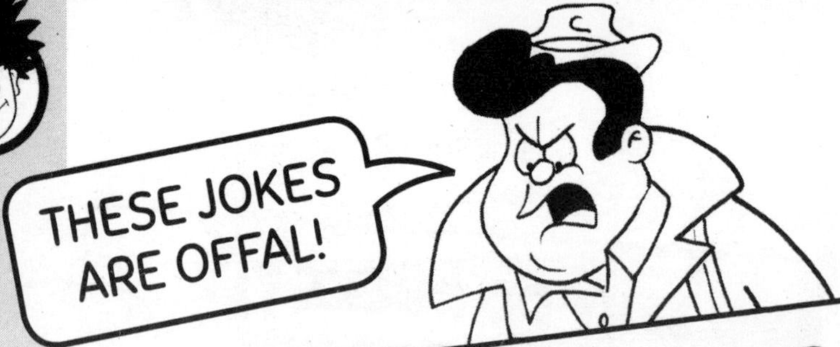
THESE JOKES ARE OFFAL!

WHY DIDN'T THE BUTCHER WANT TO SKYDIVE?

THE STEAKS WERE TOO HIGH!

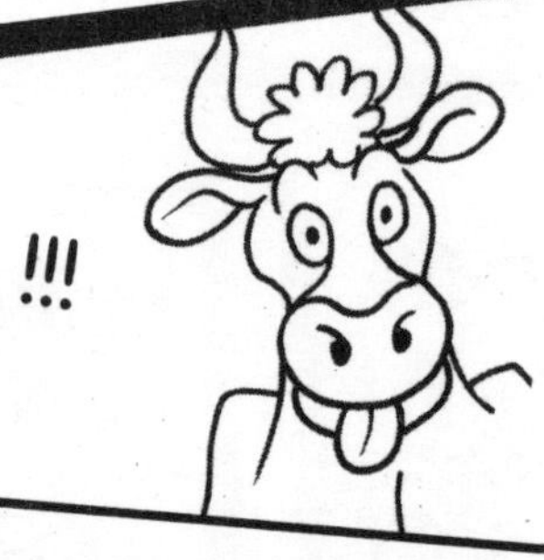
!!!

HAVE YOU HEARD THIS SHEEPDOG JOKE? . . .

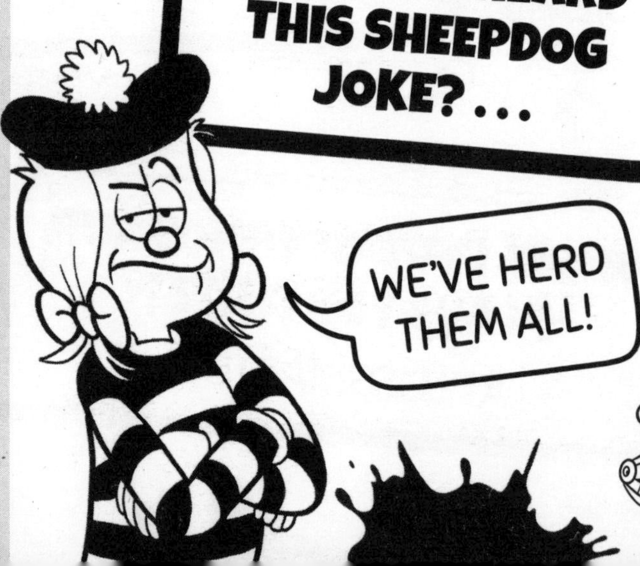
WE'VE HERD THEM ALL!

HAVE YOU HEARD THE ONE ABOUT THE CLIFFHANGER? ...

YOU FORGOT THE PUNCHLINE! OH ... WAIT ...

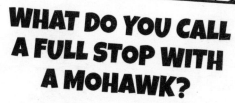

WHAT DO YOU CALL A FULL STOP WITH A MOHAWK?
PUNK–TUATION!

WHAT DO YOU CALL AN ALLIGATOR IN A VEST?
AN IN–VEST–IGATOR!

13

MINNIE THE MINX

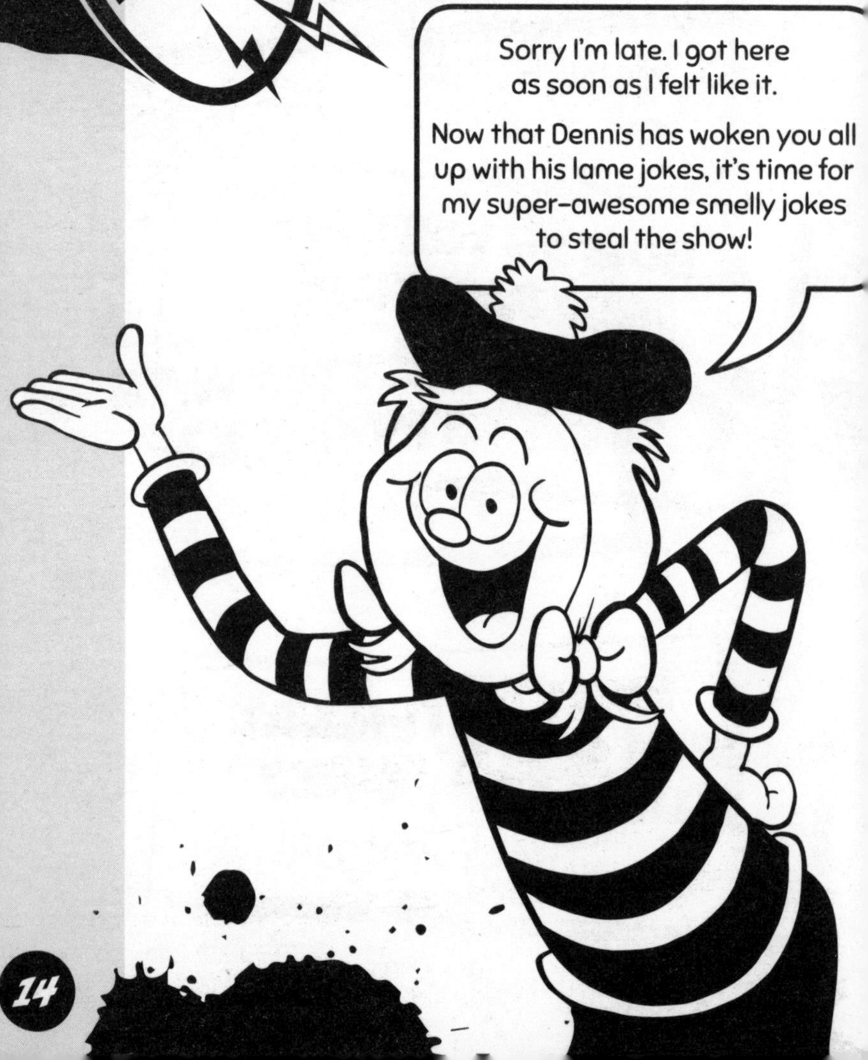
Sorry I'm late. I got here as soon as I felt like it.
Now that Dennis has woken you all up with his lame jokes, it's time for my super-awesome smelly jokes to steal the show!

WHY ARE NINJA FARTS SO DANGEROUS?

THEY'RE SILENT BUT DEADLY!

HOW DO YOU STOP A SKUNK FROM SMELLING?

HOLD ITS NOSE!

WHAT DO YOU CALL A SMELLY FAIRY?

STINKERBELL!

WHAT DO YOU CALL A CAT WHO LIKES TO EAT BEANS?

PUSS 'N TOOTS!

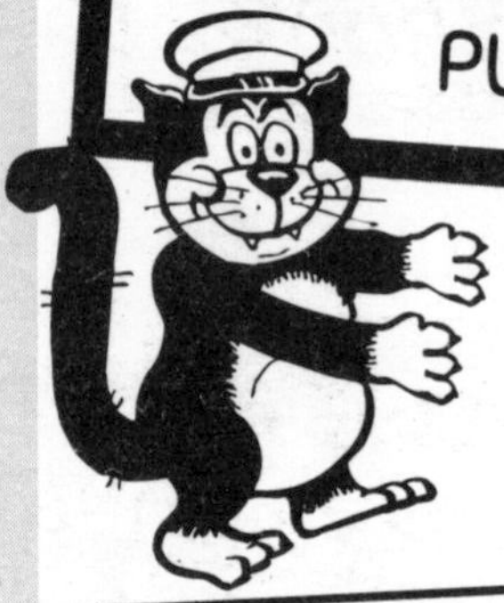

WHAT'S THE SMELLIEST CITY IN AMERICA?

PHEW YORK!

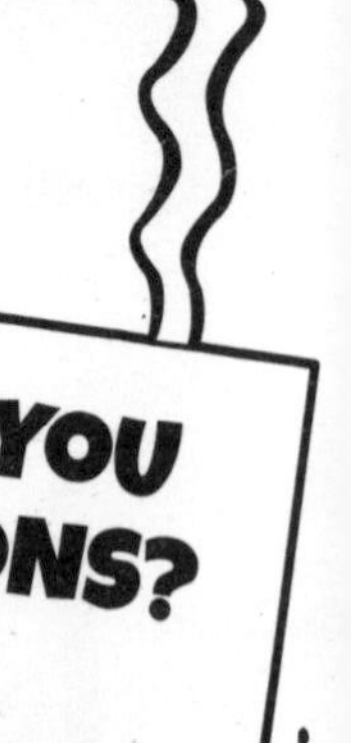

WHAT DO YOU GET IF YOU EAT BEANS WITH ONIONS?

TEARGAS!

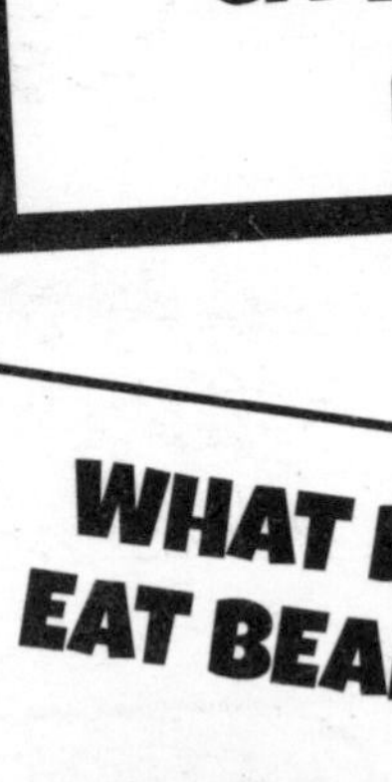
WINDY BEANS

WHAT DID THE POO SAY TO THE FART?

YOU BLEW ME AWAY!

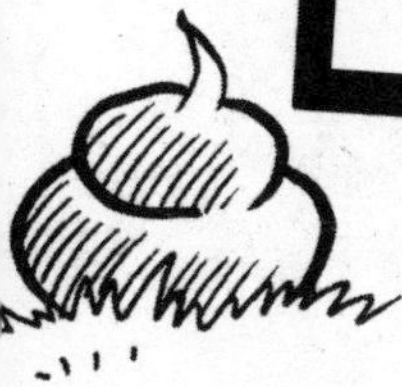

HOW CAN YOU TELL IF A CLOWN HAS FARTED?

THEY SMELL FUNNY!

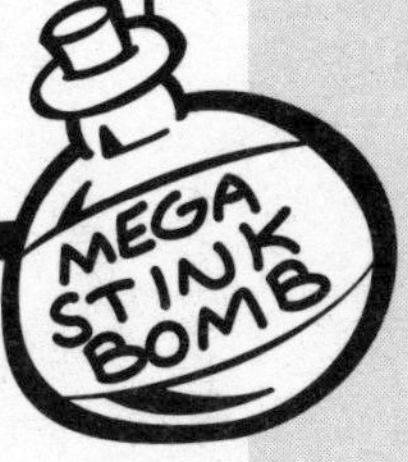
MEGA
STINK
BOMB

WHEN SHOULD YOU STOP TELLING FART JOKES?

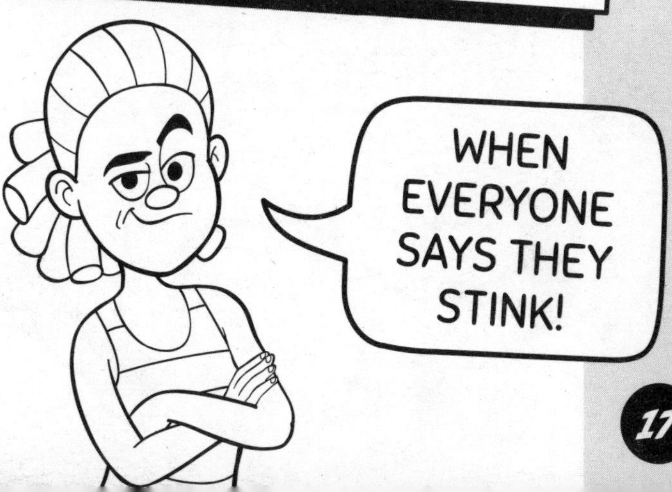
WHEN EVERYONE SAYS THEY STINK!

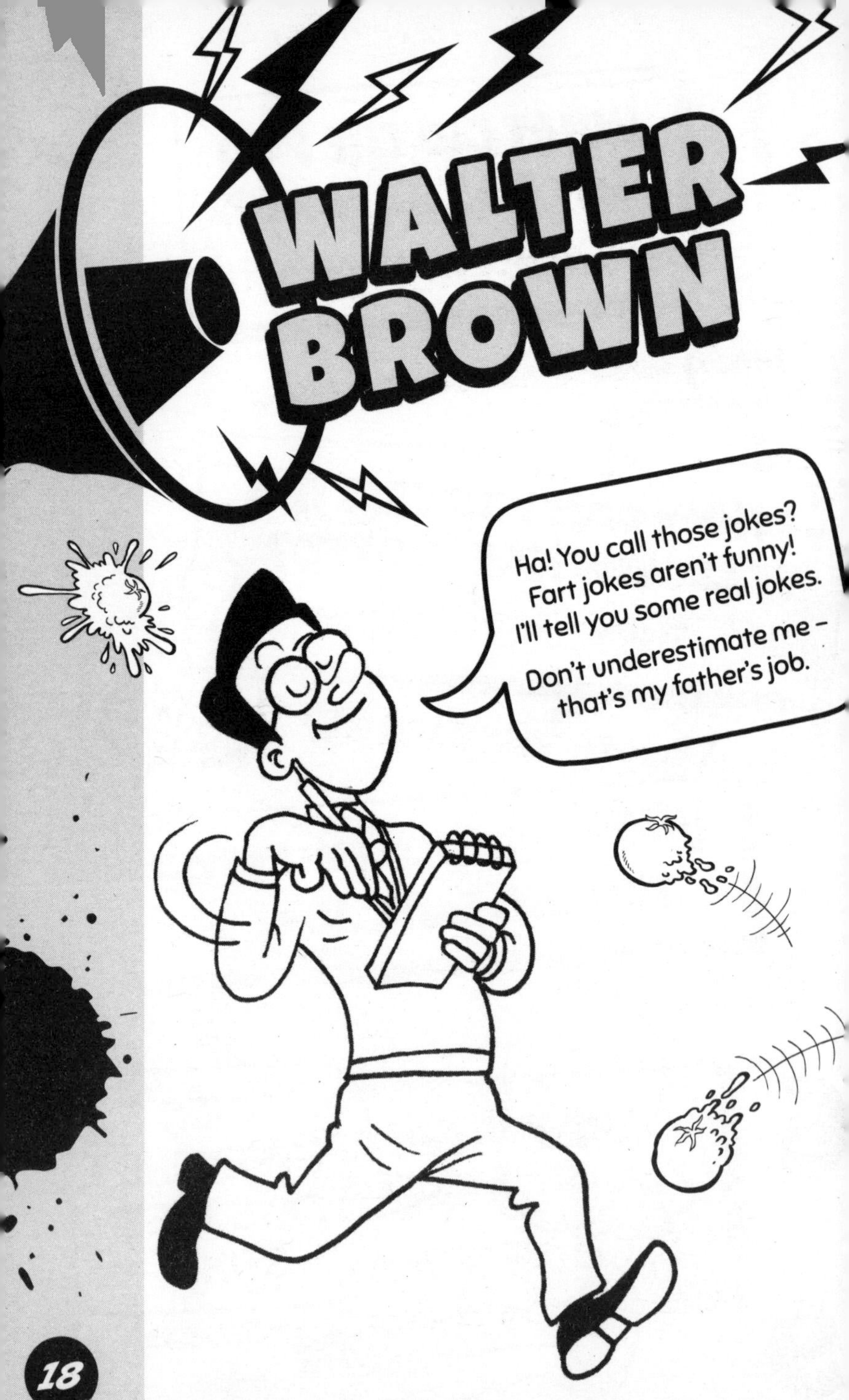
WALTER BROWN
Ha! You call those jokes? Fart jokes aren't funny! I'll tell you some real jokes.
Don't underestimate me – that's my father's job.

I'D TELL YOU A CHEMISTRY JOKE . . .

BUT I KNOW I WOULDN'T GET A REACTION!

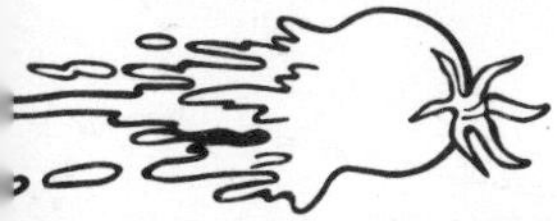

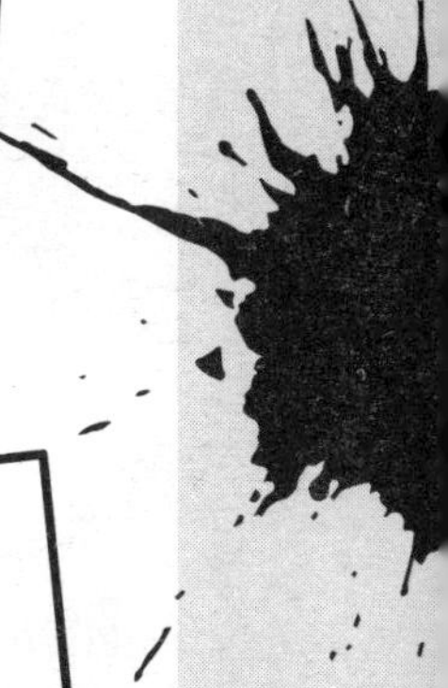

TEACHER: HOW DO YOU SPELL 'LONDON'?

CHILD: L . . . O . . . I . . .

TEACHER: THERE'S NO 'I' IN LONDON!

CHILD: YES THERE IS, I WENT ON IT WITH MY MUM!

7

6

WHY IS SIX AFRAID OF SEVEN?

BECAUSE SEVEN ATE NINE!

9

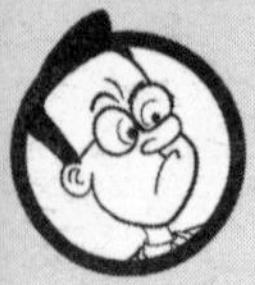

HAVE YOU GOT ANY BOOKS ON TURTLES?

HARDBACK?

YES, WITH LITTLE HEADS.

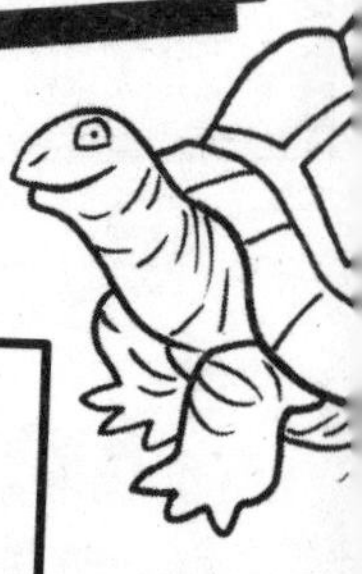

WHAT'S ORANGE AND BAD FOR YOUR TEETH?

A BRICK!

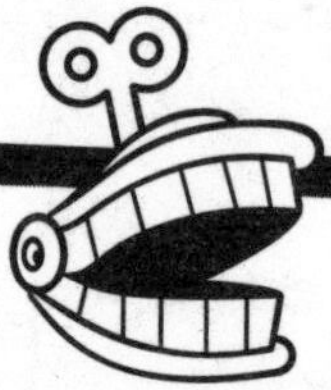

I BOUGHT THE WORLD'S WORST THESAURUS YESTERDAY . . .

NOT ONLY IS IT TERRIBLE,
IT'S TERRIBLE!

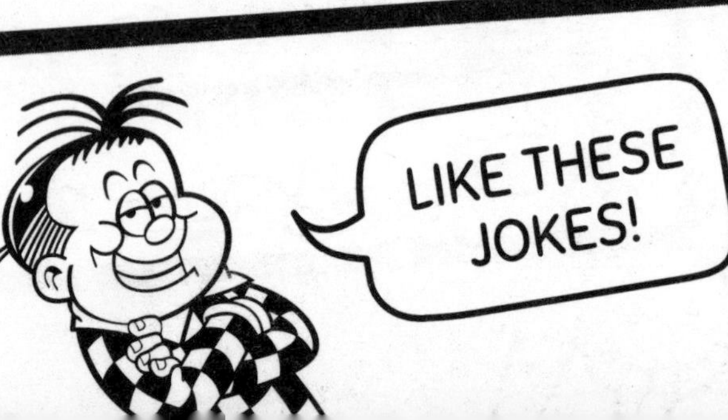
LIKE THESE JOKES!

WHAT DO YOU DO WHEN YOUR TEACHER ROLLS THEIR EYES AT YOU?

PICK THEM UP AND ROLL THEM BACK!

TEACHER: IF YOU GOT £20 FROM 5 PEOPLE, WHAT DO YOU GET?

STUDENT: A NEW BIKE!

KNOCK KNOCK.

WHO'S THERE?

INTERRUPTING COW.

INTERRUPTING C–

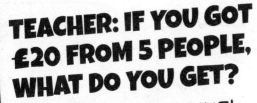

MOO!

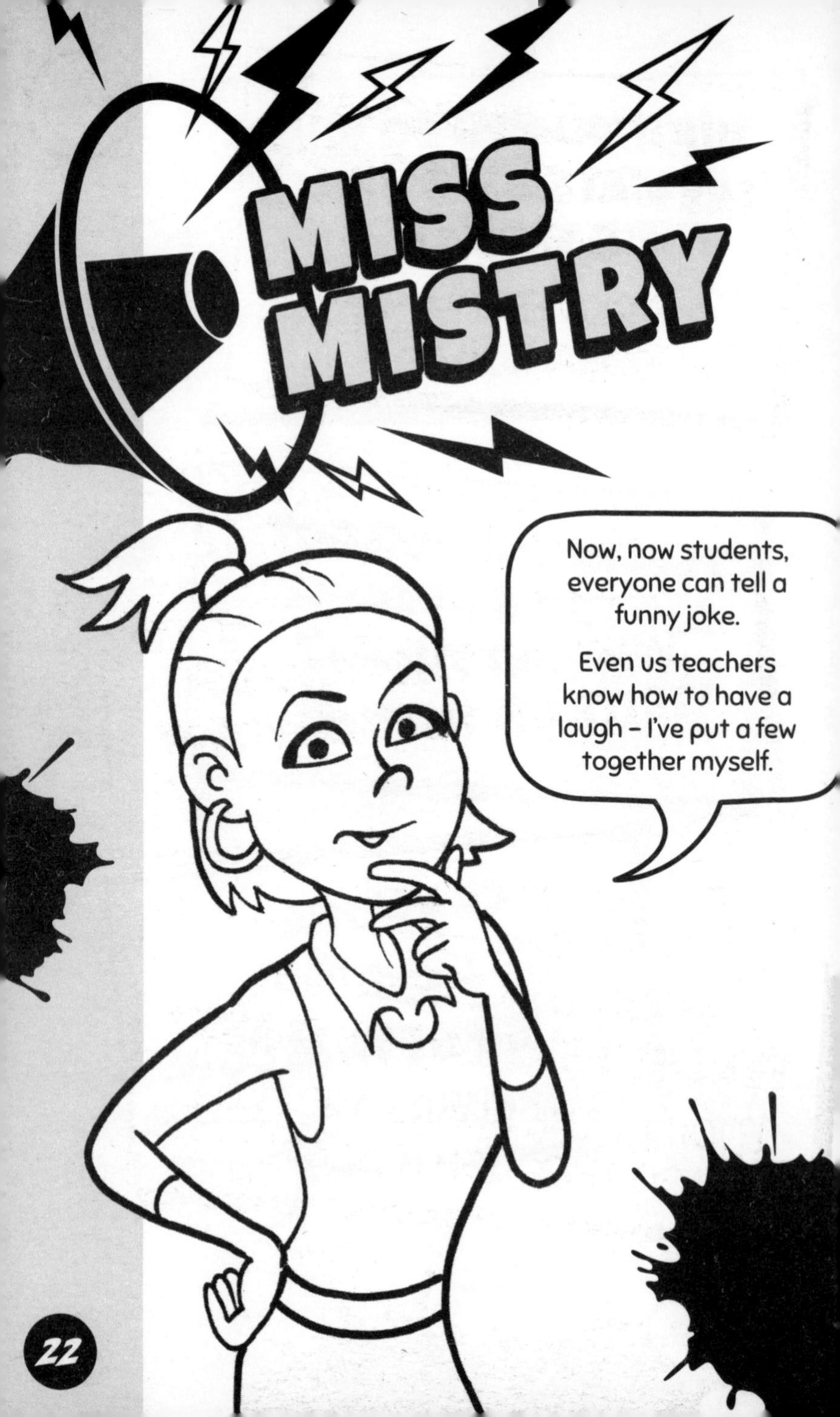
MISS MISTRY
Now, now students, everyone can tell a funny joke.
Even us teachers know how to have a laugh – I've put a few together myself.

WHAT HAPPENED TO THE MATHS TEACHER'S GARDEN?

THE PLANTS ALL GREW SQUARE ROOTS!

WHY DID THE TEACHER WRITE ON THE WINDOW?

SO THE LESSON WAS CLEAR!

WHAT DID THE GHOST TEACHER SAY TO THE CLASS?

LOOK AT THE BOARD AND I WILL GO THROUGH IT AGAIN!

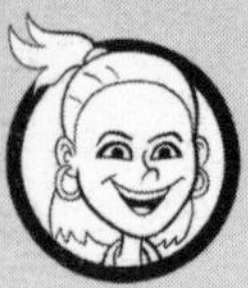

WHAT DO ENGLISH TEACHERS AND JUDGES HAVE IN COMMON?

THEY BOTH HAND OUT LONG SENTENCES!

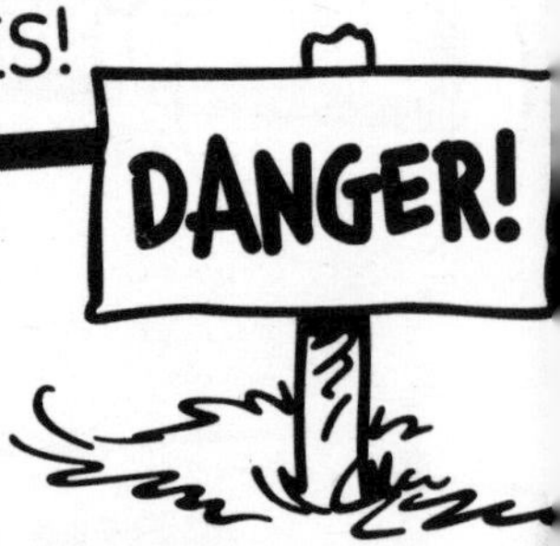
DANGER!

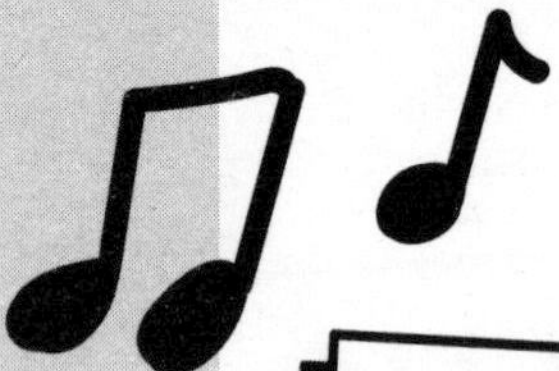

WHY DID THE MUSIC TEACHER NEED A LADDER?

TO REACH THE HIGH NOTES!

WHY DID THE TEACHER WEAR SUNGLASSES?

THE PUPILS WERE SO BRIGHT!

WHAT DO YOU SAY WHEN YOU ARE COMFORTING AN ENGLISH TEACHER?

THERE, THEIR, THEY'RE.

WHY ARE TEACHERS SO RUDE ON VACATION?

BECAUSE NOBODY LIKES THEM?

BECAUSE THEY HAVE NO CLASS!

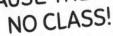

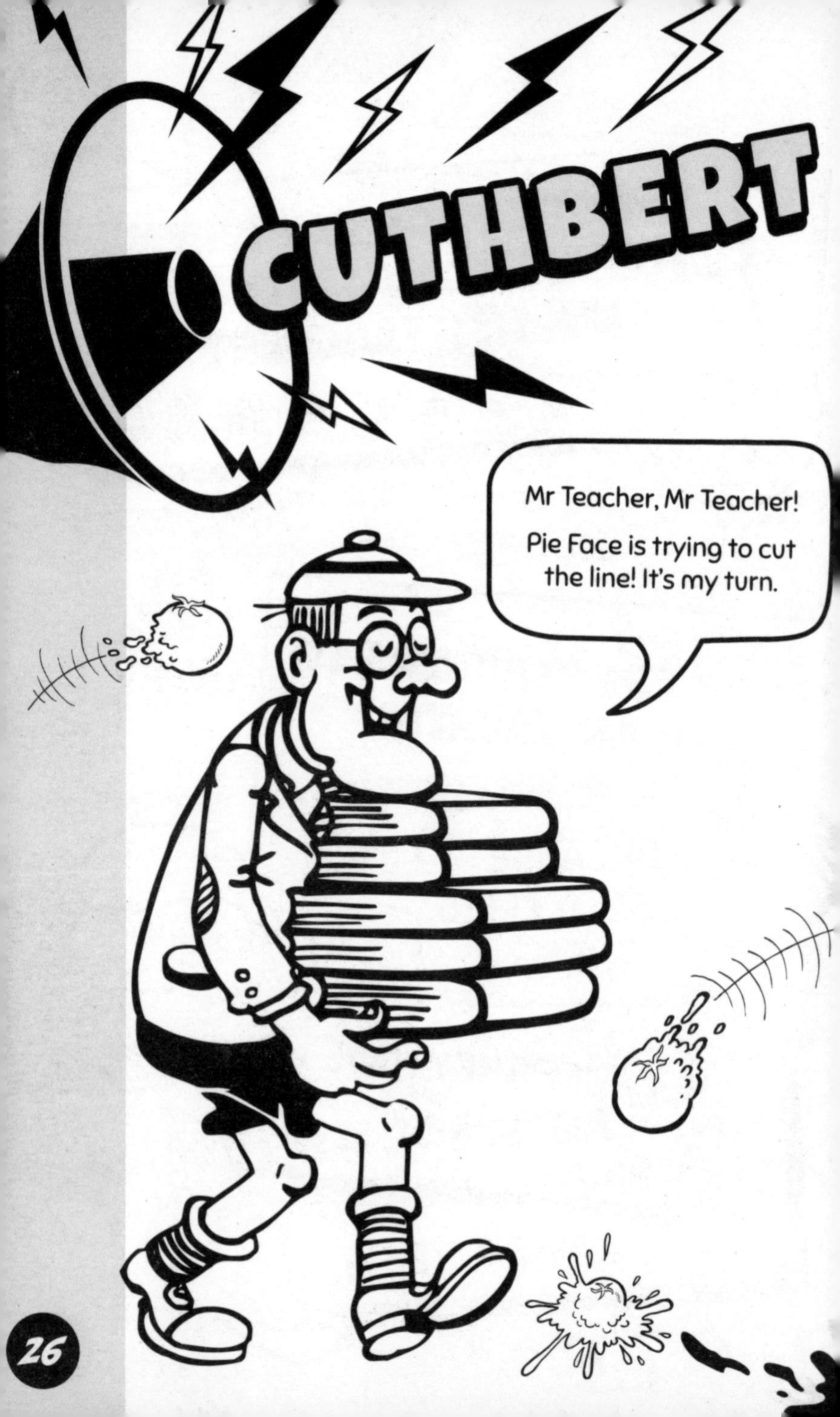
CUTHBERT
Mr Teacher, Mr Teacher!
Pie Face is trying to cut the line! It's my turn.

HOW DO YOU GET STRAIGHT A'S AT SCHOOL?

USE A RULER!

A A A A A A A A

IF I HAD 6 ORANGES IN ONE HAND AND 7 APPLES IN THE OTHER, WHAT WOULD I HAVE?

BIG HANDS!

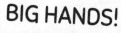

2 + 4 = ?

WHAT IS BLACK, WHITE AND HORRIBLE?

A MATHS TEST!

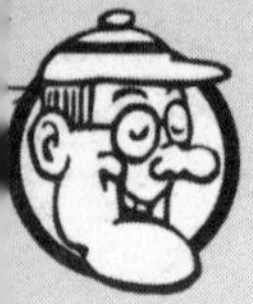

DO YOU KNOW HOW MANY TEACHERS WORK AT THIS SCHOOL?

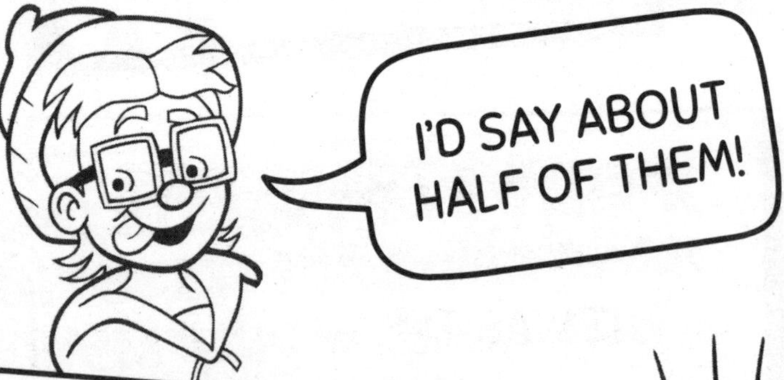
I'D SAY ABOUT HALF OF THEM!

WHY DID THE ECHO GET DETENTION?

FOR ANSWERING BACK!

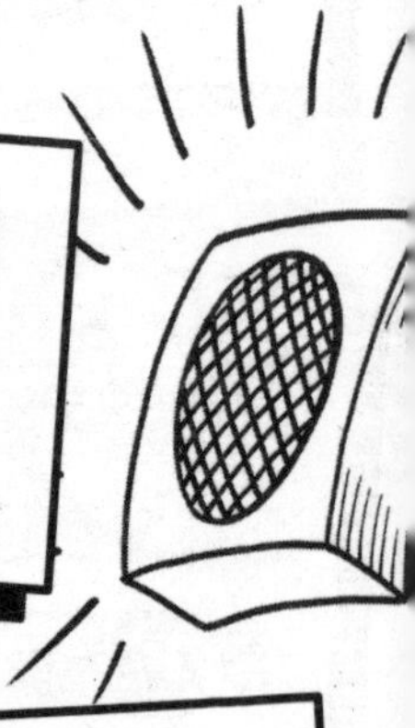

WHY DID THE SCHOOL BAN SCISSORS?

TO STOP PEOPLE CUTTING CLASS!

WHAT SCHOOL SUBJECT IS THE FRUITIEST?

HISTORY – IT'S FULL OF DATES!

WHY DID THE BICYCLE HAVE A NAP?

IT WAS TWO-TYRED.

WHAT'S THE WORST THING YOU CAN FIND IN BASH STREET SCHOOL'S CANTEEN?

THE FOOD!

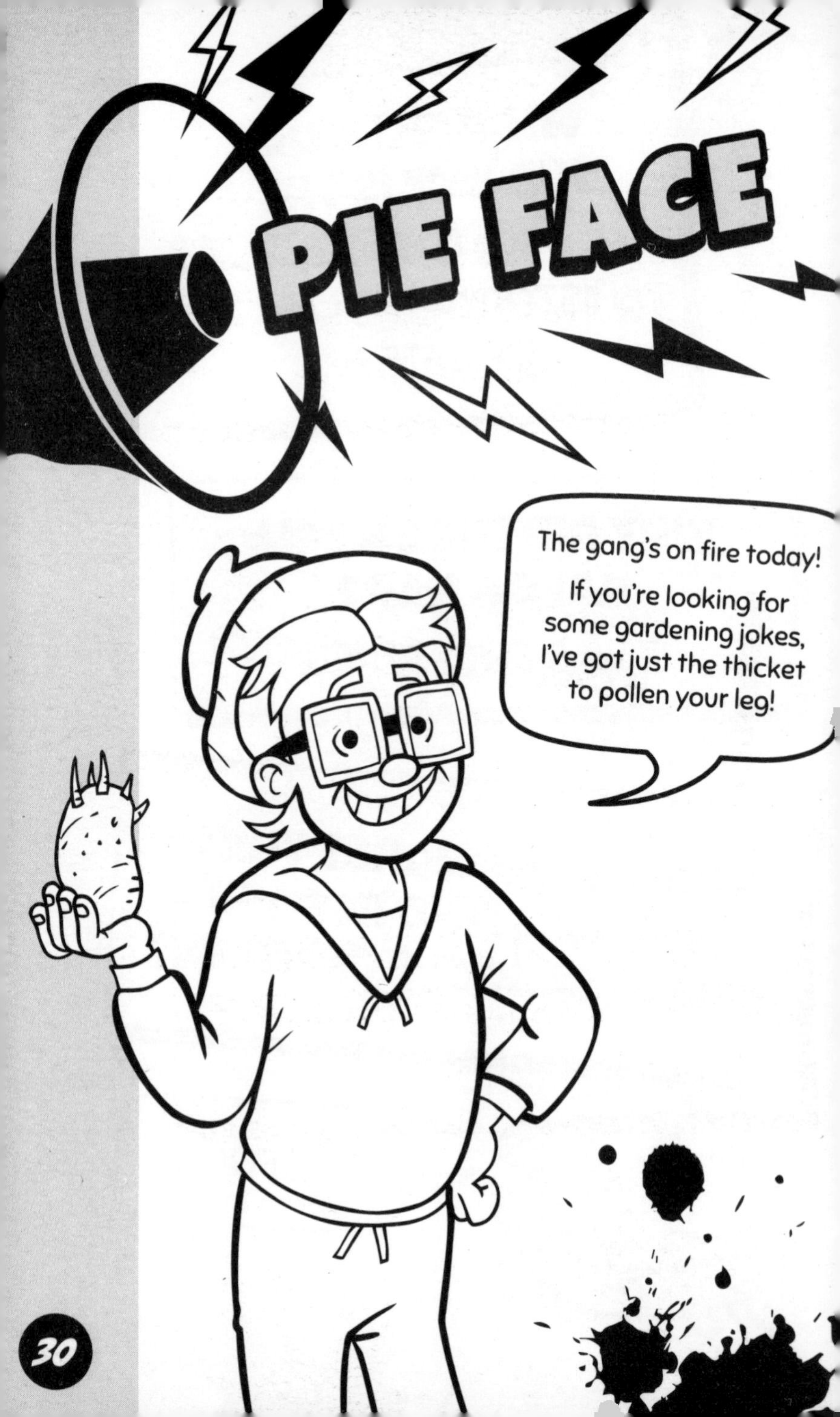
PIE FACE
The gang's on fire today! If you're looking for some gardening jokes, I've got just the thicket to pollen your leg!

WHAT DID THE TREE SAY TO THE LUMBERJACK?

LEAF ME ALONE!

WHICH FLOWERS LIKE KISSING THE MOST?

TU-LIPS!

WHAT DOES A FLOWER CALL THEIR BEST FRIEND?

BUD!

WHAT DID THE DAFFODIL SAY WHEN THE DAISY CRIED?

GET CLOVER IT!

WHAT DID THE FLOWER SAY TO HIS MUM WHEN HE GAVE HER A GIFT?

I HOPE THISTLE CHEER YOU UP!

WHAT DO YOU CALL A GIRL WITH A FROG ON HER HEAD?

LILY!

YOUR SISTER!

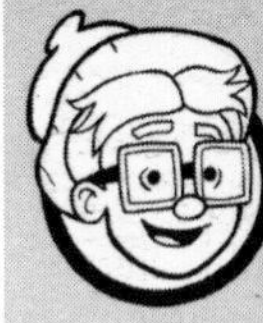

WHY ARE FLOWERS NEVER LONELY?

BECAUSE OF THEIR LITTLE BUD-DIES!

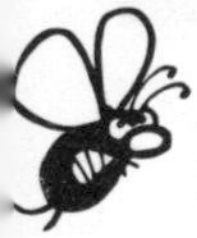

WHY IS A FLOWER LIKE THE LETTER A?

BECAUSE A BEE GOES AFTER IT!

WHAT FLOWERS MAKE A REALLY BAD GIFT?

CAULI-FLOWERS!

WHAT DID THE FLOWER SAY AFTER TELLING A JOKE?

I'M ONLY POLLEN YOUR LEG!

RALF THE JANITOR

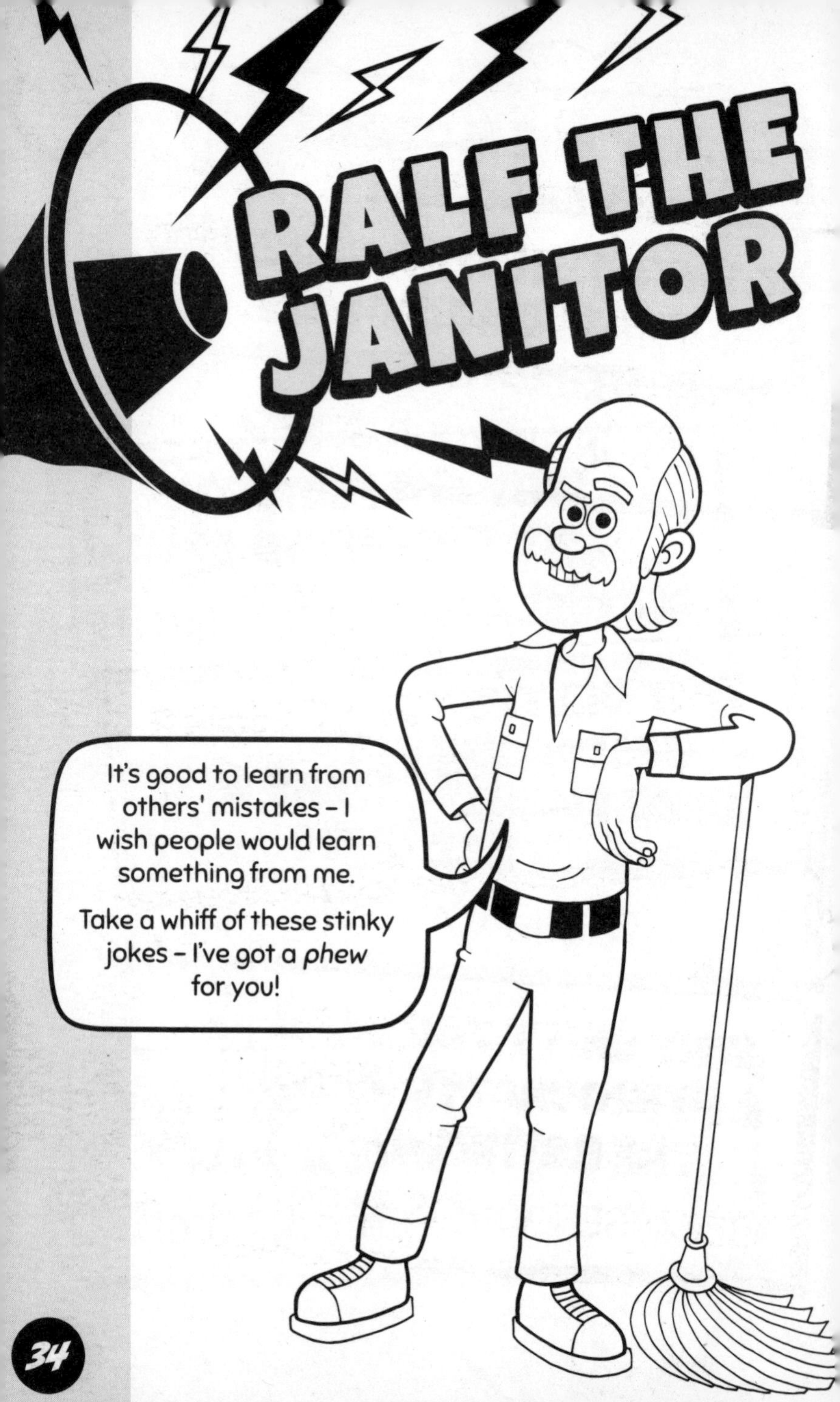
It's good to learn from others' mistakes – I wish people would learn something from me.
Take a whiff of these stinky jokes – I've got a *phew* for you!

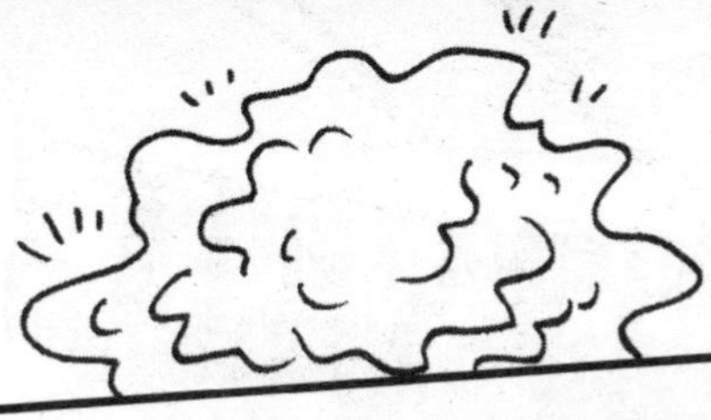

SCIENTISTS HAVE DISCOVERED THAT DIARRHOEA IS HEREDITARY . . .

IT RUNS IN YOUR GENES!

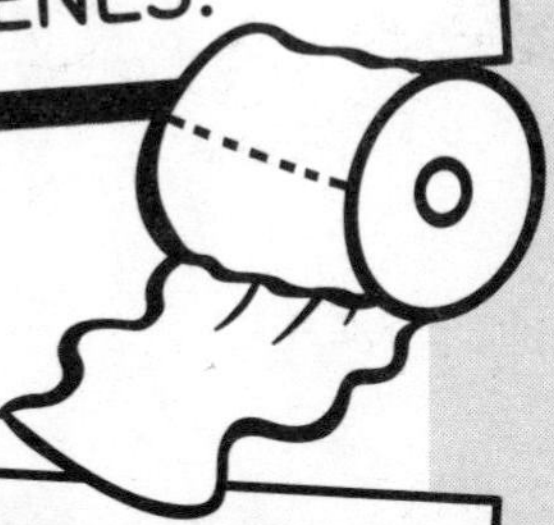

WHY DID THE TOILET PAPER ROLL DOWN THE HILL?

TO GET TO THE BOTTOM!

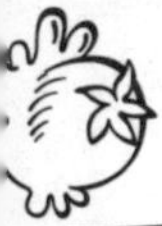

WHY CAN'T YOU HEAR A PTERODACTYL USING THE BATHROOM?

BECAUSE THE 'P' IS SILENT!

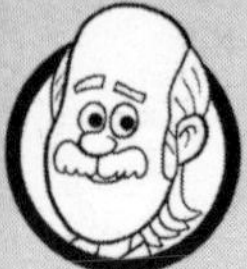

WHAT DID ONE TOILET SAY TO THE OTHER?

YOU LOOK A LITTLE FLUSHED!

WHAT'S BROWN AND SOUNDS LIKE A BELL?

DUNG!

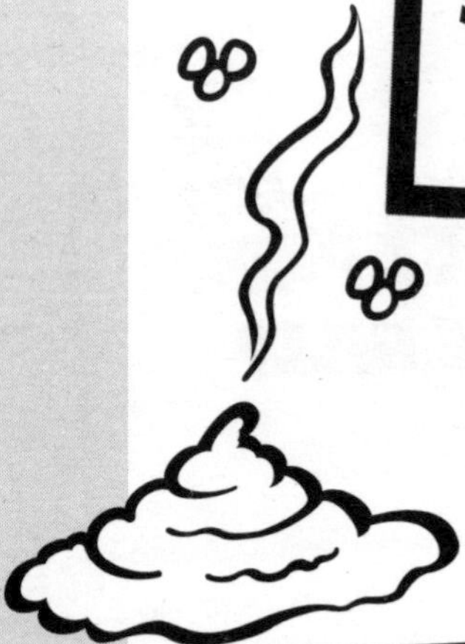

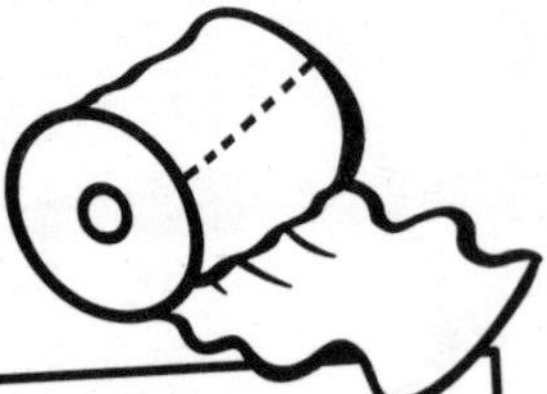

WHY DIDN'T THE TOILET ROLL MAKE IT ACROSS THE ROAD?

IT GOT STUCK IN THE CRACK!

THERE ARE TWO REASONS YOU SHOULDN'T DRINK FROM THE TOILET.

NUMBER ONE AND NUMBER TWO!

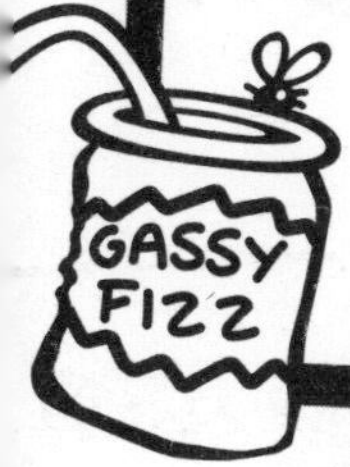
GASSY FIZZ

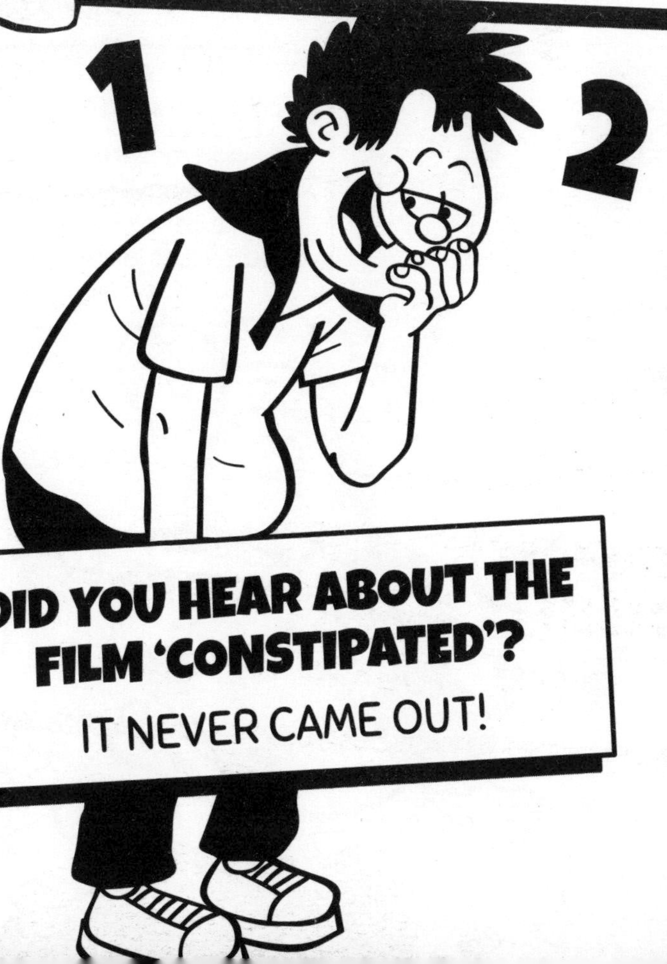
1
2

DID YOU HEAR ABOUT THE FILM 'CONSTIPATED'?

IT NEVER CAME OUT!

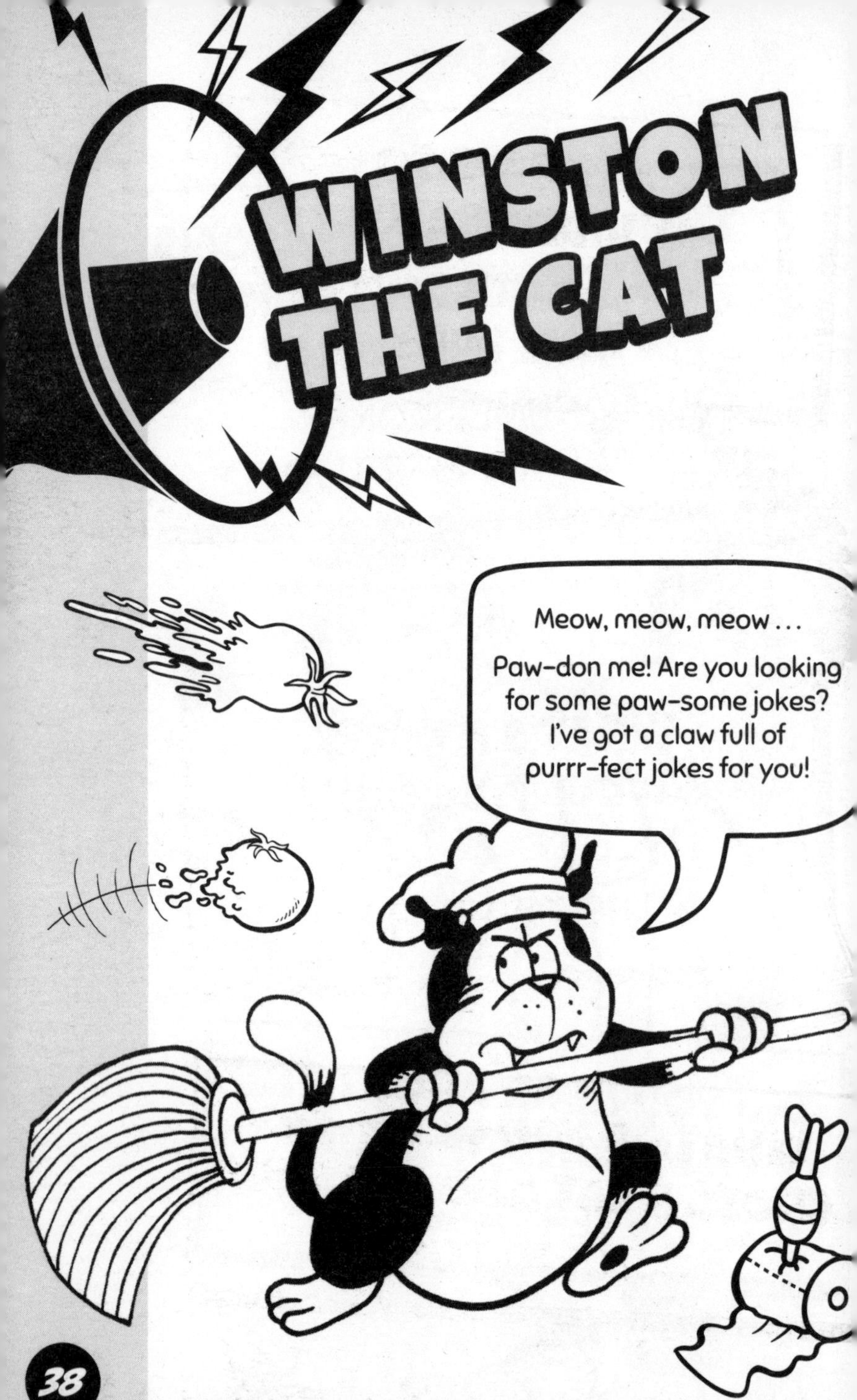
WINSTON THE CAT
Meow, meow, meow ...
Paw-don me! Are you looking for some paw-some jokes? I've got a claw full of purrr-fect jokes for you!

WHY ARE CATS SO GOOD AT VIDEO GAMES?

BECAUSE THEY HAVE NINE LIVES!

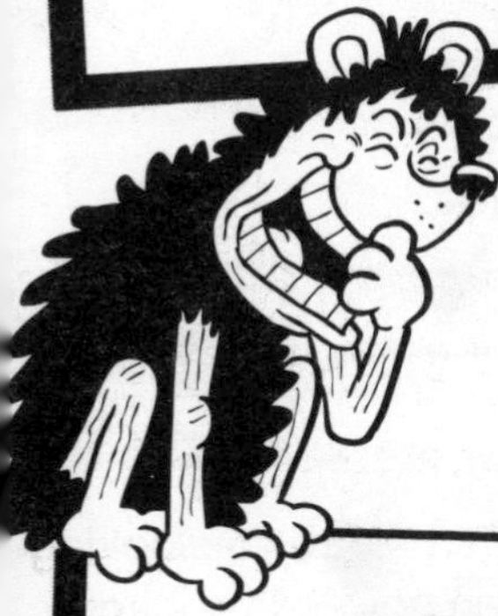

WHAT'S A CAT'S FAVOURITE BOOK?

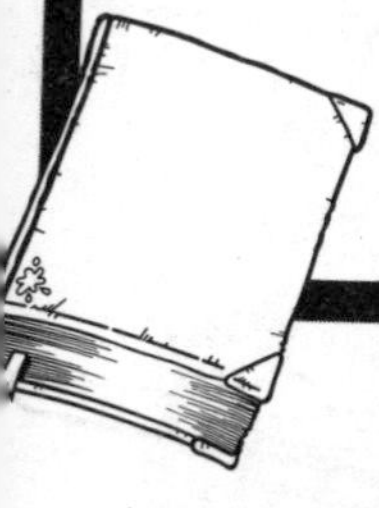

THE PRINCE AND THE PAW-PURR!

WHAT DO YOU GET IF YOU CROSS A CAT AND A SQUID?

AN OCTO-PUSS!

WHAT'S A CAT'S FAVOURITE NURSERY RHYME?

THREE BLIND MICE!

WHY WAS THE MOUSE AFRAID OF SWIMMING?

CATFISH!

DOES ANYONE EVEN UNDERSTAND WHAT HE'S SAYING?

WHICH MUSICAL INSTRUMENT IS BEST AT CATCHING FISH?

A CLARI-NET!

DOCTOR, DOCTOR! I KEEP THINKING I'M A CAT!

HOW LONG HAS THIS BEEN GOING ON?

SINCE I WAS A KITTEN!

WHEN IS IT BAD LUCK TO SEE A BLACK CAT?

WHEN YOU'RE A MOUSE!

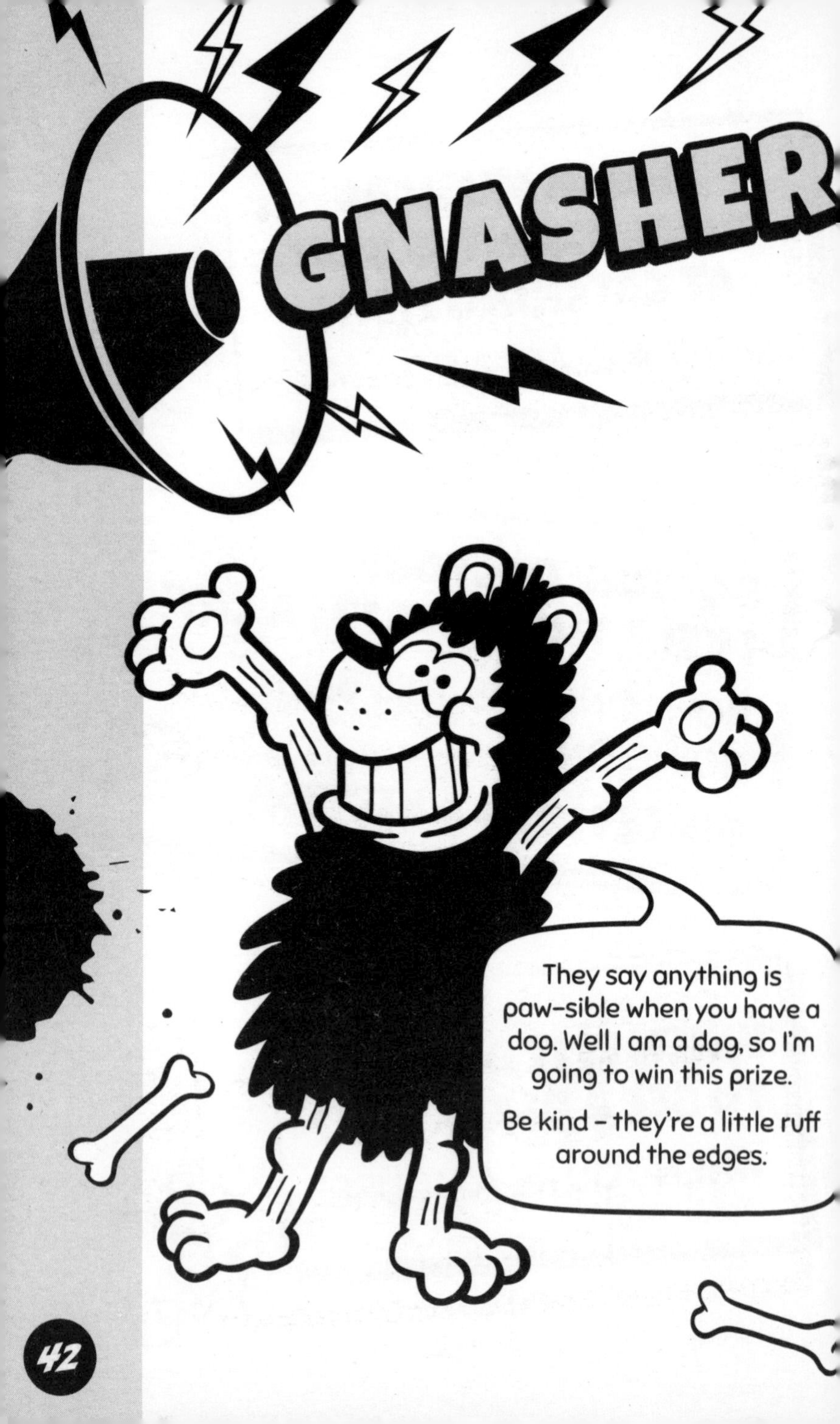
GNASHER
They say anything is paw-sible when you have a dog. Well I am a dog, so I'm going to win this prize.
Be kind – they're a little ruff around the edges.

WHERE DOES A DOG GO TO GET ANOTHER TAIL?

THE RE-TAIL SHOP!

WHAT DO YOU CALL A SNOWMAN'S DOG?

A SLUSH PUPPY!

DID YOU HEAR ABOUT THE VAMPIRE WHO GOT A PET DOG?

HE'D ALWAYS WANTED A BLOODHOUND!

WHAT GOES TICK-TOCK WOOF-WOOF?

DENNIS WHEN YOU ASK FOR HIS HOMEWORK?

A WATCHDOG!

DID YOU HEAR ABOUT THE DOG WHO ATE NOTHING BUT GARLIC?

HIS BARK WAS WORSE THAN HIS BITE!

DID YOU HEAR ABOUT THE DOG WHO WENT TO SEE THE FLEA CIRCUS?

HE STOLE THE SHOW!

WHY WILL A DOG NEVER WIN STRICTLY?

THEY HAVE TWO LEFT FEET!

WHO DELIVERS YOUR DOG'S CHRISTMAS PRESENTS?

SANTA PAWS!

DENNIS MENACE SR.

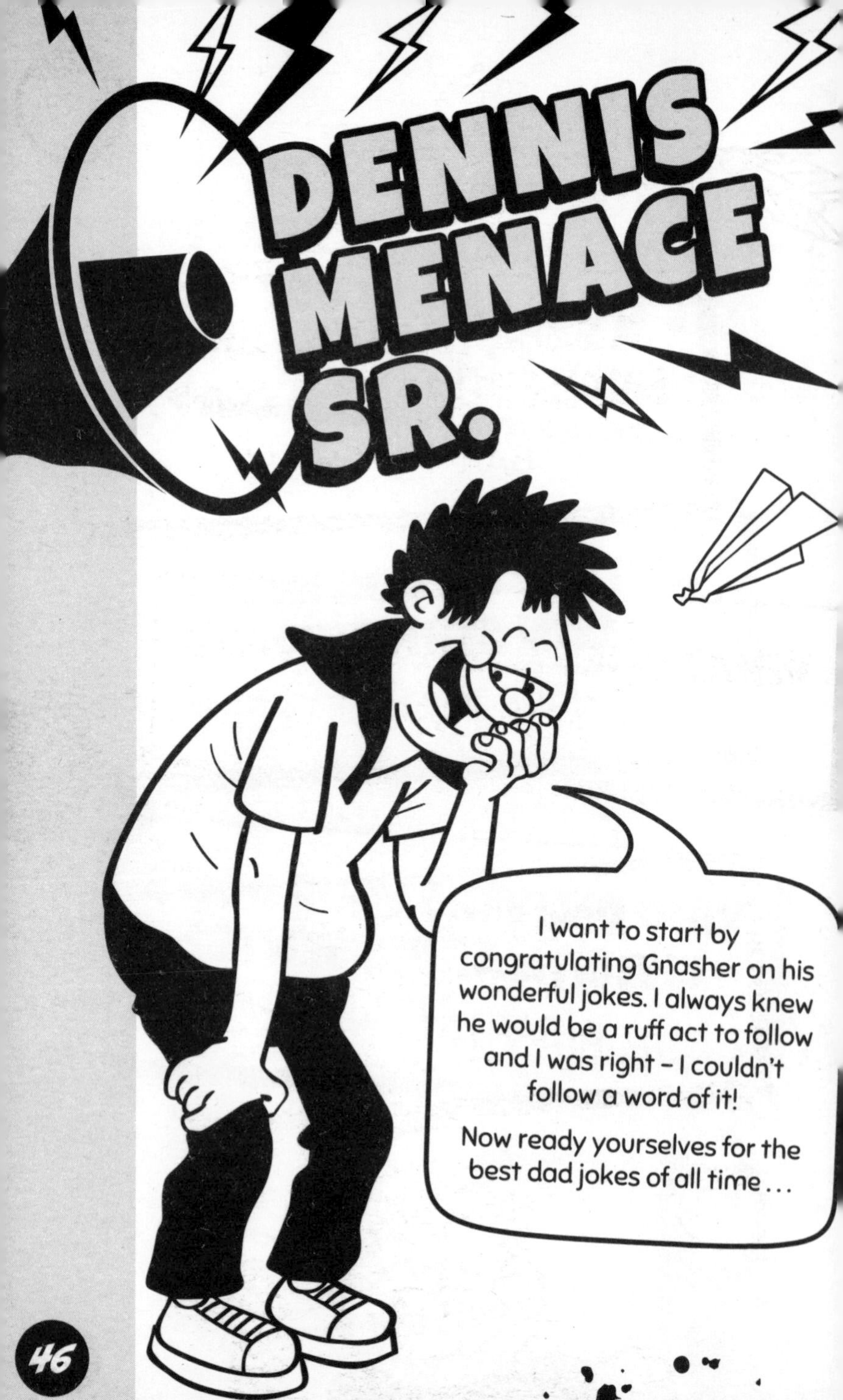
I want to start by congratulating Gnasher on his wonderful jokes. I always knew he would be a ruff act to follow and I was right – I couldn't follow a word of it!
Now ready yourselves for the best dad jokes of all time . . .

A SHEEP, A DRUM AND A SNAKE FELL OFF A CLIFF...
BAA–DUM–SSS!

WHAT DOES A HOUSE WEAR?
ADDRESS!

DOGS CAN'T GO THROUGH MRIs...
BUT CAT SCAN!

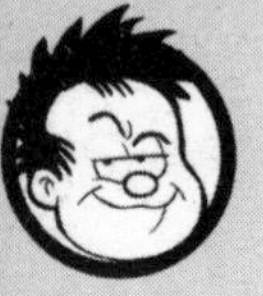

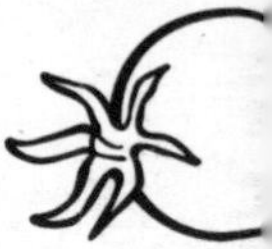

WHY IS CORN SUCH A GOOD LISTENER?

BECAUSE IT'S ALL EARS!

I WOULDN'T BUY ANYTHING WITH VELCRO...

IT'S A TOTAL RIP OFF!

WHY SHOULDN'T YOU WRITE WITH A BROKEN PENCIL?

BECAUSE IT'S POINTLESS!

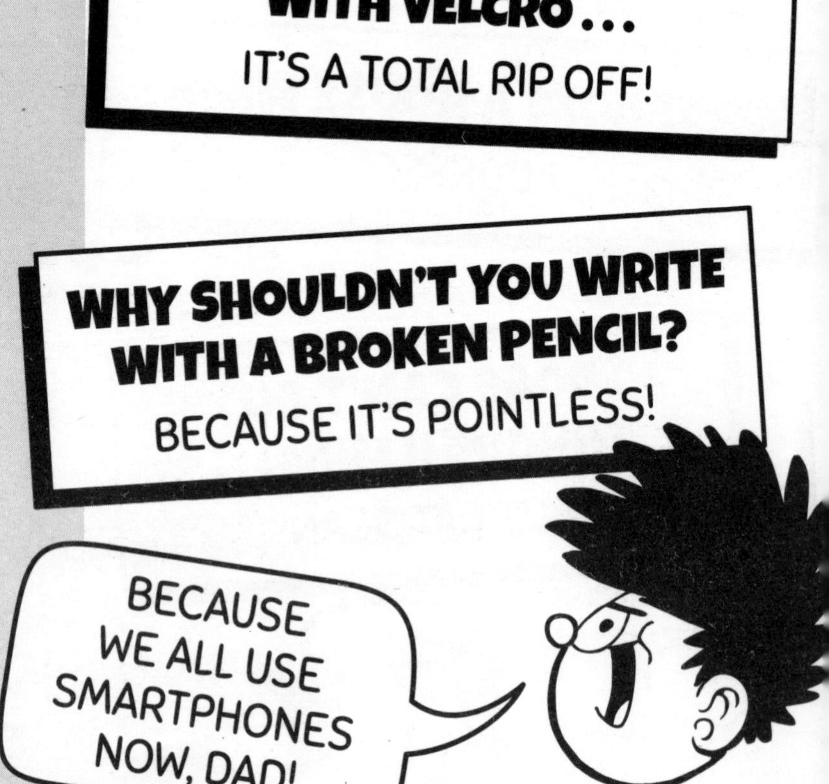
BECAUSE WE ALL USE SMARTPHONES NOW, DAD!

WHAT DO YOU CALL A BEAR WITHOUT ANY TEETH?

A GUMMY BEAR!

WHERE DO YOU LEARN TO MAKE ICE CREAM?

SUNDAE SCHOOL!

WHAT DID THE DRUMMER NAME HIS TWIN DAUGHTERS?

ANNA ONE, ANNA TWO!

BEA MENACE

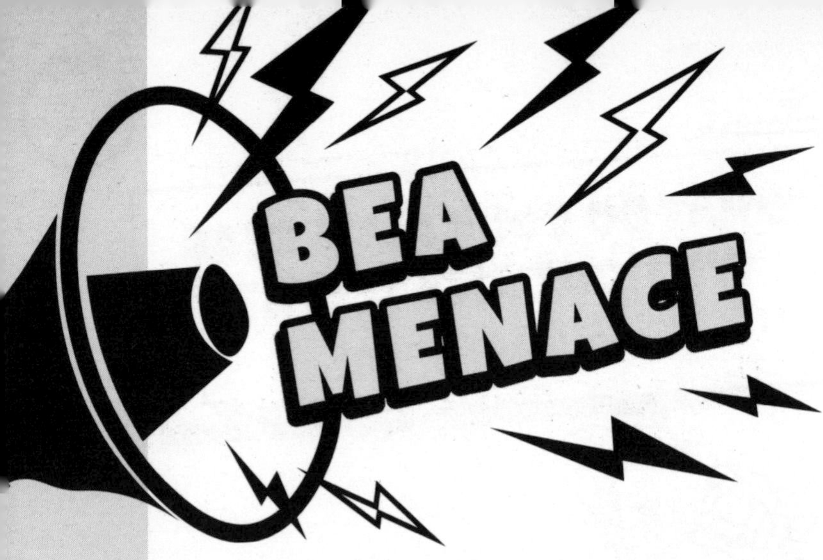

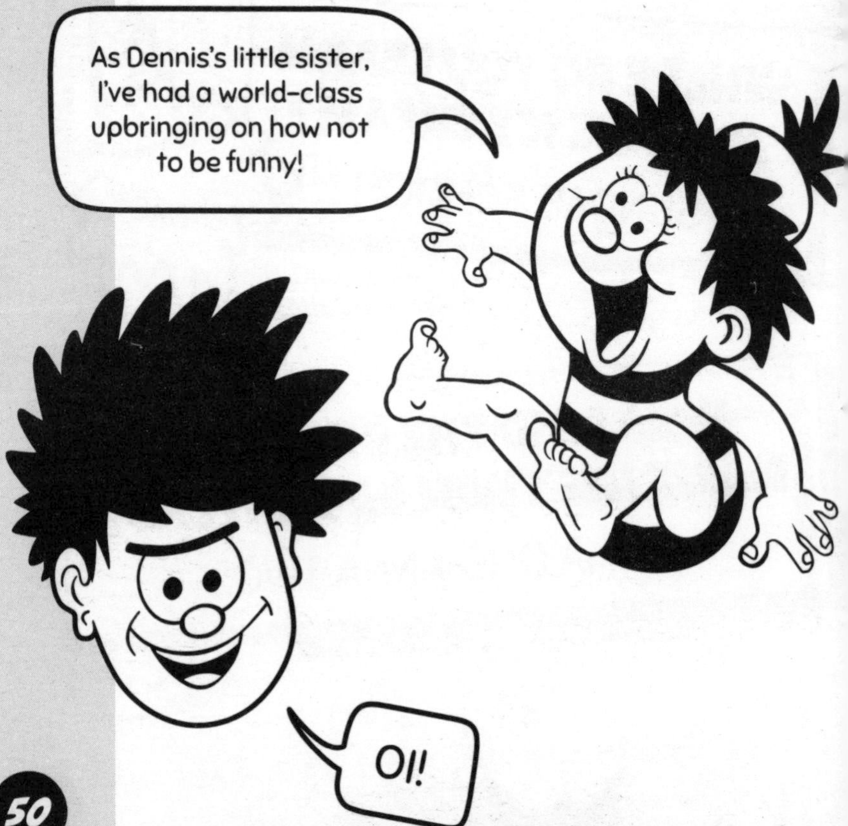

As Dennis's little sister, I've had a world-class upbringing on how not to be funny!
OI!

WHAT DID MUMMY PASTA SAY TO BABY PASTA?

IT'S PASTA YOUR BEDTIME!

MY DOG MINTON ATE TWO SHUTTLECOCKS...

BAD MINTON!

WHAT'S A FROG'S FAVOURITE DRINK?

CROAK-A-COLA!

GASSY FIZZ

WHY DON'T YOU MAKE A JOKE ANGRY?
BECAUSE IT ALWAYS HAS A PUNCHLINE!

TWO FISH WERE IN A TANK. ONE SAID TO THE OTHER . . .
DO YOU KNOW HOW TO DRIVE THIS THING?!

WHY DO GORILLAS HAVE BIG NOSTRILS?
BECAUSE THEY HAVE BIG FINGERS!

HOW DO YOU FRY A BLACK-AND-WHITE BEAR?

WITH A PAN–DUH!

HOW DO YOU MAKE A TISSUE DANCE?

PUT A LITTLE BOOGEY IN IT!

SOME PEOPLE HAVE DIFFICULTY SLEEPING . . .

BUT I CAN DO IT WITH MY EYES SHUT!

OLIVE & OLIVE

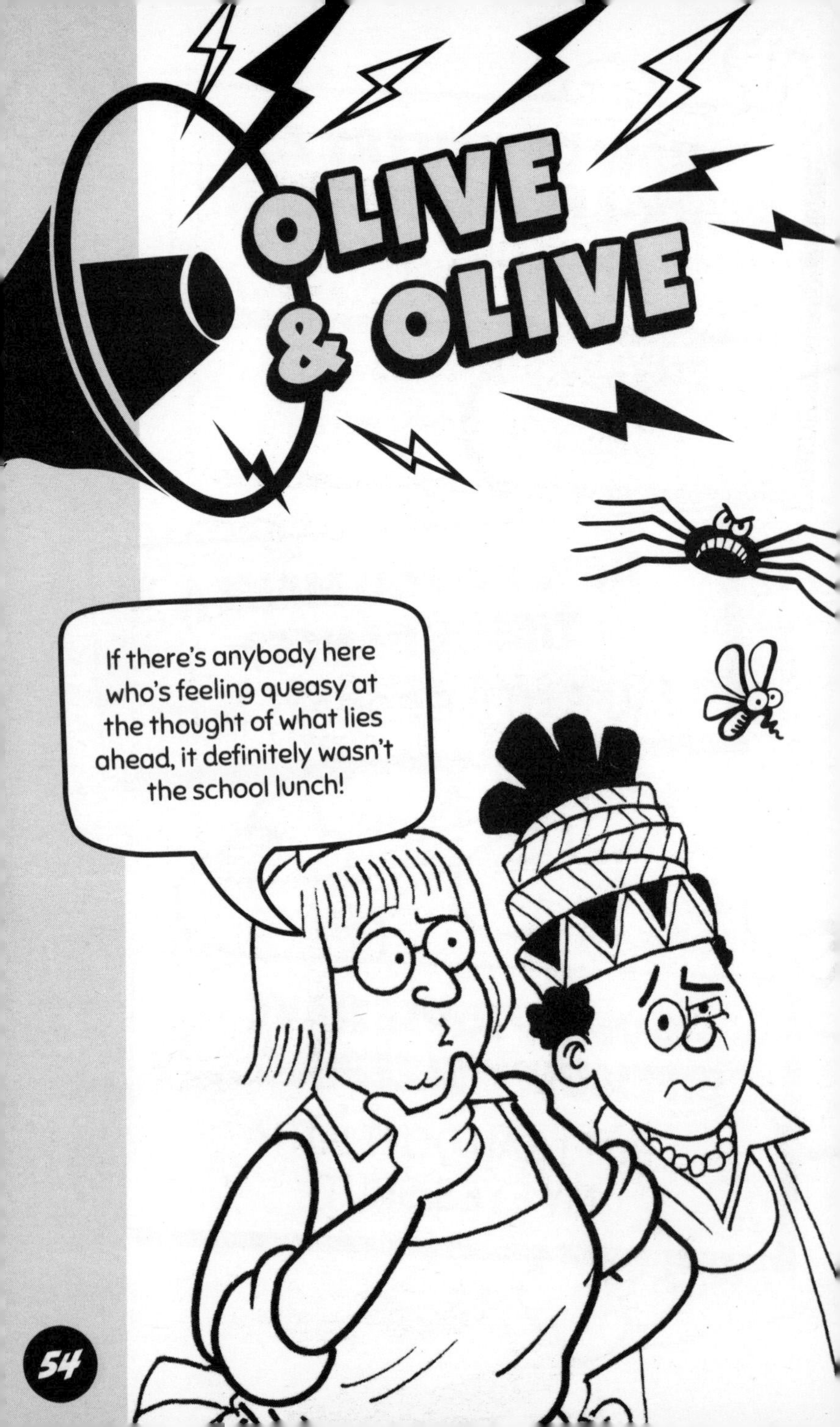
If there's anybody here who's feeling queasy at the thought of what lies ahead, it definitely wasn't the school lunch!

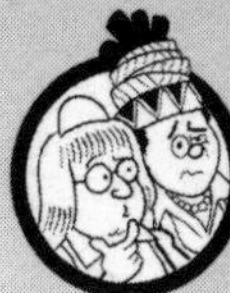

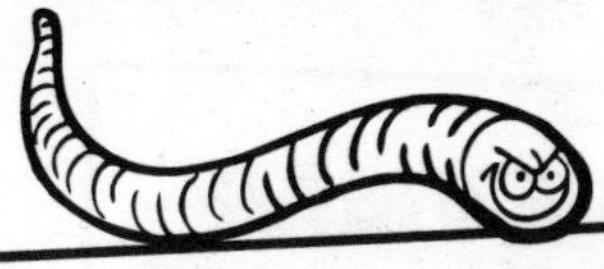

WHAT DID THE KNIFE AND FORK SAY AS THEY DROVE AWAY FROM THE CUTLERY DRAWER?

SEE YOU SPOON!

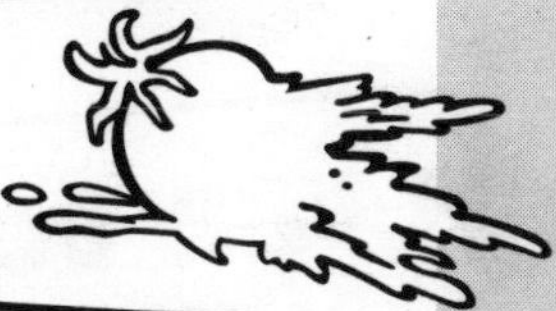

WHAT'S AN EMPEROR'S FAVOURITE FOOD?

CAESAR SALAD!

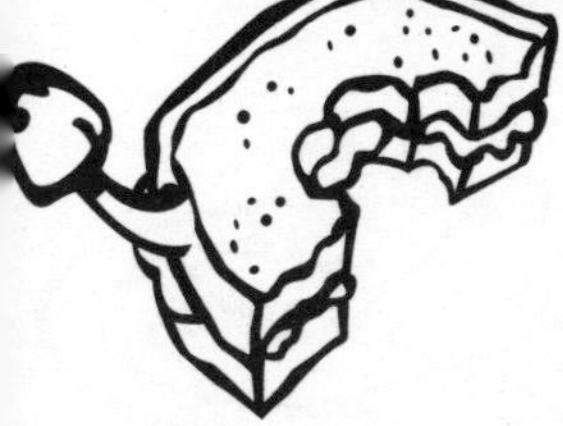

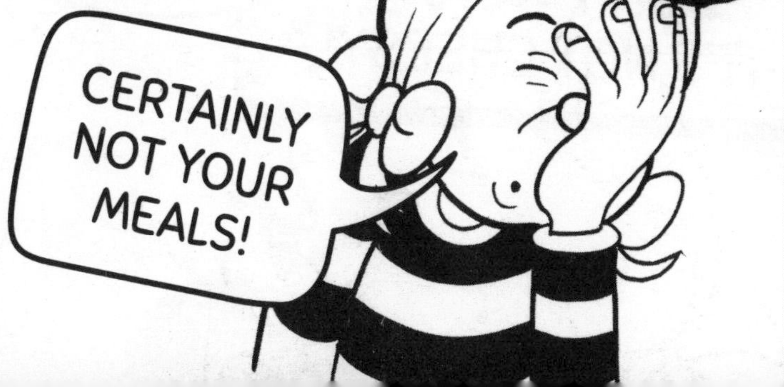
CERTAINLY NOT YOUR MEALS!

WHAT DID THE VICAR SAY TO THE VEGETABLE CONGREGATION?

LETTUCE PRAY!

WHY DO PICKLES ALWAYS ENJOY THEMSELVES?

THEY RELISH EVERY MOMENT!

CAN I TELL YOU A VEGAN JOKE?

DON'T WORRY, IT'S NOT CHEESY!

WHAT DO YOU GET WHEN YOU CROSS A CHEETAH WITH A BURGER?

FAST FOOD!

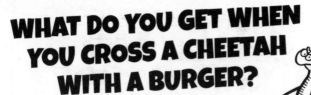

WHAT DOES A THESAURUS HAVE FOR BREAKFAST?

SYNONYM BUNS!

WHY WAS THE BAGEL SO GOOD AT GOLF?

IT ALWAYS GOT A HOLE IN ONE!

WHAT CEREAL GOES TO THE GYM TWICE A DAY?

SHREDDED WHEAT!

HOW TO WRITE A JOKE

A WORD FROM OUR SPONSOR HARI CHANDRA OF HAR HAR'S JOKE SHOP, BEANOTOWN . . .

There are millions of jokes in use, with thousands of new ones created and shared every single day. This is important, because the truth is that every joke becomes old as soon as it's shared.

Most jokes work in the same way – they make you expect one thing, then surprise you with something different. Everyone loves

SURPRISES!

THE SCIENCE BIT!

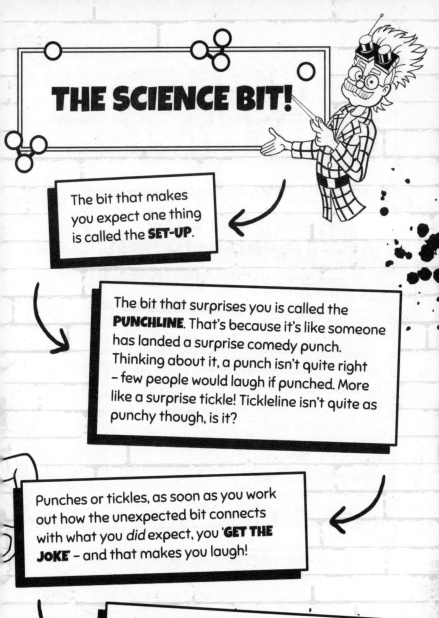

The bit that makes you expect one thing is called the **SET-UP**.

The bit that surprises you is called the **PUNCHLINE**. That's because it's like someone has landed a surprise comedy punch. Thinking about it, a punch isn't quite right – few people would laugh if punched. More like a surprise tickle! Tickleline isn't quite as punchy though, is it?

Punches or tickles, as soon as you work out how the unexpected bit connects with what you *did* expect, you '**GET THE JOKE**' – and that makes you laugh!

Jokes are like puzzles for your brain, and the reward you get for solving the puzzle is a good chuckle!

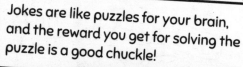

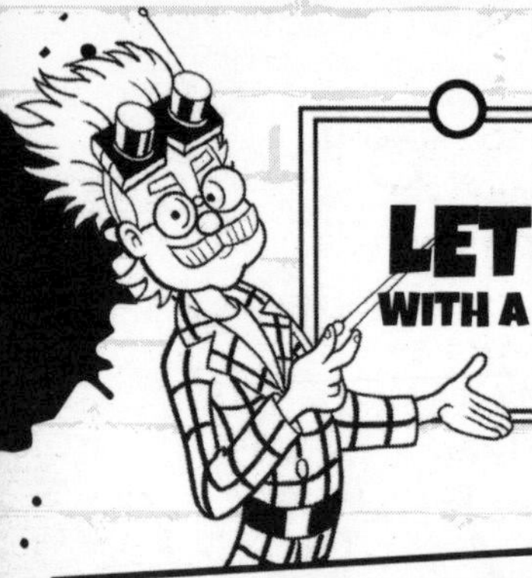

LET'S EXPERIMENT

WITH A JOKE TO TEST OUT THE THEORY!

WHY DID THE LION COMPLAIN WHEN HE WAS SERVED COOKED VEGGIES?

This is the **SET-UP** for the joke. Remember, the set-up's job is to make you EXPECT something. So, what do you expect to hear next?

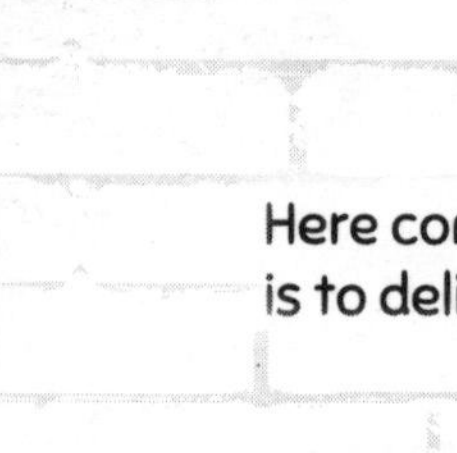

You probably expect the lion to demand a tasty wildebeest instead of all those boiled sprouts, carrots and cabbage, right?

Here comes the **PUNCHLINE** and its job is to deliver the unexpected bit . . .

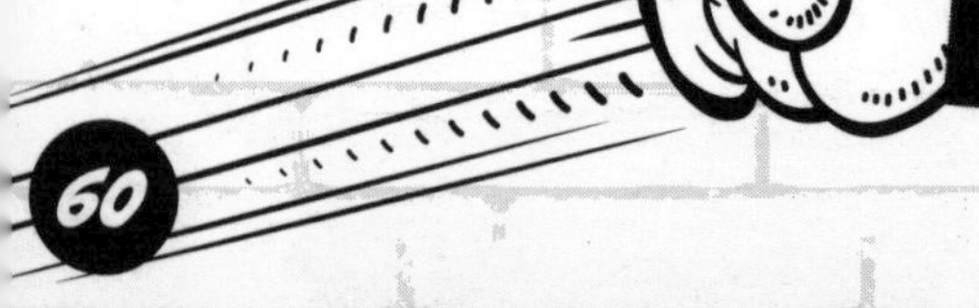

HE PREFERS THEM ROAR!

The secret is that ROAR and RAW are something called '**HOMOPHONES**' – words that sound the same but have different spellings and meanings.

These are great for writing and telling jokes because you can trick people by swapping homophones to surprise them! Your brain recognises this happening, and it tries to find a connection.

A lion complaining that it doesn't like cooked vegetables is funny because you don't typically think of lions choosing vegetables at all for dinner.

You perhaps also think of the lion complaining to a waiter – again, hilarious!

The noise a lion makes when they're feeling a bit grumpy would most likely be a ROAR!

This is a silly joke. It's silly because it takes two things and smashes them together in an unexpected way.

SEE WHAT JOKES YOU CAN COME UP WITH THIS WAY!

ANOTHER GREAT WAY TO START WRITING JOKES IS BY ATTEMPTING TO CREATE A KNOCK-KNOCK GAG. THESE JOKES ARE ALWAYS CREATED THE SAME WAY, MAKING THEM PERFECT FOR BEGINNERS!

They're little conversations between two people separated by a door:

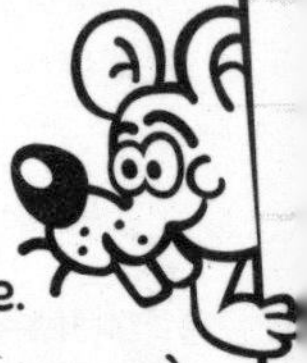

- The first and second lines are always the same.
- The third line is always a noun (someone's first name).
- The fourth line always asks for their surname.
- The fifth line is always a phrase that expands on the person's name in an unexpected way.

KNOCK-KNOCK

WHO'S THERE?

THEODORE.

THEODORE WHO?

THEODORE WASN'T OPEN, SO I HAD TO KNOCK!

The name on this joke is 'Theodore' and the phrase is 'Theodore wasn't open, so I had to knock'. This joke works because 'Theodore' sounds very similar to 'the door' but means something different.

HERE'S ANOTHER EXAMPLE:

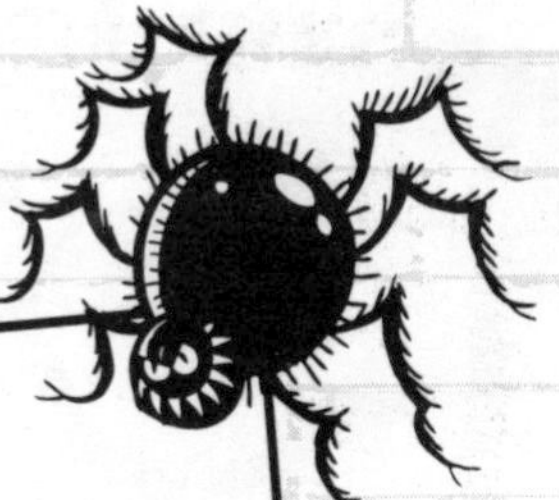

KNOCK-KNOCK
WHO'S THERE?
ALISON.
ALISON WHO?
ALISON WONDERLAND!

What not try writing knock-knock jokes using your own name? Ask classmates to try writing some too!

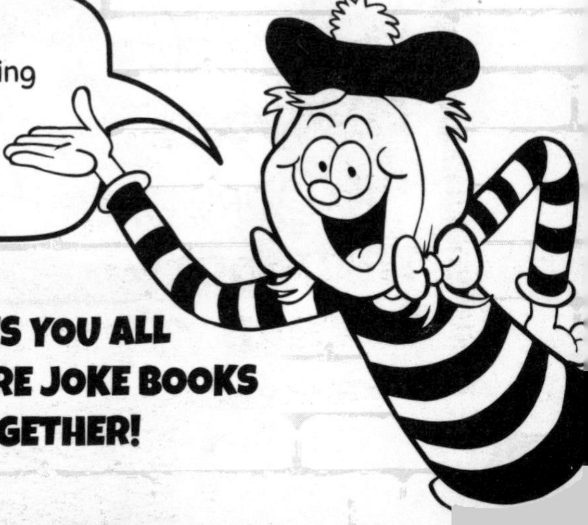

THE MORE JOKES YOU ALL WRITE, THE MORE JOKE BOOKS WE CAN FILL TOGETHER!

DASHER

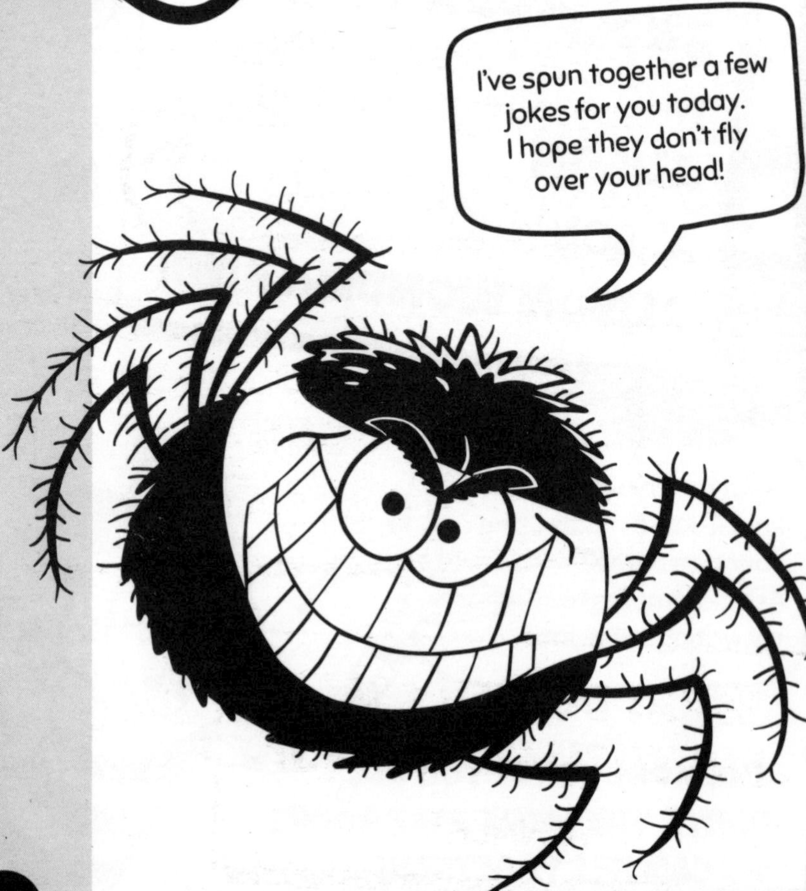
I've spun together a few jokes for you today. I hope they don't fly over your head!

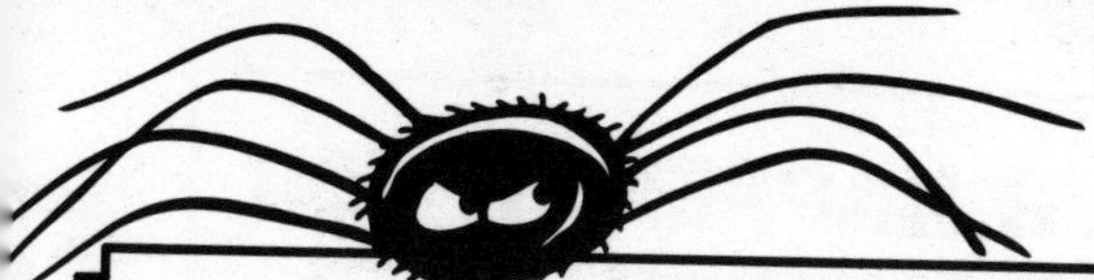

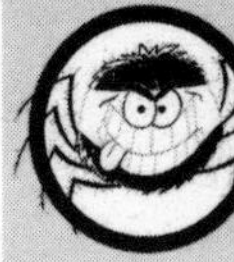

WHY DO SPIDERS SPIN WEBS?

BECAUSE THEY CAN'T KNIT!

WHAT DOES A WASP SAY WHEN IT'S HAVING AN IDENTITY CRISIS?

TO BEE OR NOT TO BEE!

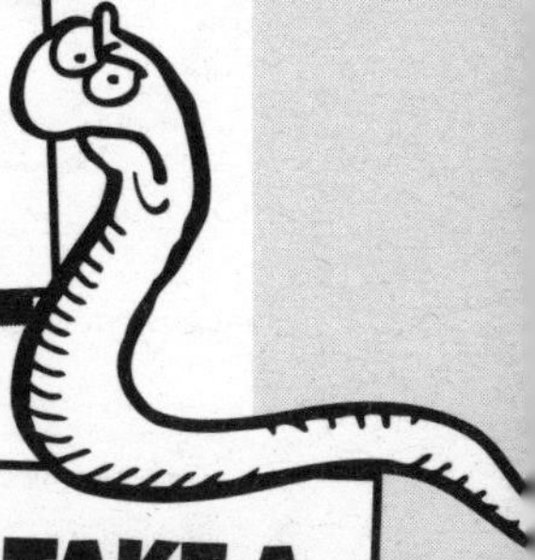

WHERE DO YOU TAKE A SICK HORNET?

TO THE WASP–ITAL!

WHAT DO YOU CALL A FLY WITH NO WINGS?

A WALK!

WHAT HAPPENS IF YOU EAT CATERPILLARS?

YOU GET BUTTERFLIES IN YOUR TUMMY!

WHAT INSECT IS THE MOST UNTIDY?

THE LITTERBUG!

WHY DID THE SNAIL CROSS THE ROAD?

TO GET AWAY FROM THESE JOKES?

I'LL LET YOU KNOW WHEN HE GETS HERE!

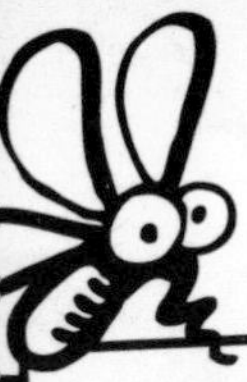

WHAT INSECT RUNS AWAY FROM EVERYTHING?

A FLEA!

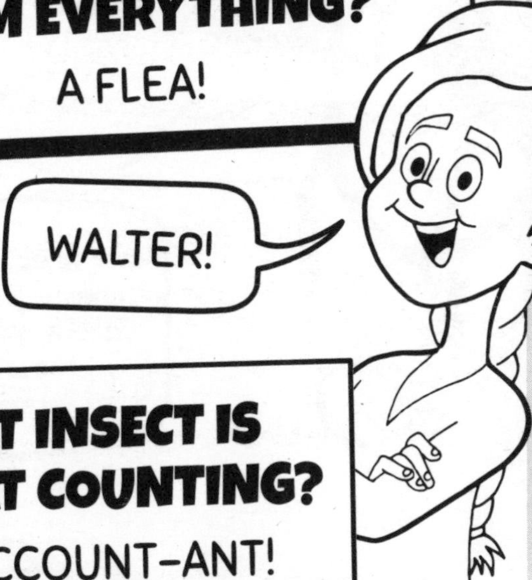
WALTER!

WHAT INSECT IS GOOD AT COUNTING?

THE ACCOUNT–ANT!

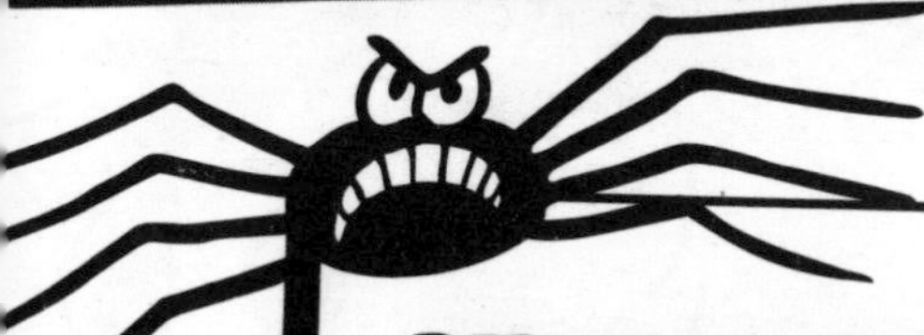

DID YOU HEAR ABOUT THE SPIDER WHO ATE THE FLY?

HE WAS A REAL BUZZ KILL!

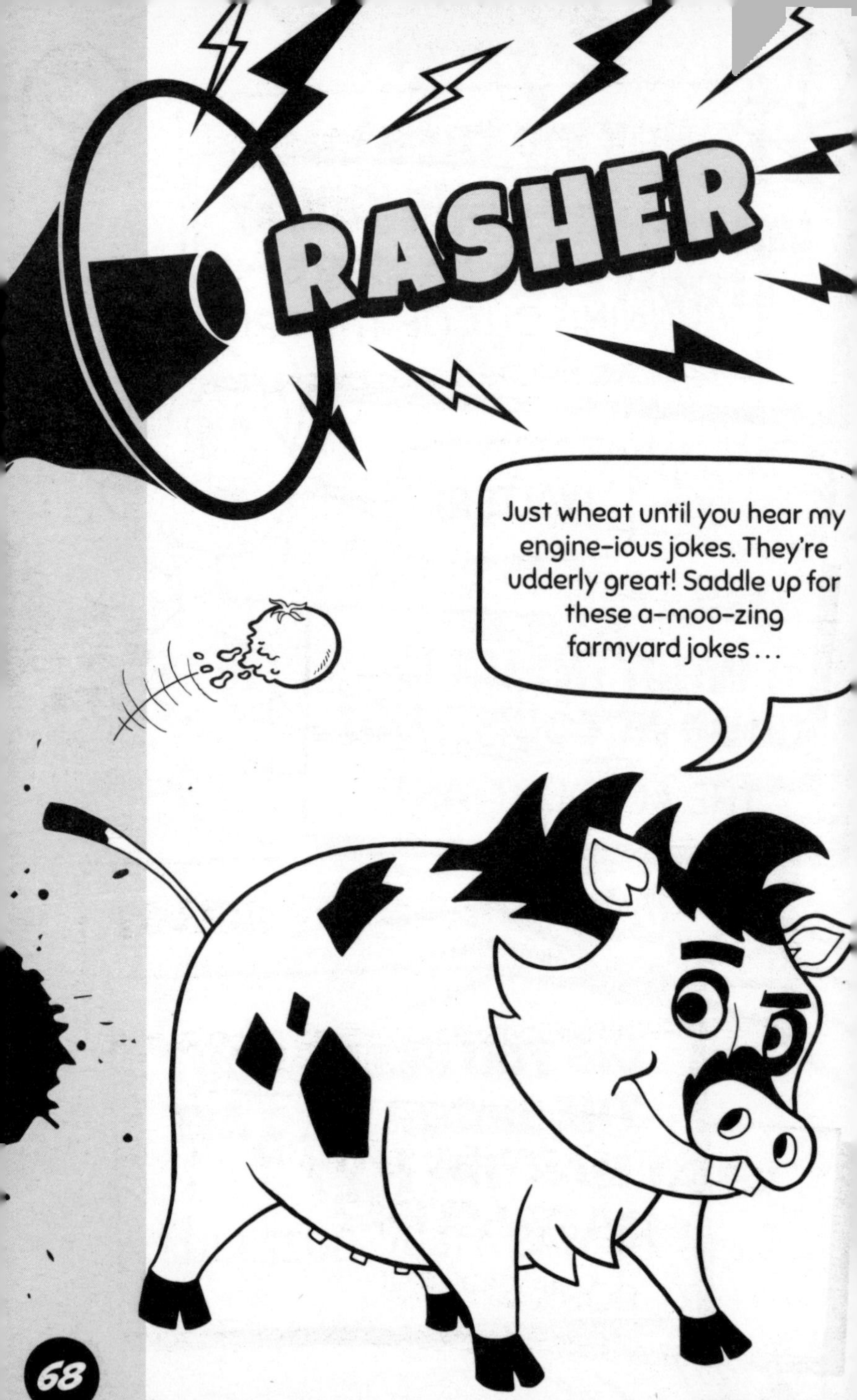
RASHER
Just wheat until you hear my engine-ious jokes. They're udderly great! Saddle up for these a-moo-zing farmyard jokes . . .

WHY DID THE FARMER CALL HIS PIG 'INK'?

BECAUSE IT WAS ALWAYS RUNNING OUT OF THE PEN!

WHY ARE PIGS BAD DRIVERS?

THEY'RE ALL ROAD HOGS!

HOW DO HORSES SAY HELLO?

HAY!

WHAT MARTIAL ART DO PIGS PRACTISE?

PORK CHOPS!

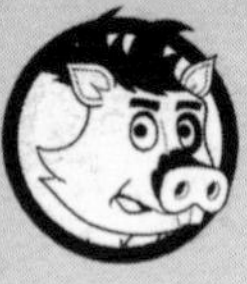

WHAT'S A SCARECROW'S FAVOURITE FRUIT?

STRAW–BERRIES!

WHY DID THE CHICK GET SENT OFF DURING THE FOOTBALL GAME?

IT COMMITTED A FOWL!

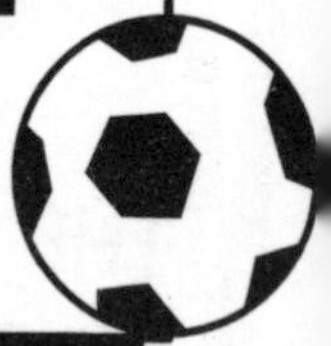

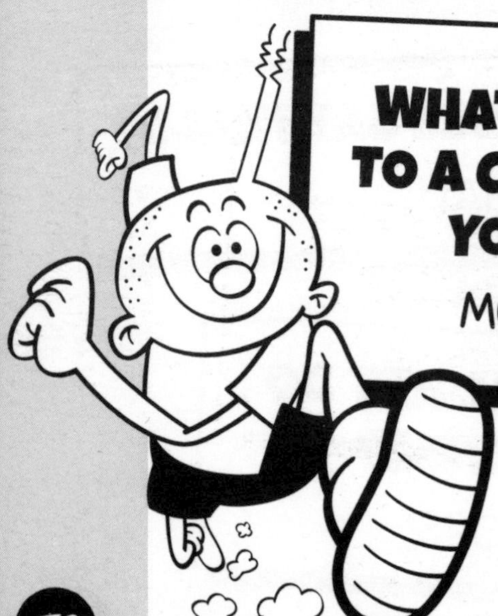

WHAT DO YOU SAY TO A COW THAT'S IN YOUR WAY?

MOOOOOVE!

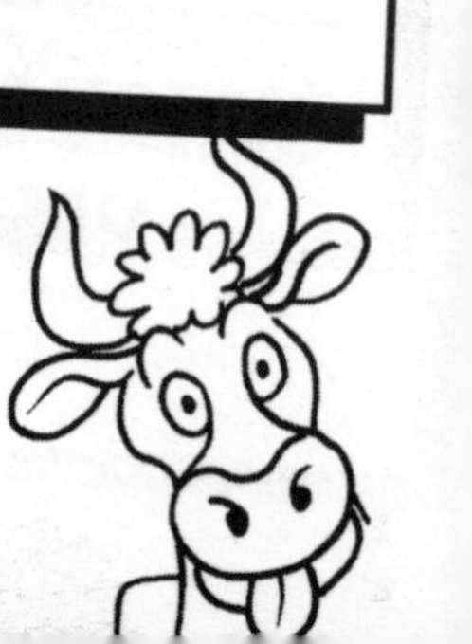

WHERE DOES A FARMER GET HIS MEDICINE?

THE FARM-ACIST!

WHAT DOES A FARMER TALK ABOUT WHILE MILKING HIS COWS?

UDDER NONSENSE!

WHO TELLS THE BEST FARMER JOKES?

COMEDI-HENS!

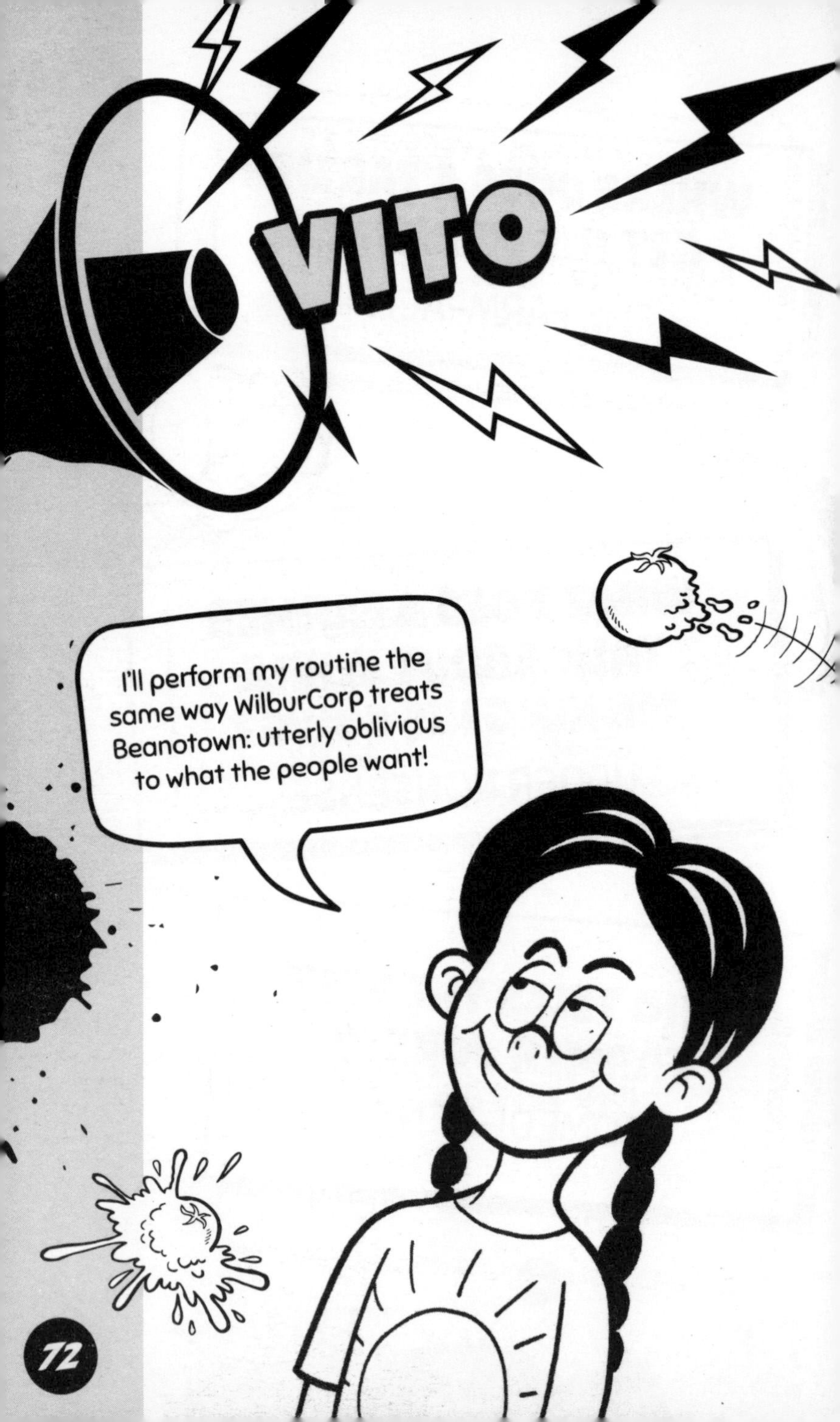
VITO
I'll perform my routine the same way WilburCorp treats Beanotown: utterly oblivious to what the people want!

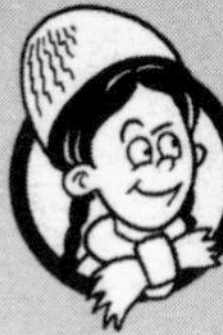

WHAT DO YOU CALL DOGS WHO DIG UP ANCIENT ARTEFACTS?

BARKAEOLOGISTS!

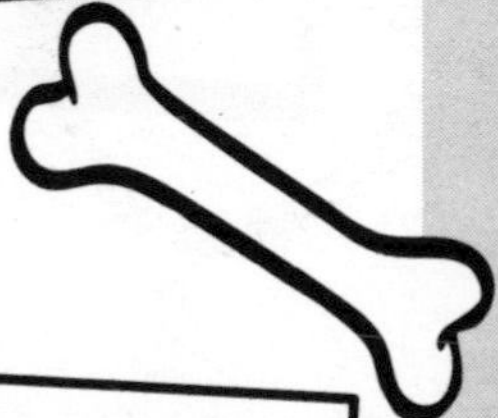

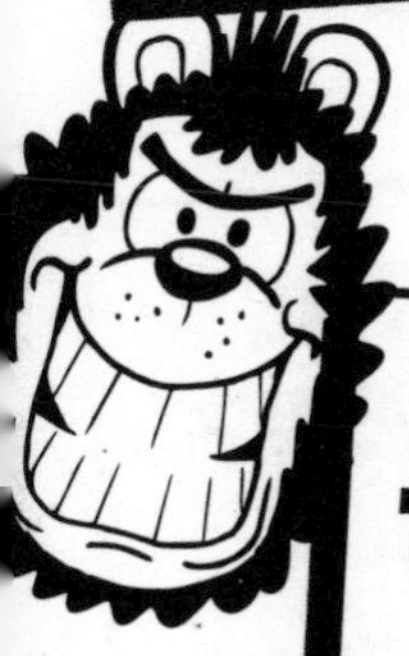

HOW DO BIKES HELP THE ENVIRONMENT?

BY RE-CYCLING!

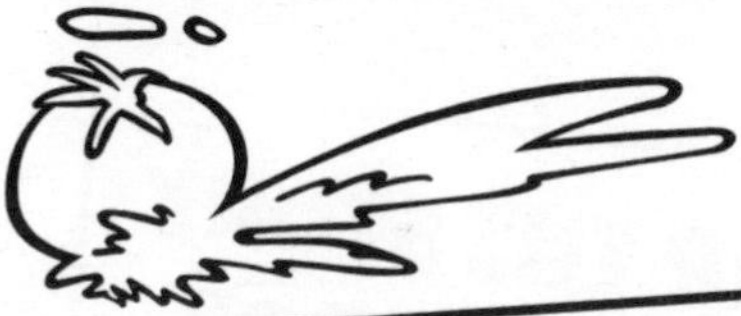

WHY IS MAGMA SO TRENDY?

IT WAS LAVA
BEFORE IT WAS COOL!

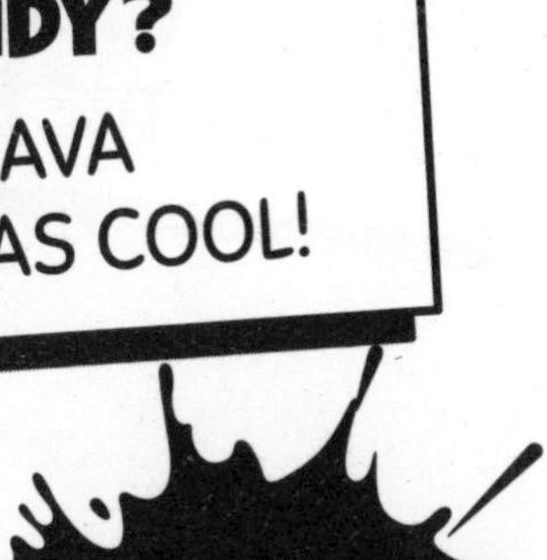

WHAT DO CLOUDS DO WHEN THEY BECOME RICH?

THEY MAKE IT RAIN!

WHY DID THE WHALE BLUSH?

IT SAW THE OCEAN'S BOTTOM!

DID YOU HEAR THE STORY ABOUT THE TORNADO?

THERE WAS A TWIST AT THE END!

WHY WAS THE GEOLOGIST SO CALM?

SHE WAS VERY DOWN TO EARTH!

SHE'D FALLEN ASLEEP DURING THIS SET!

HOW DOES THE RAIN TIE ITS SHOES?

WITH A RAIN-BOW!

WHAT'S THE BEST WAY TO ORGANISE A SPACE PARTY?

PLAN-ET EARLY!

FREDDY BROWN

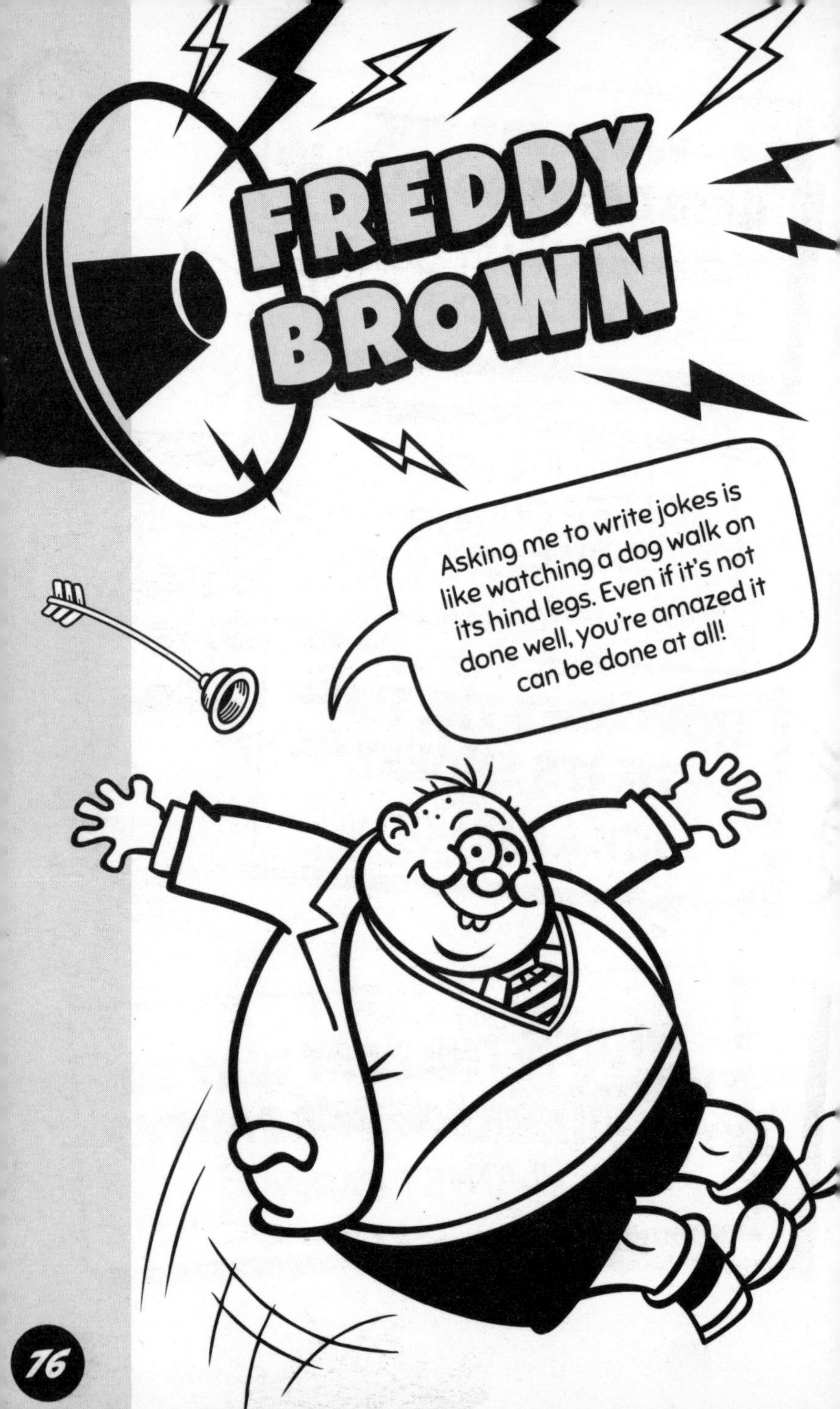
Asking me to write jokes is like watching a dog walk on its hind legs. Even if it's not done well, you're amazed it can be done at all!

WHAT ALWAYS SITS IN A CORNER BUT CAN MOVE ALL ROUND THE WORLD?

A STAMP!

WHAT DID THE LLAMA SAY WHEN ASKED IF THEY WANTED TO GO ON HOLIDAY?

ALPACA MY BAGS!

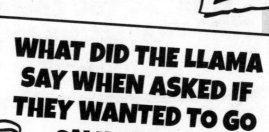

WHAT DO YOU CALL A TURKEY ON THE DAY AFTER THANKSGIVING?

LUCKY!

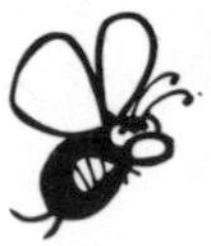

WHERE DO BEES GO ON THEIR HOLIDAYS?

STINGAPORE!

WHAT DO YOU CALL A TIME-TRAVELLING COW?

DOCTOR MOO!

WHAT IS BROWN, HAIRY AND WEARS SUNGLASSES?

A COCONUT ON ITS SUMMER HOLIDAY!

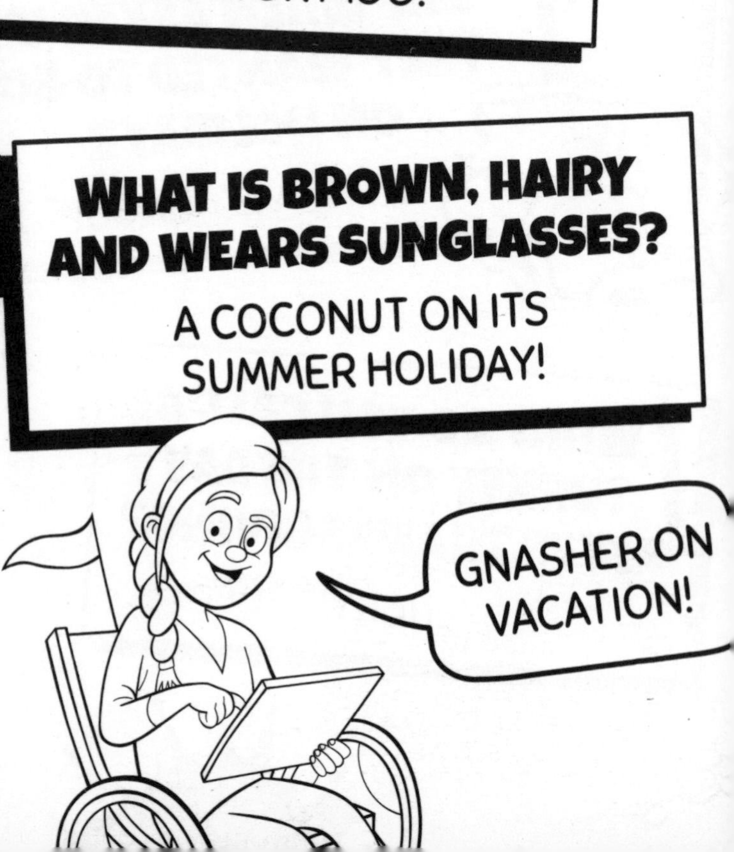
GNASHER ON VACATION!

WHAT'S RED, WHITE AND GREEN?

SANTA CLAUS WHEN HE'S TRAVEL SICK!

HOW DO YOU KNOW ELEPHANTS LOVE TO TRAVEL?

THEY ALWAYS PACKS THEIR TRUNKS!

WHY WAS THE BROOM LATE FOR ITS FLIGHT?

IT OVER–SWEPT!

CALAMITY JAMES

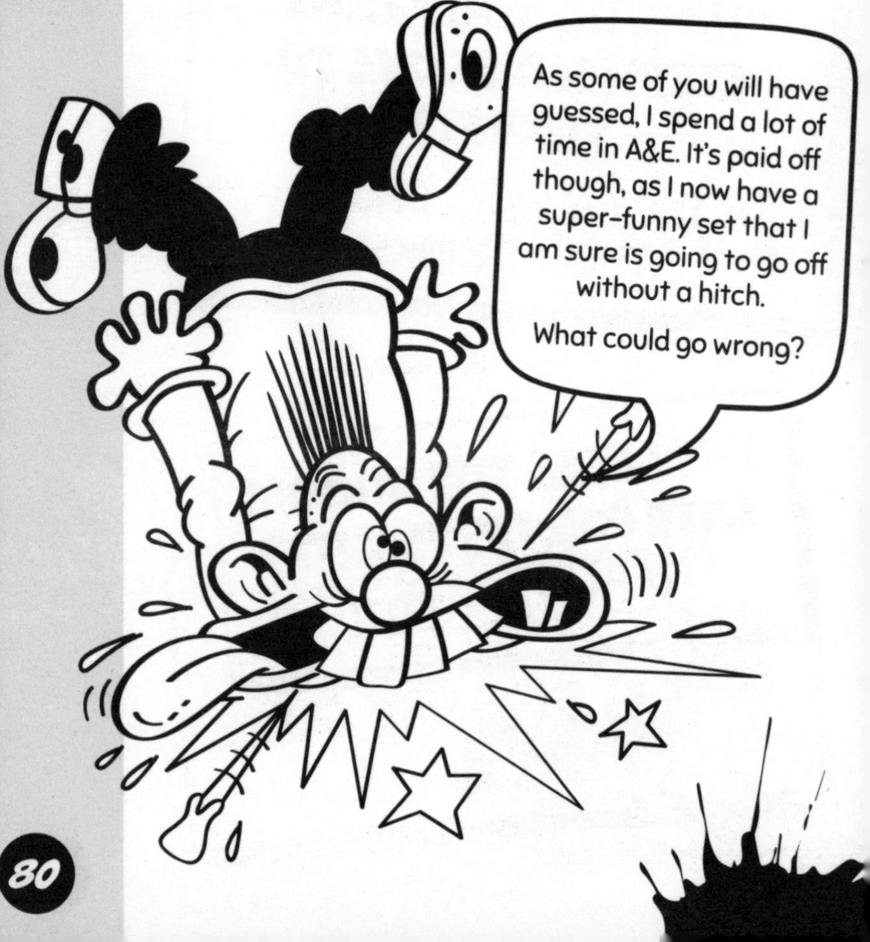
As some of you will have guessed, I spend a lot of time in A&E. It's paid off though, as I now have a super-funny set that I am sure is going to go off without a hitch.
What could go wrong?

WHICH IS FASTER, HOT OR COLD?

HOT. YOU CAN ALWAYS CATCH A COLD!

WHY DO NURSES CREEP AROUND AT NIGHT?

SO THEY DON'T WAKE THE SLEEPING PILLS!

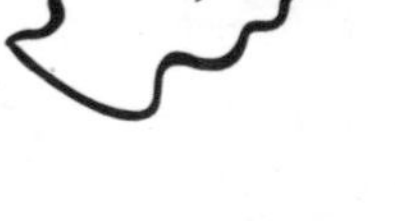

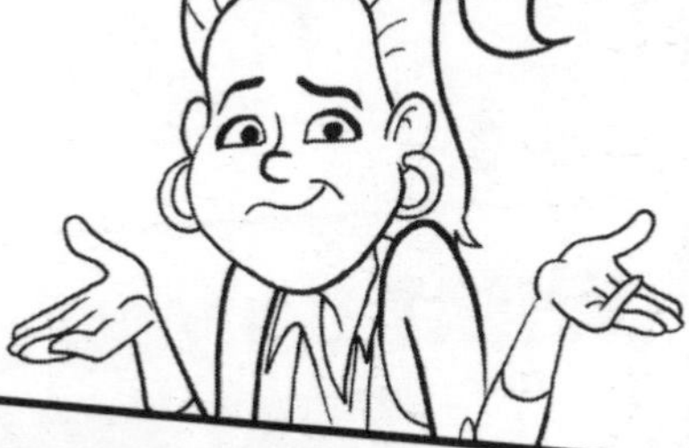

WHAT'S THE WORST PLACE IN THE HOSPITAL TO PLAY HIDE AND SEEK?

THE ICU!

I SOMETIMES GET HEARTBURN WHEN I EAT BIRTHDAY CAKE...

YOU'RE SUPPOSED TO TAKE THE CANDLES OFF FIRST!

WHAT DO YOU CALL A DUCK THAT WORKS IN A HOSPITAL?

A HEALTH QUACKTITIONER!

DID YOU HEAR ABOUT THE PATIENT WHO LOST HIS WHOLE LEFT SIDE?

THEY WERE ALL RIGHT IN THE END!

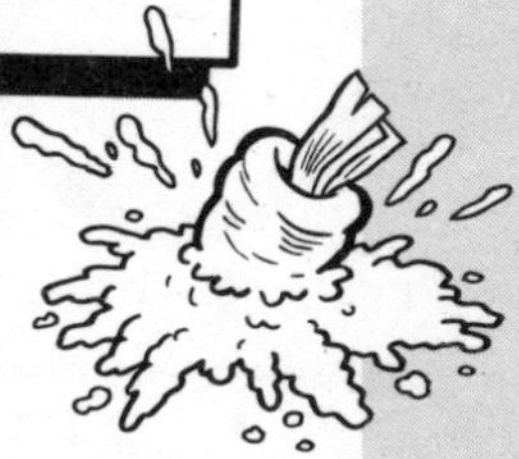

WHY DO NURSES CARRY RED PENS?

IN CASE THEY HAVE TO DRAW BLOOD!

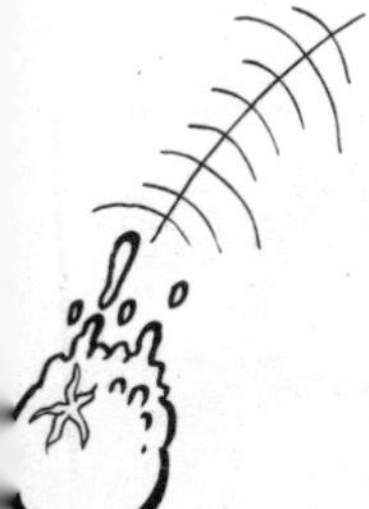

NEVER LIE TO AN X-RAY TECHNICIAN...

THEY CAN SEE STRAIGHT THROUGH YOU!

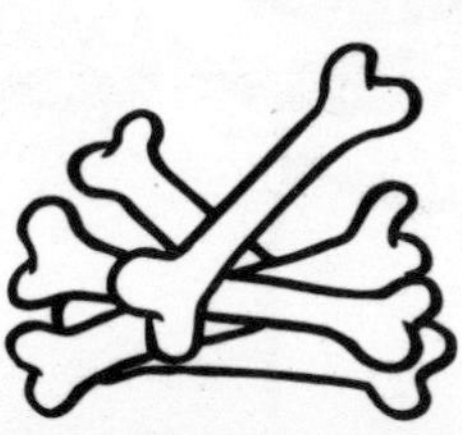

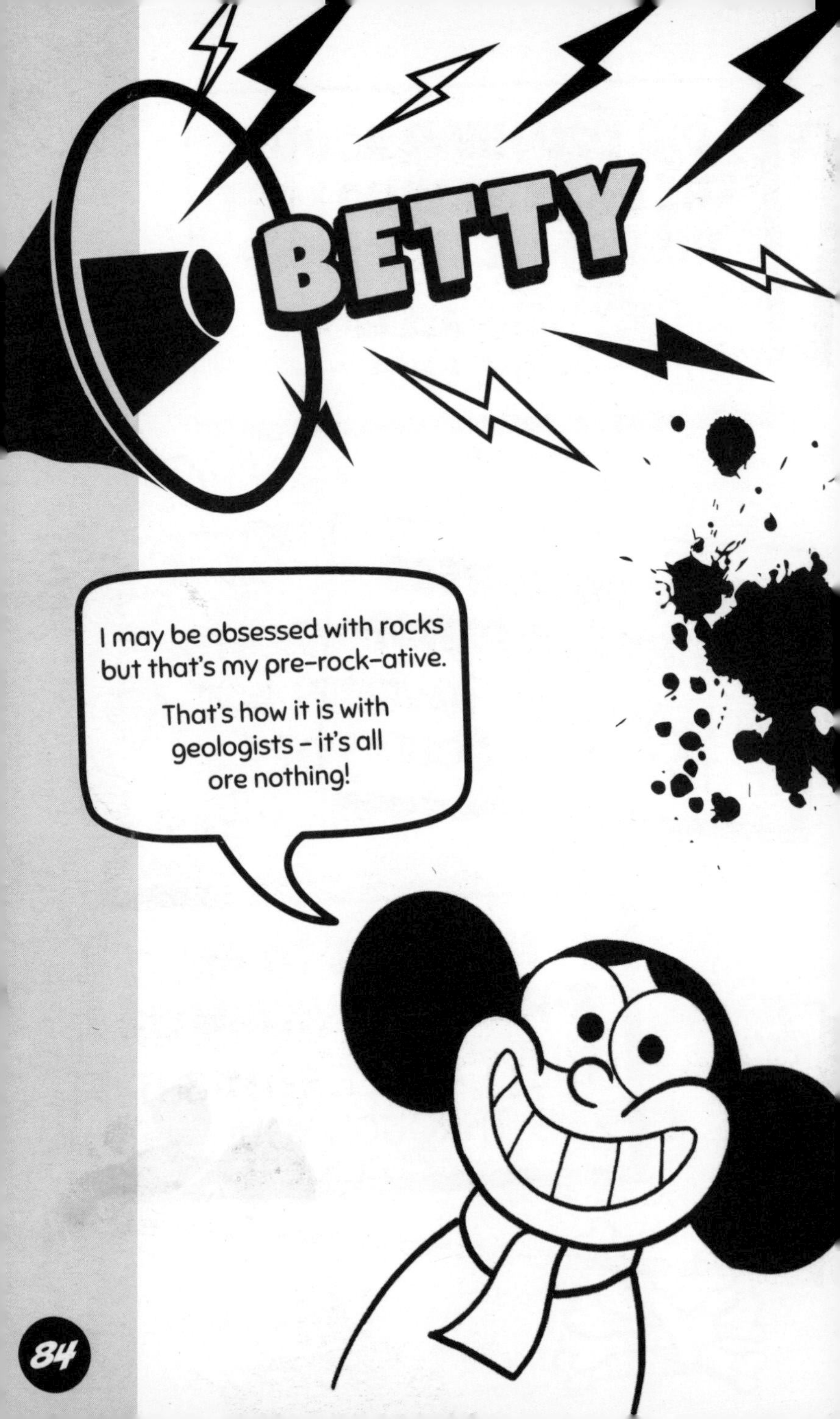
BETTY
I may be obsessed with rocks but that's my pre-rock-ative.
That's how it is with geologists – it's all ore nothing!

WHAT DID THE SEA SAY TO THE SHORE?

NOTHING, IT JUST WAVED!

WHY ARE MOUNTAINS THE FUNNIEST PLACE TO TRAVEL TO?

BECAUSE THEY'RE HILL AREAS!

HOW DOES A FOX KNOW WHEN IT'S GOING TO RAIN?

IT CHECKS THE WEATHER FUR-CAST!

WHAT'S THE BEST THING ABOUT SWITZERLAND?

I DON'T KNOW,
BUT THE FLAG IS A BIG PLUS!

YOU'RE NOT
TELLING
JOKES THERE!

IF YOU LIVE IN AN IGLOO, WHAT'S THE WORST THING ABOUT GLOBAL WARMING?

NO PRIVACY!

WHAT DO YOU CALL THE LITTLE RIVERS THAT FLOW INTO THE NILE?

JUVE-NILES!

WHAT DO FASHIONABLE MOUNTAINS WEAR WHEN IT'S COLD?

AN ICE CAP!

WHY IS THE OCEAN SO STRONG?

BECAUSE IT HAS LOTS OF MUSSELS!

WHAT DO YOU CALL A COUNTRY POPULATED ENTIRELY BY DONKEYS?

AN ASS-ASINATION!

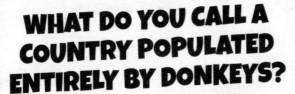

BASH STREET SCHOOL!

SERGEANT SLIPPER

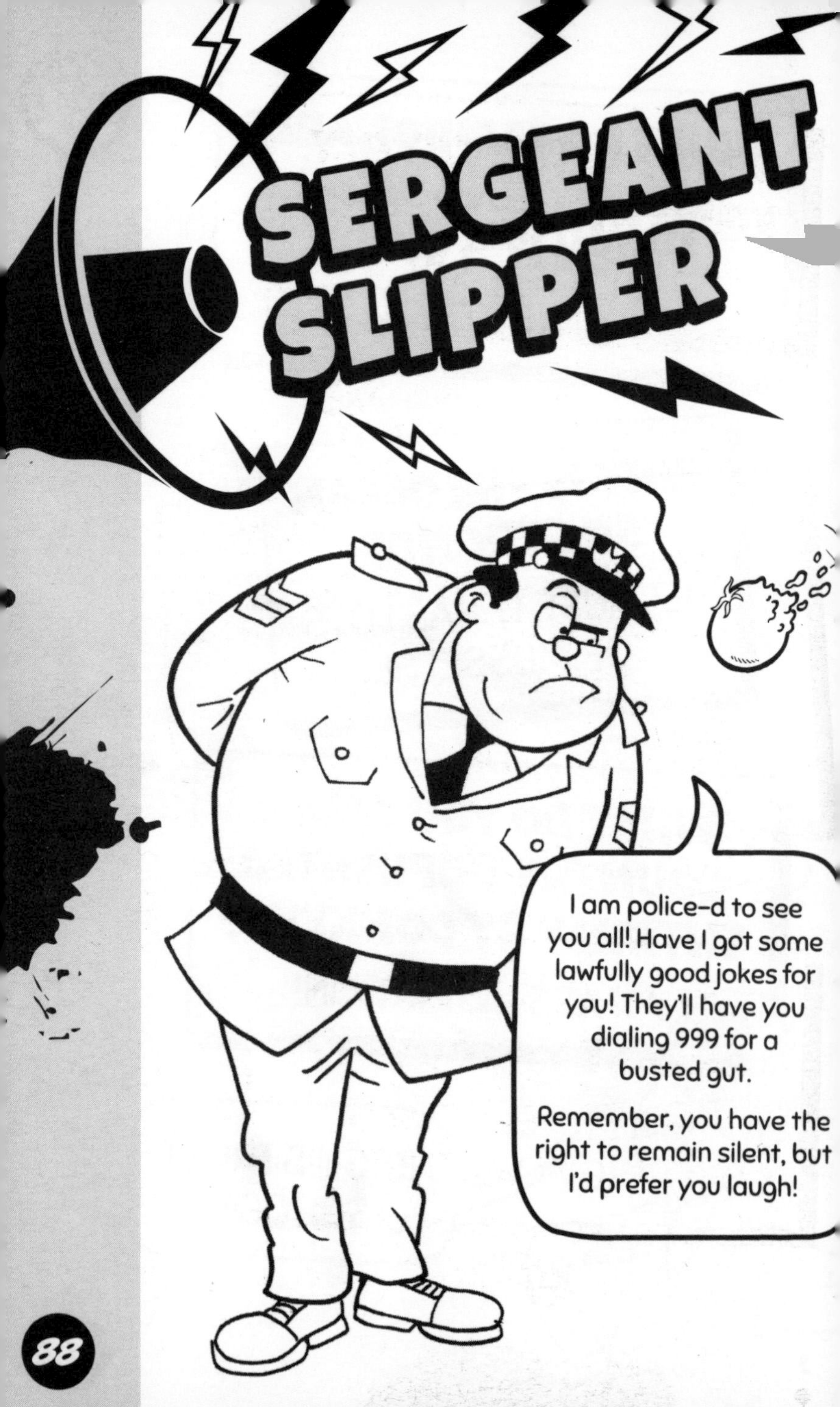
I am police-d to see you all! Have I got some lawfully good jokes for you! They'll have you dialing 999 for a busted gut.
Remember, you have the right to remain silent, but I'd prefer you laugh!

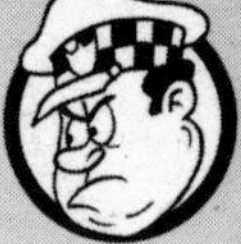

WHY DID THE CAT GET FINED BY THE POLICE?

IT LITTER-ED!

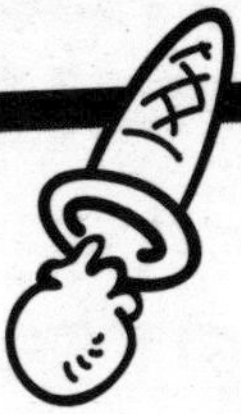

WHAT DID THE POLICE OFFICER SAY TO HIS TUMMY?

YOU'RE UNDER A VEST!

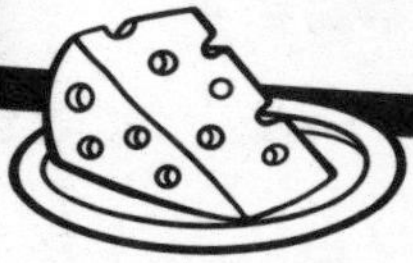

WHY DID THE POLICE ARREST THE DUVET?

THEY KNEW IT WAS COVERING SOMETHING UP!

SOMEONE KEEPS ON STEALING WHEELS FROM POLICE CARS...

THEY'RE WORKING TIRELESSLY TO CATCH THEM!

WHY WAS THE ARTIST UPSET?

THEY HAD TO SIT THROUGH THIS SET?

SHE WAS BEING FRAMED FOR MURDER!

DID YOU HEAR ABOUT THE THIEF WHO STOLE A LAMP?

HE GOT A VERY LIGHT SENTENCE!

SOMEONE STOLE SOME DOGS FROM A DOG WALKER...

THE POLICE HAVE NO LEADS!

WHICH POLICE UNIT GETS RID OF FLIES?

THE SWAT TEAM!

MRS SPLINT

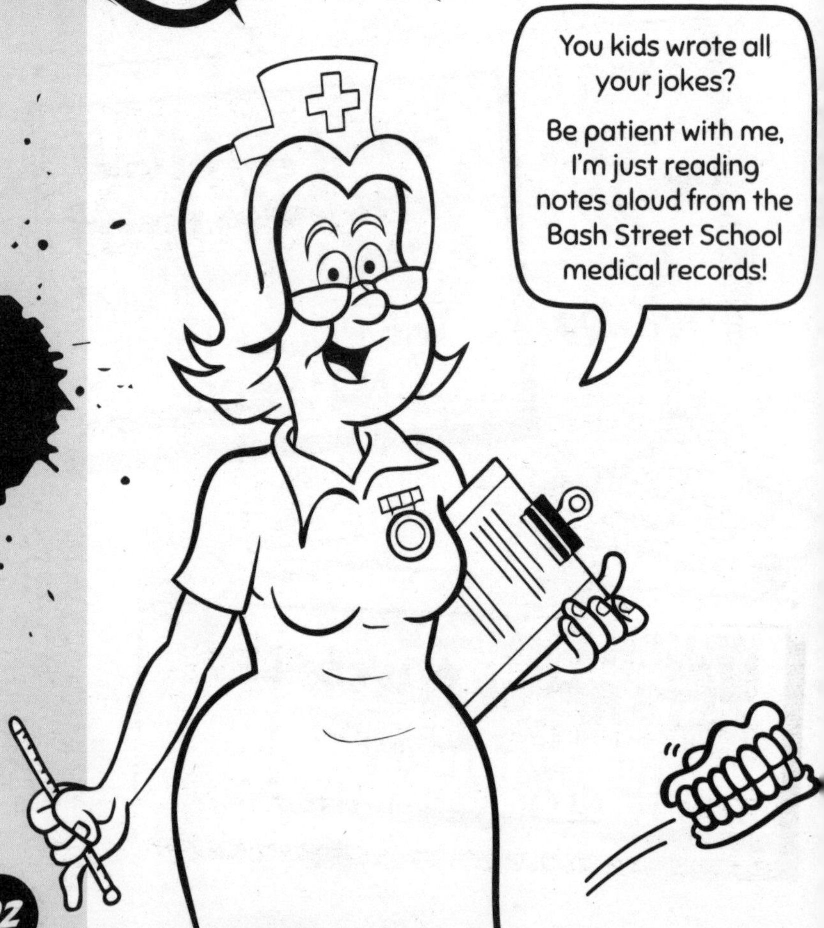
You kids wrote all your jokes?
Be patient with me, I'm just reading notes aloud from the Bash Street School medical records!

MRS SPLINT, MRS SPLINT, I THINK I'M A BRAIN!

DON'T WORRY, IT'S ALL IN YOUR HEAD.

MRS SPLINT, MRS SPLINT, THERE'S A PUPIL OUTSIDE THAT SAYS HE'S INVISIBLE.

WELL, TELL HIM I CAN'T SEE HIM RIGHT NOW!

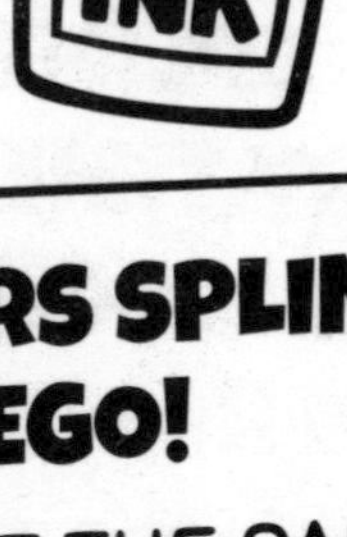
INVISIBLE
INK

MRS SPLINT, MRS SPLINT, I STOOD ON A LEGO!

TRY TO BLOCK OUT THE PAIN!

MRS SPLINT, MRS SPLINT, CAN YOU GIVE ME SOMETHING FOR MY WIND?

YES, HERE'S A KITE!

MRS SPLINT, MRS SPLINT, HOW LONG CAN A PERSON LIVE WITHOUT A BRAIN?

I DON'T KNOW ... HOW OLD ARE YOU?

MRS SPLINT, MRS SPLINT, EVERY TIME I DRINK A CUP OF TEA, I GET A STABBING PAIN IN MY EYE!

TRY TAKING THE SPOON OUT FIRST!

MRS SPLINT, MRS SPLINT, WILL THIS CREAM CLEAR UP MY SPOTS?

I DON'T MAKE RASH PROMISES!

MRS SPLINT, MRS SPLINT, AAA, EEE, I, OH! YOU . . .

I THINK YOU MAY HAVE IRRITABLE VOWEL SYNDROME!

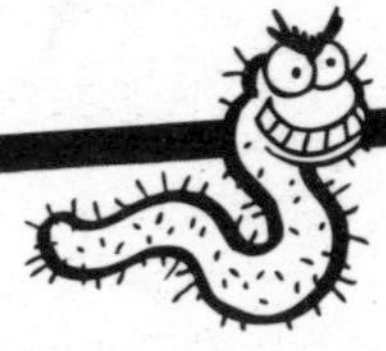

MRS SPLINT, MRS SPLINT, EVERY TIME I STAND UP QUICKLY I SEE MICKEY MOUSE, DONALD DUCK AND GOOFY!

HOW LONG HAVE YOU BEEN GETTING THESE DISNEY SPELLS?!

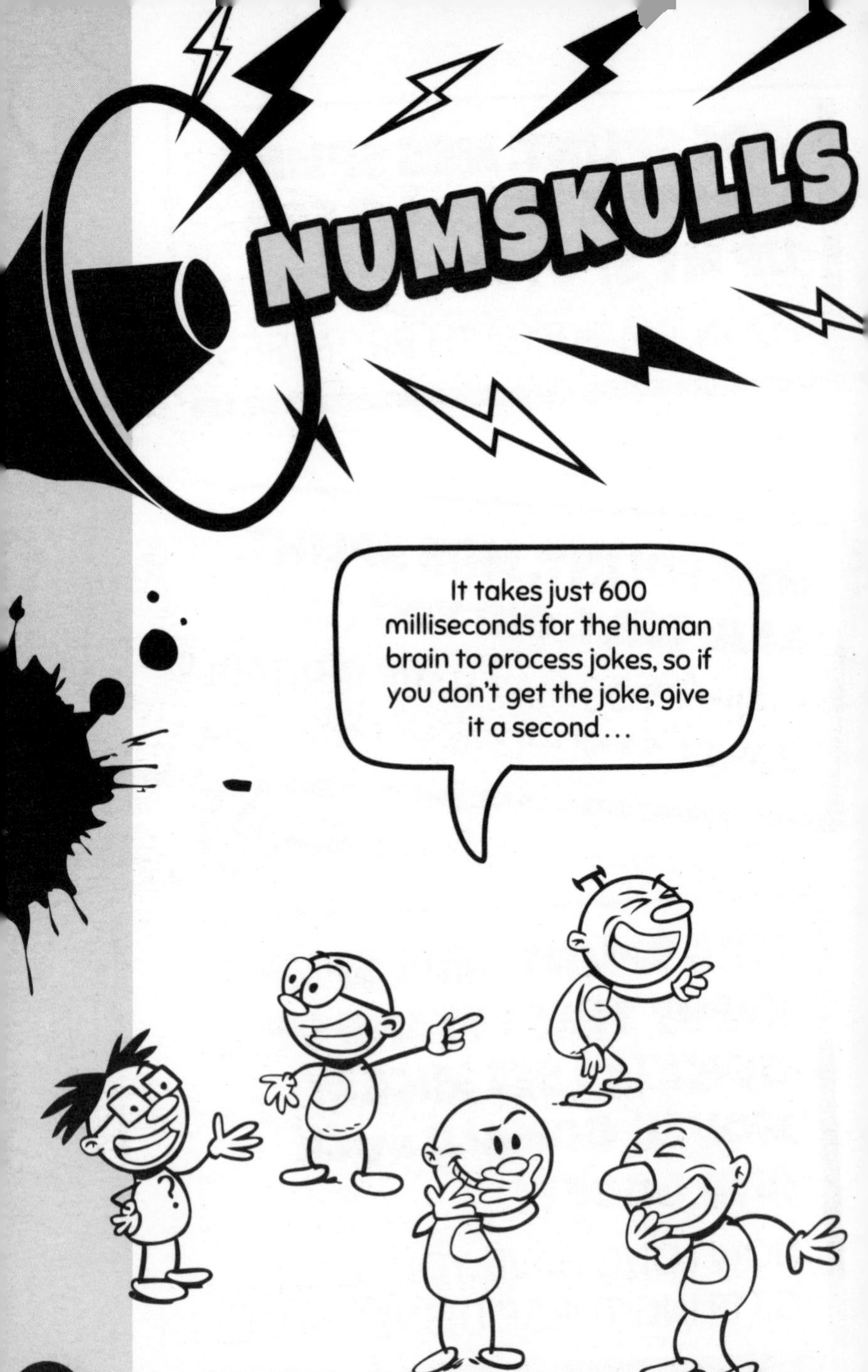
NUMSKULLS
It takes just 600 milliseconds for the human brain to process jokes, so if you don't get the joke, give it a second...

WHAT HAS FIVE FINGERS BUT ISN'T YOUR HAND?

MY HAND!

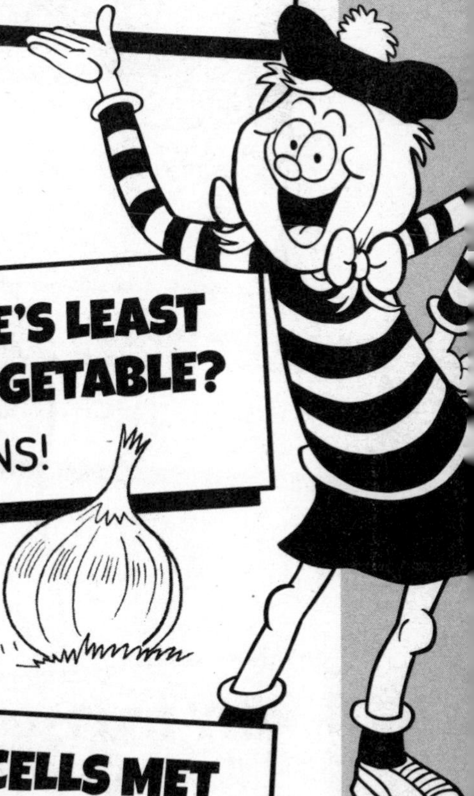

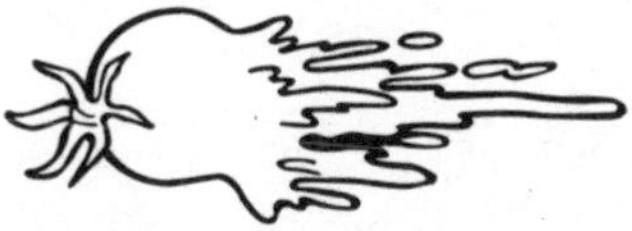

WHAT'S A TOE'S LEAST FAVOURITE VEGETABLE?

BUNIONS!

TWO BLOOD CELLS MET AND FELL IN LOVE . . .

ALAS, IT WAS ALL IN VEIN!

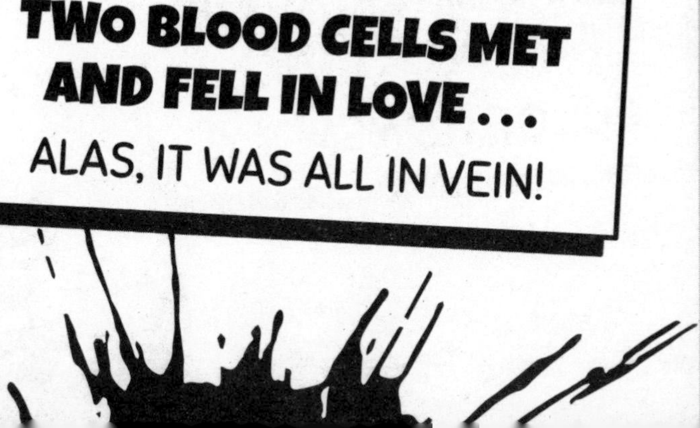

WHAT IS AN ANATOMIST'S FAVOURITE BOAT?

A BLOOD VESSEL!

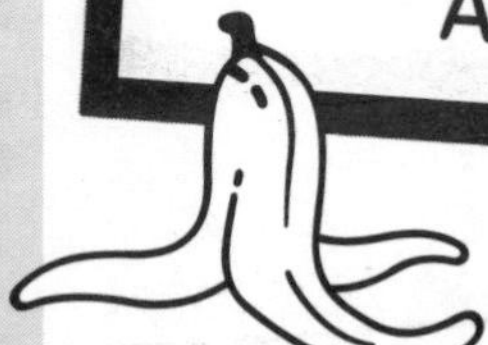

WHAT BONE ALWAYS LIES?

THE FIB-ULA!

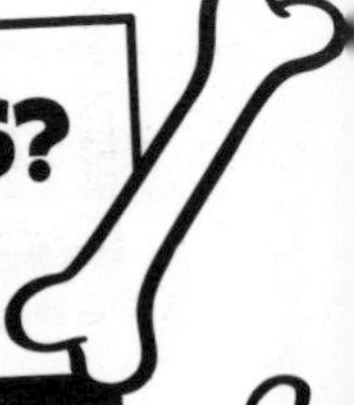

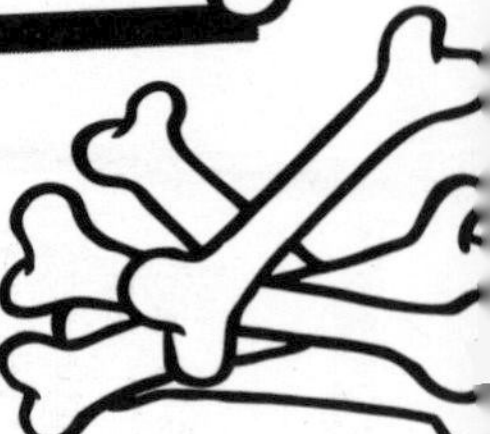

WHY DID THE BRAIN GO FOR A RUN?

TO JOG ITS MEMORY!

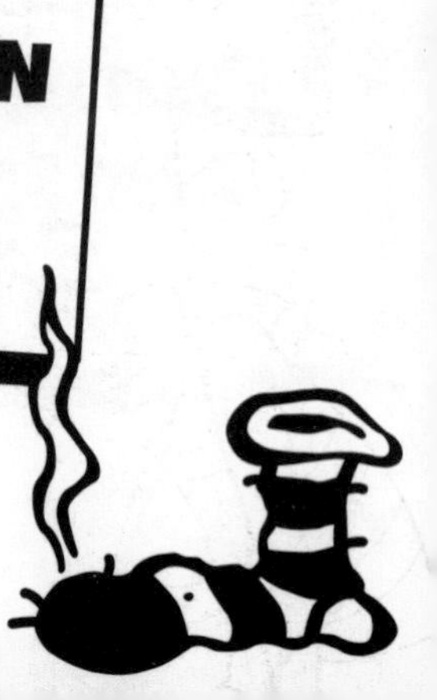

WHY ARE HEARTS SO GOOD AT DANCING?

THEY LOVE FEELING THE BEAT!

WHY WAS THE NOSE TIRED?

IT NEVER STOPPED RUNNING!

WHICH OF YOUR BONES IS THE BEST AT JOKES?

THE FUNNY BONE!

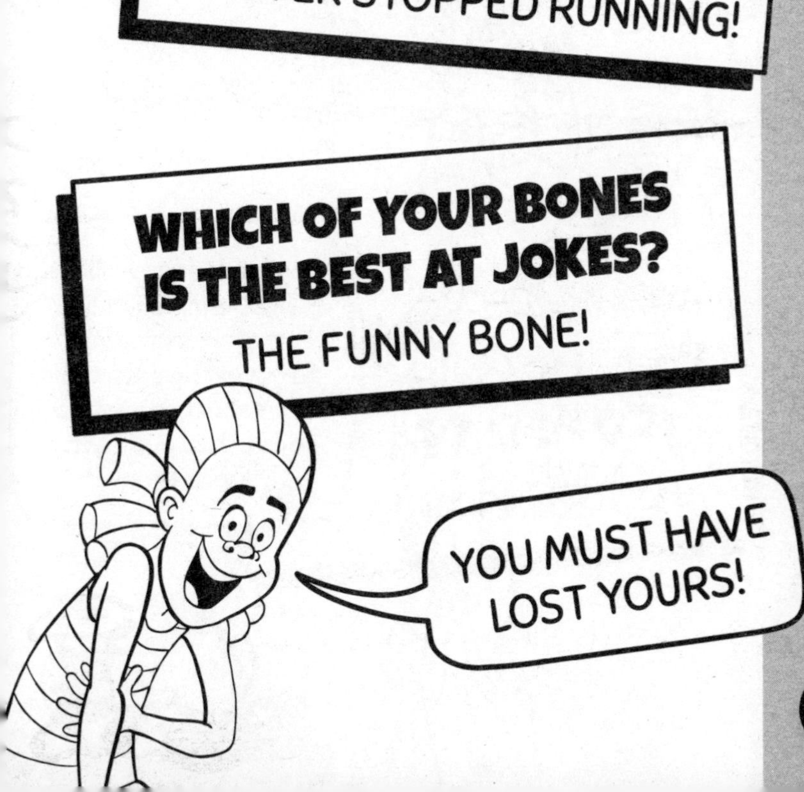
YOU MUST HAVE LOST YOURS!

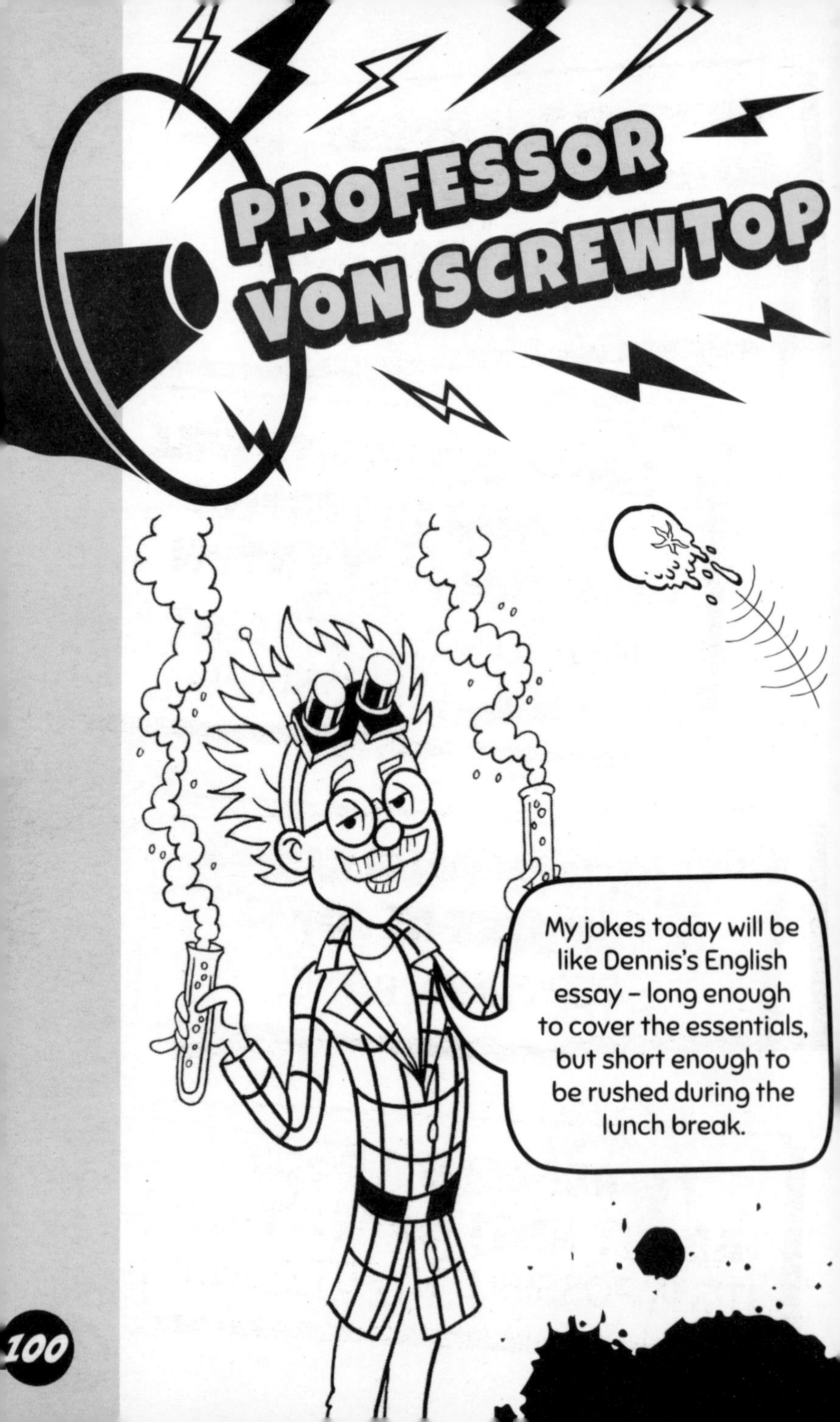
PROFESSOR VON SCREWTOP
My jokes today will be like Dennis's English essay – long enough to cover the essentials, but short enough to be rushed during the lunch break.

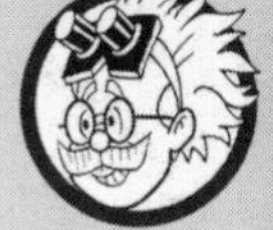

WHY DID THE ROBOT GO BACK TO SCHOOL?

HER SKILLS WERE A LITTLE RUSTY!

I HOPE SCIENTISTS WILL BE ABLE TO PERFECT HUMAN CLONING SOON . . .

IF NOT, I WON'T BE ABLE TO LIVE WITH MYSELF!

HOW OFTEN CAN YOU JOKE ABOUT CHEMISTRY?

PERIODICALLY!

I'M READING A BOOK ABOUT ANTI-GRAVITY . . .

IT'S IMPOSSIBLE TO PUT DOWN!

WHAT DO YOU DO WITH A SICK CHEMIST?

IF YOU CAN'T HELIUM AND YOU CAN'T CURIUM, THEN YOU MAY AS WELL BARIUM!

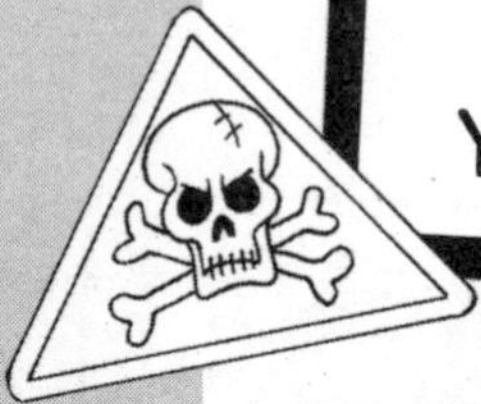

WHY WAS THE THERMOSTAT SO SMART?

IT HAD SEVERAL DEGREES!

WHAT'S THE DULLEST ELEMENT?

BOHRIUM!

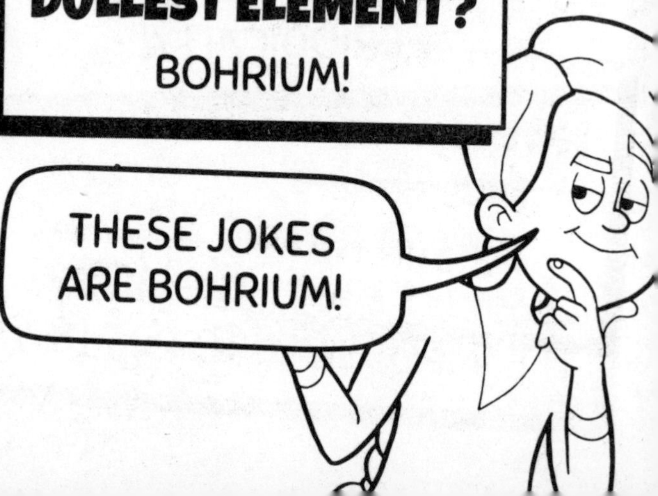
THESE JOKES ARE BOHRIUM!

WHY DO PEOPLE HATE GRAVITY?

IT'S ALWAYS PULLING THEM DOWN!

WHAT DID ONE PHYSICIST SAY WHEN HE WANTED TO FIGHT ANOTHER PHYSICIST?

LET ME ATOM!

HOW DO BRAINS SAY HELLO?

A BRAIN WAVE!

RUBI VON SCREWTOP

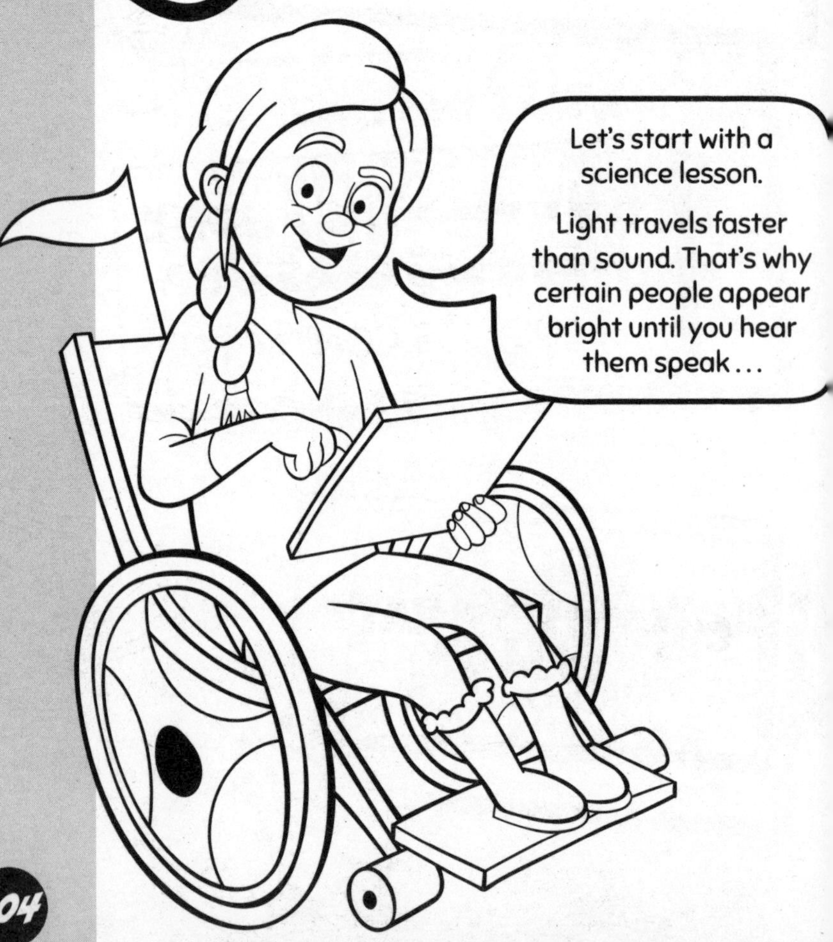
Let's start with a science lesson.
Light travels faster than sound. That's why certain people appear bright until you hear them speak . . .

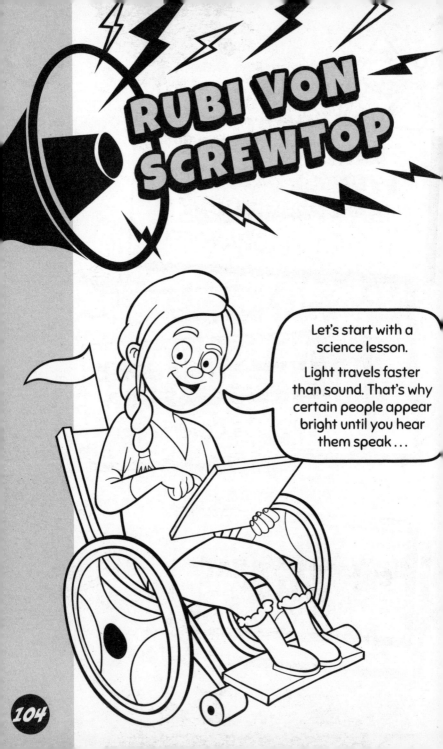

WHY SHOULD YOU NEVER USE 'BEEF STEW' AS A PASSWORD?

IT'S NOT STROGANOFF!

WHY WAS THE PHONE WEARING GLASSES?

IT LOST ITS CONTACTS!

WHAT DO COMPUTERS EAT?

MICROCHIPS!

WHY DID THE POWERPOINT CROSS THE ROAD?

TO GET TO THE NEXT SLIDE!

WHERE DO BIRDS STORE THEIR PHOTOS?

ON THE CLOUD!

WHAT DO BABY COMPUTERS CALL THEIR FATHERS?

DA-TA!

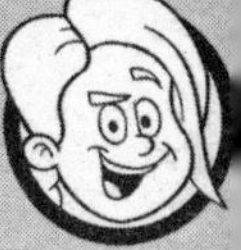

WHAT DO YOU CALL AN ONLINE POTATO?

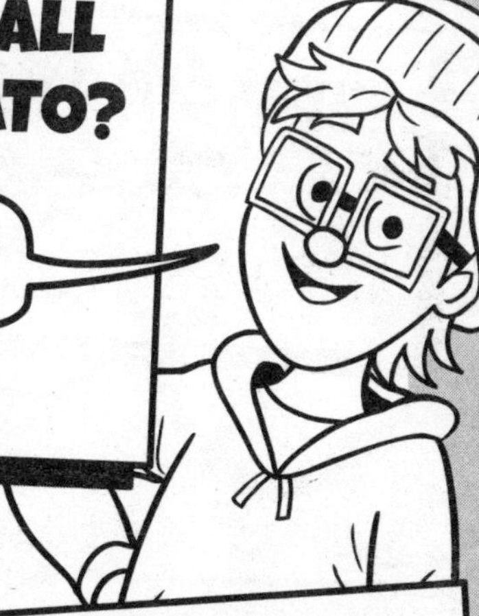
MY PARENTS?

A YOU-TUBER!

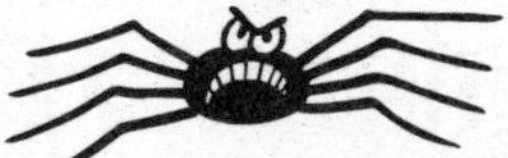

WHY SHOULD YOU NEVER GO CAMPING ON THE INTERNET?

THERE'S TOO MANY BUGS!

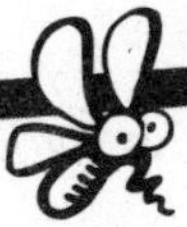

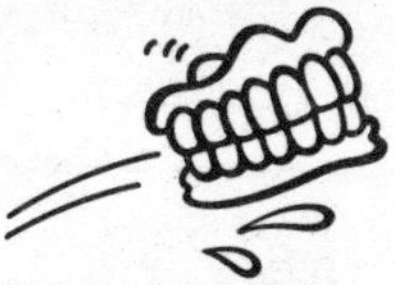

WHY COULDN'T THE VOLCANO GET ONLINE?

IT COULDN'T FIND A GOOD HOTSPOT!

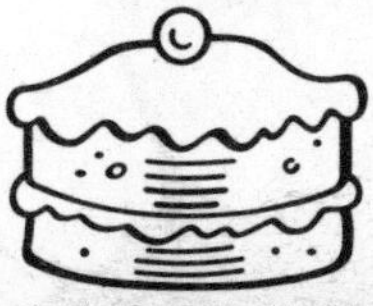

STEVIE STAR

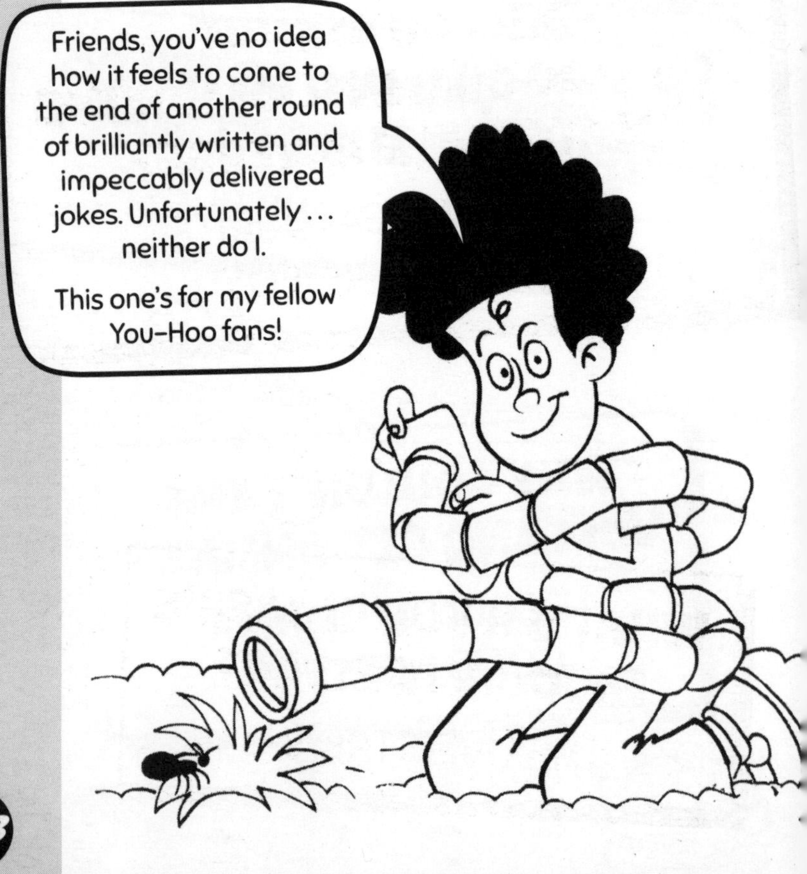
Friends, you've no idea how it feels to come to the end of another round of brilliantly written and impeccably delivered jokes. Unfortunately . . . neither do I.
This one's for my fellow You-Hoo fans!

WHAT DO YOU CALL A REALLY SATISFIED YOU-HOOER?

A CONTENT CREATOR!

DID YOU SEE THE YOU-HOO CHANNEL OF BOXING MATCHES IN REVERSE?

THEY'RE MY FAVOURITE UNBOXING VIDEOS!

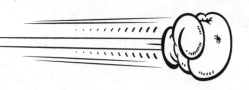

WHAT'S A YOU-HOOER'S FAVOURITE RIVER?

THE LIVE STREAM!

DID YOU SEE THE YOU-HOO VIDEO OF THE GORILLA OPENING BANANAS?

IT'S SUPER APE-PEELING!

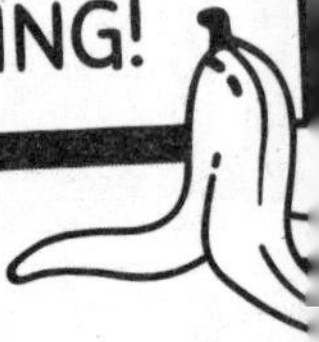

WHAT HAPPENED WHEN DRACULA UPLOADED COPYRIGHTED CONTENT TO YOU-HOO?

A COUNT SUSPENDED!

WHY WAS THE YOU-HOOER SO GOOD AT HANDLING COWS?

HE WAS USED TO MILKING CONTENT!

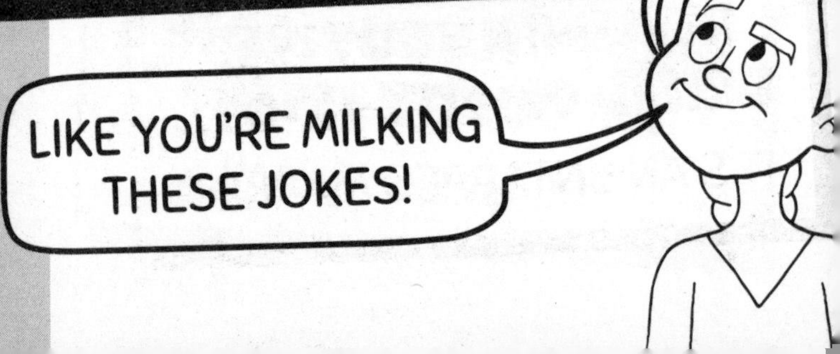
LIKE YOU'RE MILKING THESE JOKES!

I JUST STARTED A YOU-HOO CHANNEL ABOUT VIRUSES...

I'M A REAL INFLUENZA!

HOW MANY YOU-HOOERS DOES IT TAKE TO CHANGE A LIGHT BULB?

HIT LIKE AND SUBSCRIBE TO FIND OUT!

NO THANKS!

I'M GOING TO START REVIEWING BOTTLED WATER ON YOU-HOO...

IT'S AN UNTAPPED MARKET!

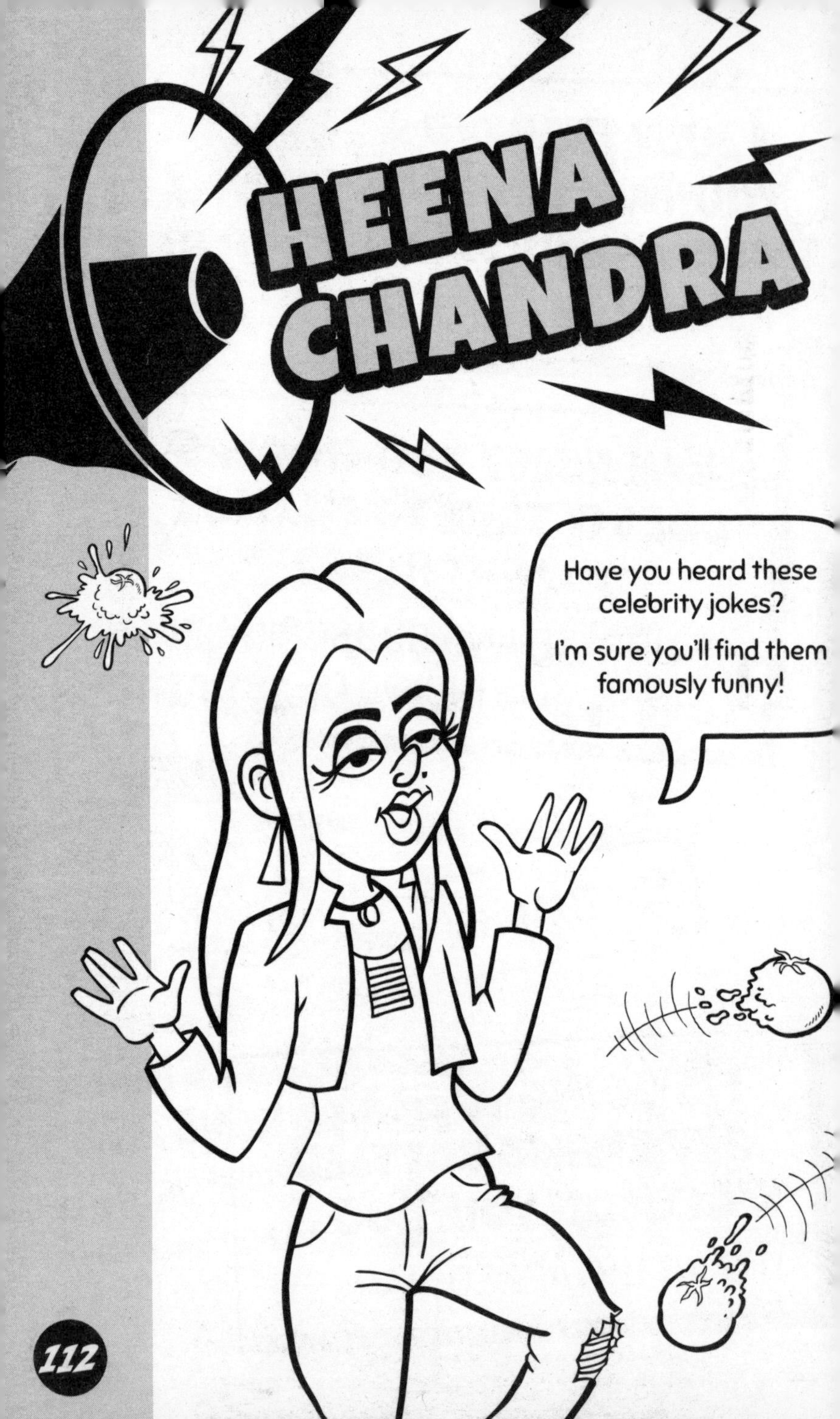
HEENA CHANDRA
Have you heard these celebrity jokes?
I'm sure you'll find them famously funny!

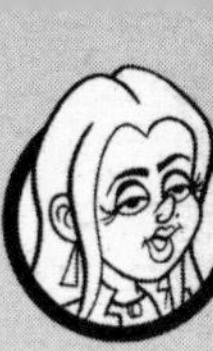

WHAT DOES A TREE DO BEFORE MEETING JOE WICKS?

IT LIMBERS UP READY TO WORK ON ITS TRUNK!

WHICH CELEB IS THE BEST AT FIXING THINGS?

SHAWN MENDES!

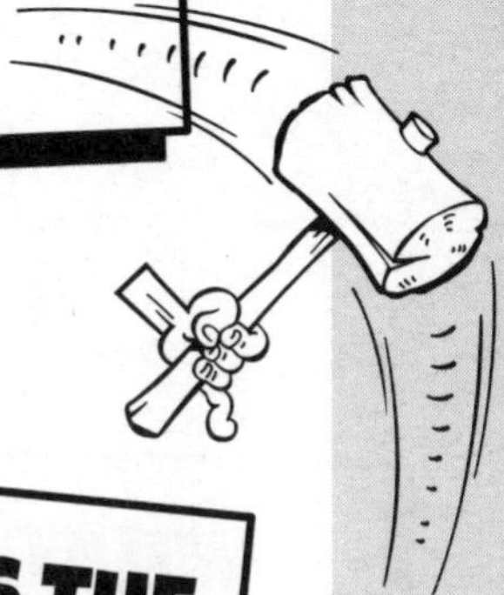

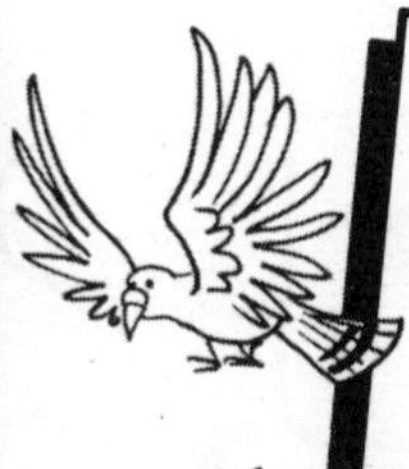

WHICH BIRD IS THE BEST AT SINGING?

THE TAYLOR SWIFT!

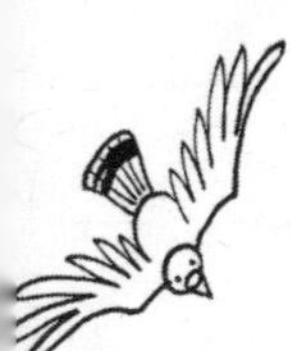

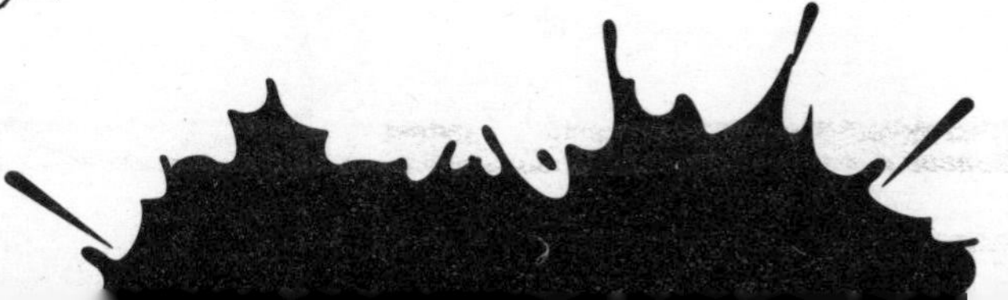

WHICH RAPPER TAKES THE MOST NAPS?

JAY ZZZZZZZ

DO YOU THINK DANIEL RADCLIFFE WOULD EVER PLAY A HOBBIT?

NO, BUT ELIJAH WOOD!

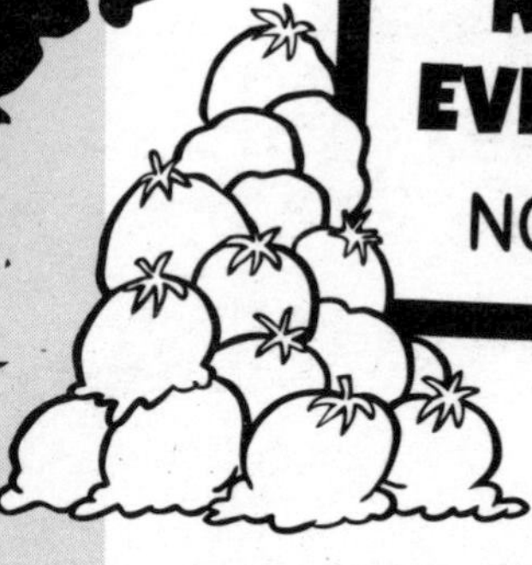

WHAT WAS DWAYNE JOHNSON CALLED WHEN HE WAS YOUNGER?

THE PEBBLE!

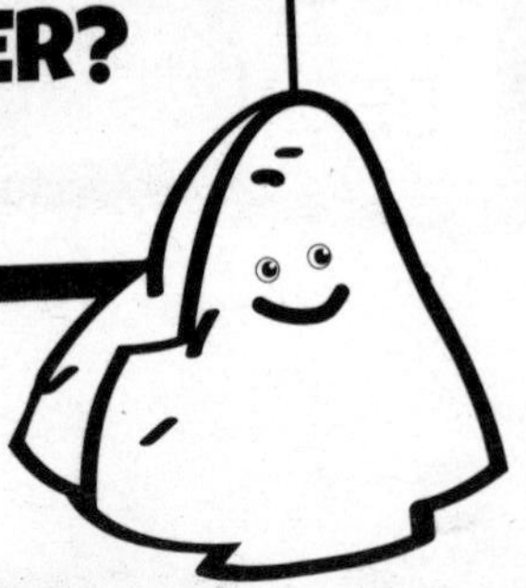

WHICH CELEB IS GOOD AT HAIRDRESSING?

HARRY STYLES!

WHAT BRAND OF LAPTOP DOES ADELE USE?

A DELL!

WHY CAN SNOOP DOGG NEVER HOLD ONTO HIS CUP OF TEA?

BECAUSE HE DROPS IT LIKE ITS HOT!

ROGER THE DODGER

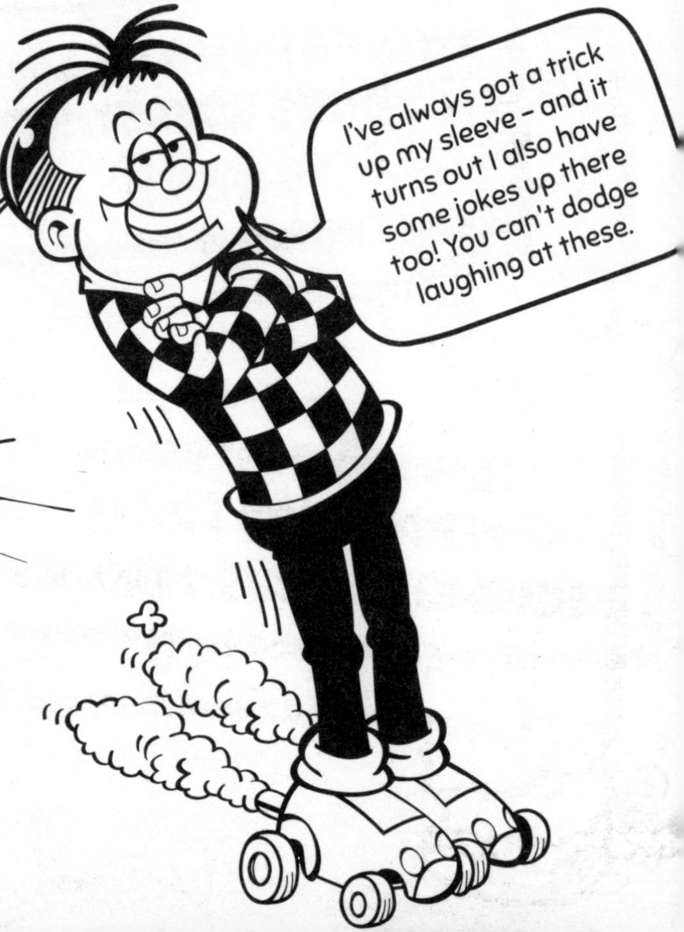
I've always got a trick up my sleeve – and it turns out I also have some jokes up there too! You can't dodge laughing at these.

WHY DID THE BOY EAT HIS HOMEWORK?

BECAUSE HIS TEACHER SAID IT WAS A PIECE OF CAKE!

WHEN'S THE BEST TIME TO BE AT SCHOOL?

HOME TIME!

HOW DO YOU STOP ELEPHANTS FROM HIDING IN YOUR FRIDGE?

PUT A MOUSSE IN THERE!

HOW DID THE COMPUTER PROGRAMMER GET OUT OF PRISON?

HE USED THE ESCAPE KEY!

WHEN SHOULD YOU TAKE A RAISIN TO DINNER?

WHEN YOU CAN'T FIND A DATE!

DO YOU KNOW WHY I STAY UP LATE ON WEEKENDS?

BECAUSE SLEEP IS FOR THE WEEK!

SOMETIMES I TUCK MY KNEES INTO MY CHEST AND LEAN FORWARDS . . .

THAT'S JUST HOW I ROLL!

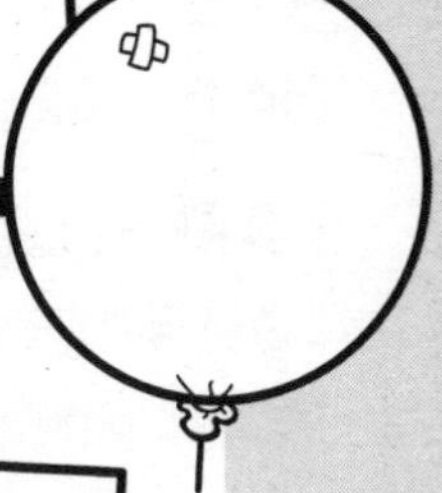

WHAT THREE LETTERS CAN YOU WRITE TO SCARE OFF BURGLARS?

I C U

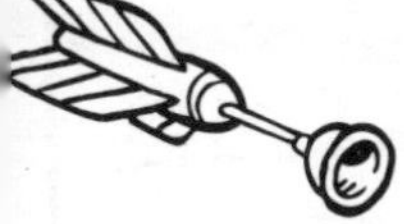

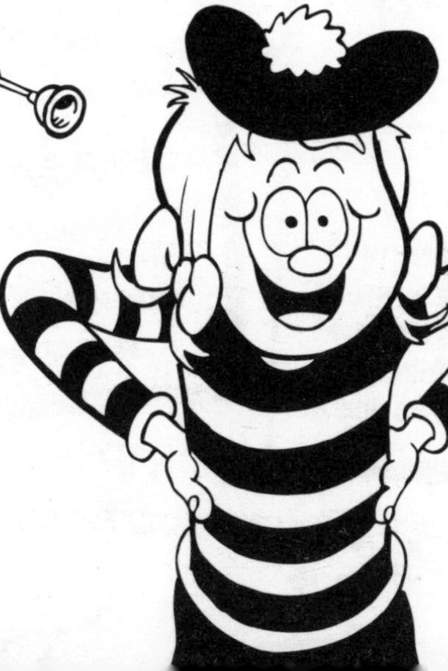

PERFECT PRANKS!

NOT ONE FOR STAND-UP COMEDY?

PRACTICAL JOKES MIGHT JUST BE THE DODGE FOR YOU! JUST PREPARE THE PRANK AND WAIT FOR THE PERFECT MOMENT TO STRIKE.

WHO POOPED?

You will need:

- One cardboard toilet roll tube

STEP 1

Finish a toilet roll and pinch the cardboard tube from inside.

STEP 2

Run the tube under the tap until the cardboard starts to get mushy.

STEP 3

Squeeze the tube tightly until you've got all the excess water out and it resembles a small poo. Now plant your fake poo somewhere for people to find it.

STEP 4

Watch your family's hysterical reactions as they scream and gag.

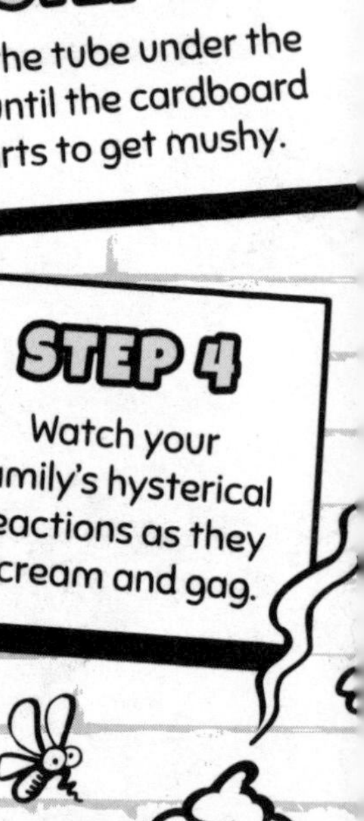

LOO-VELY CAKE!

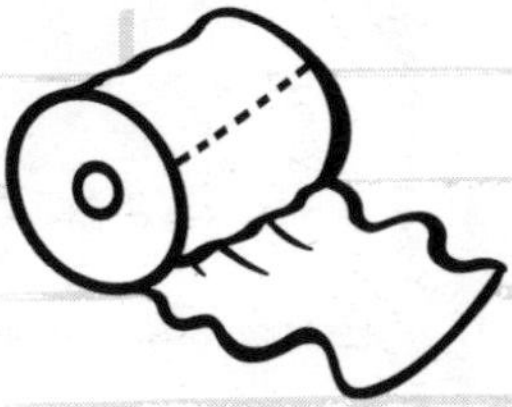

STEP 1

Place the toilet roll on a plate.

You will need:

- 1 toilet roll
- 1 plate
- Icing
- Piping bag

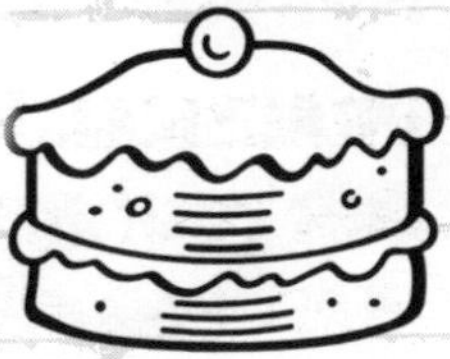

STEP 2

Cover the toilet roll with icing.

STEP 3

Use the piping bag to decorate your 'cake'.

STEP 4

Take the cake to a special occasion!

Ask a parent to prepare the prank for you – double dodge!

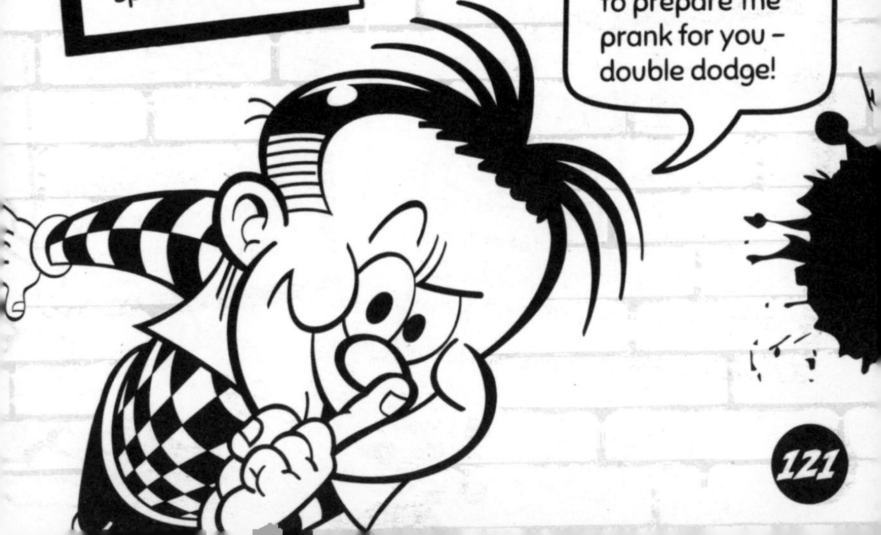

LES PRETEND

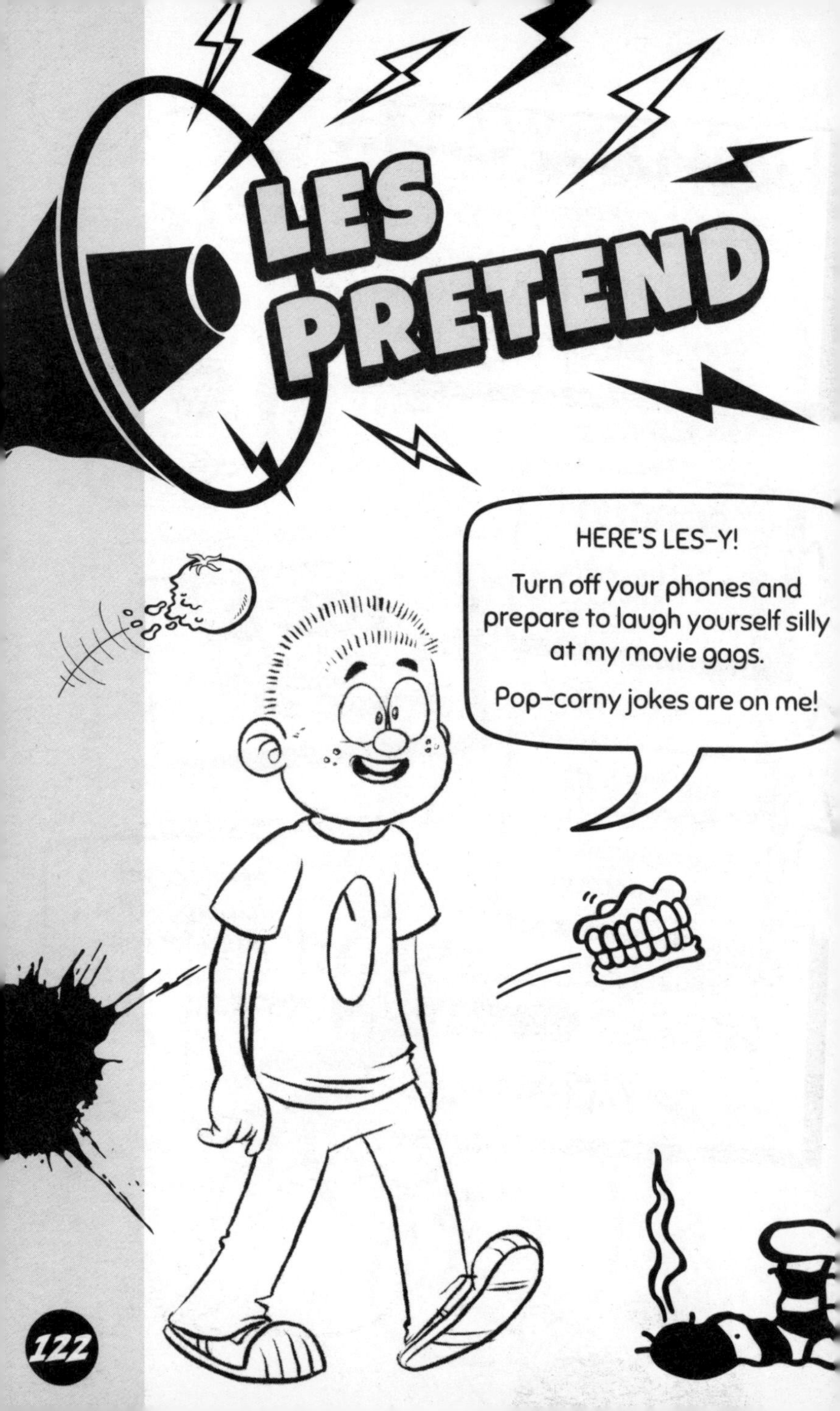
HERE'S LES–Y!
Turn off your phones and prepare to laugh yourself silly at my movie gags.
Pop–corny jokes are on me!

WHY DID CINDERELLA NOT GET PICKED FOR THE TEAM?

SHE KEPT RUNNING AWAY FROM THE BALL!

WHAT IS HARRY POTTER'S FAVOURITE SUBJECT AT HOGWARTS?

SPELLING!

WHAT DOES ARIEL LIKE TO SPREAD ON HER TOAST?

MERMA-LADE!

WHO PLAITED PRINCESS LEIA'S HAIR?

DARTH BRAIDER!

WHY IS GASTON THE CLEVEREST DISNEY VILLAIN?

HE WON THE NO-BELLE PRIZE!

WHY WOULD SNOW WHITE MAKE A GOOD JUDGE?

BECAUSE SHE'S THE FAIREST OF THEM ALL!

WHICH DISNEY PRINCESS IS THE BEST AT MAKING JOKES?

RA-PUN-ZEL!

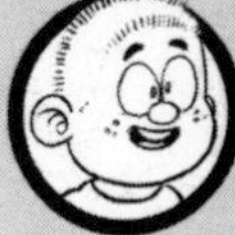

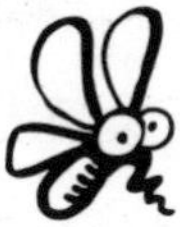

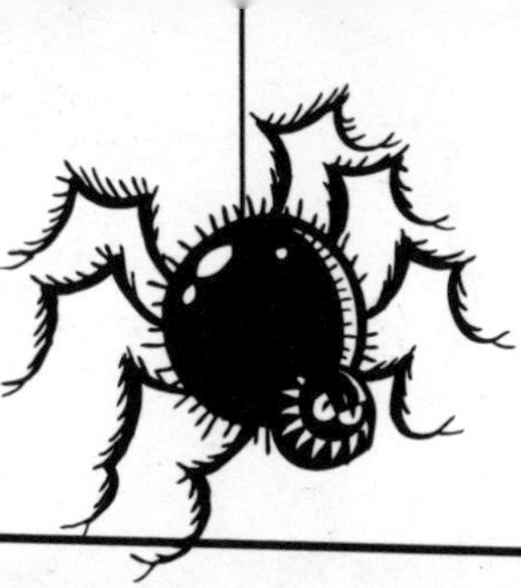

WHERE DID BLACK WIDOW AND SPIDERMAN MEET?

ON THE WEB!

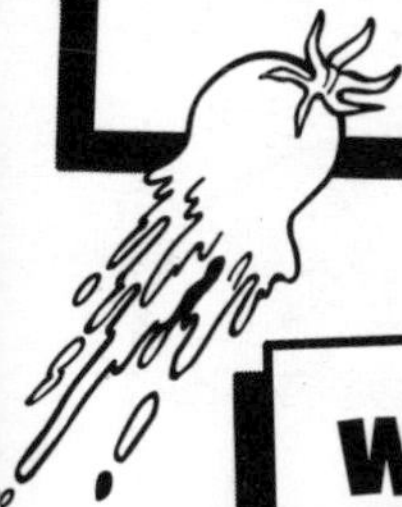

WHY DOES LOKI HATE THE DAY AFTER WEDNESDAY?

BECAUSE IT'S THOR'S DAY!

WHICH SUPERHERO LIKES WALKING?

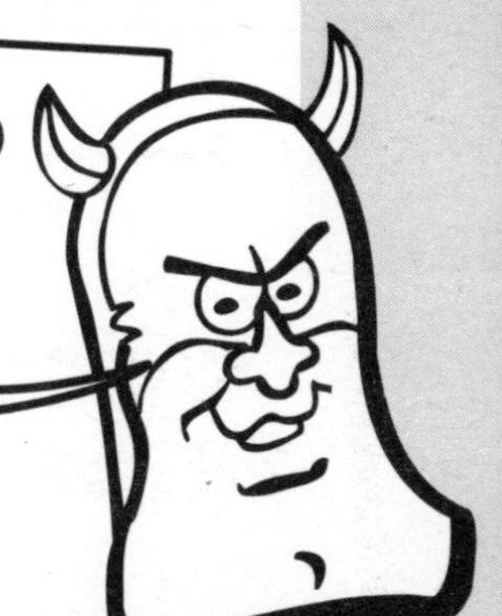
A BORING ONE?

WANDER WOMAN!

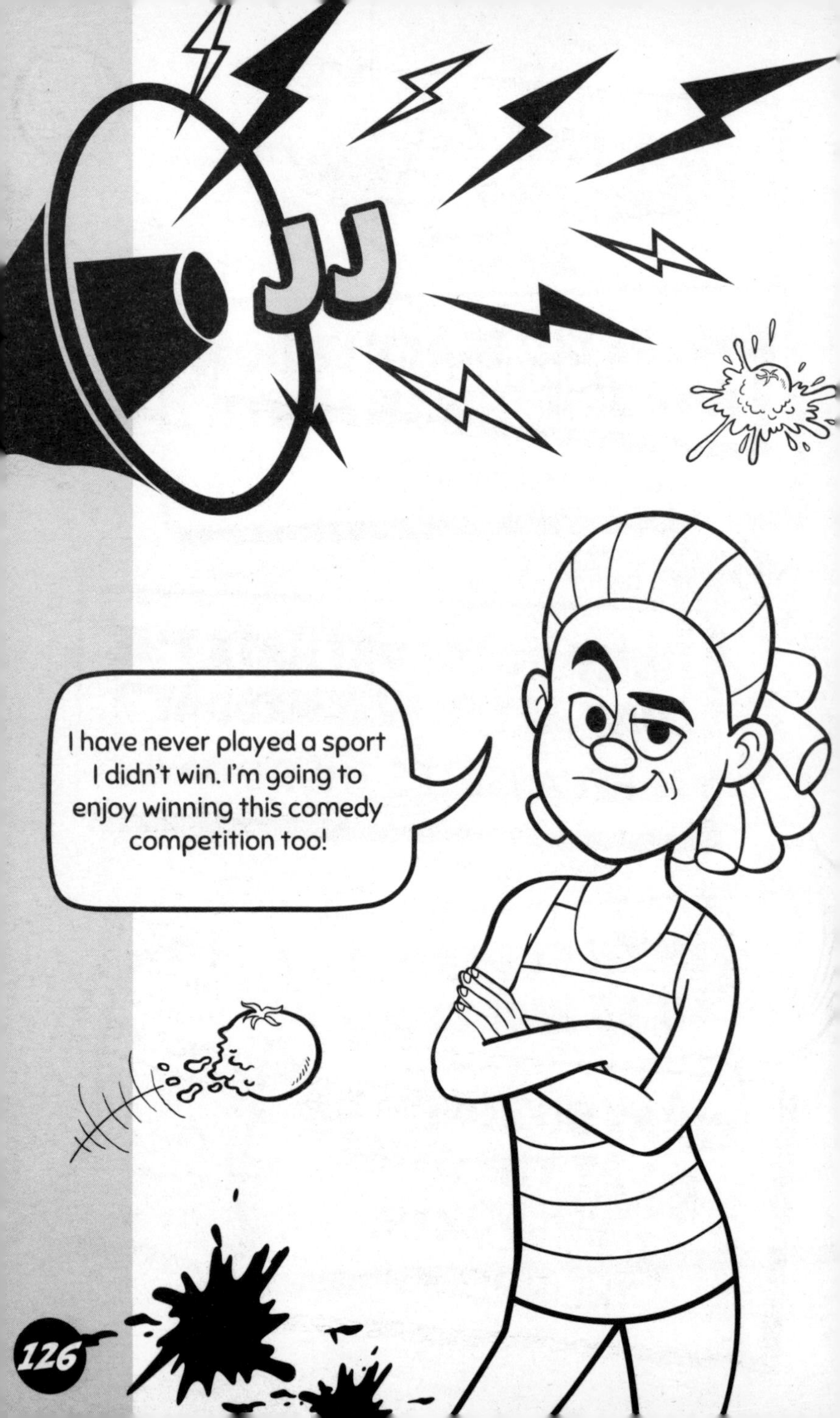
I have never played a sport I didn't win. I'm going to enjoy winning this comedy competition too!

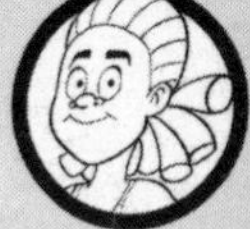

WHY ARE MATHEMATICIANS SO FIT?

THEY'RE ALWAYS WORKING OUT!

WHY DID THE PUMPKIN GO TO THE GYM?

IT WANTED TO BE A JACKED-O'-LANTERN!

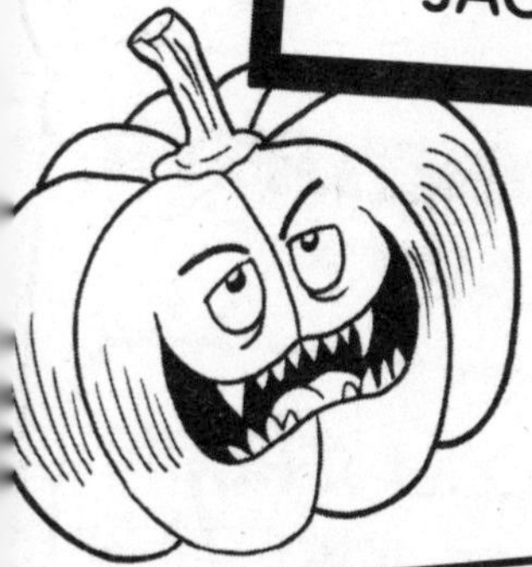

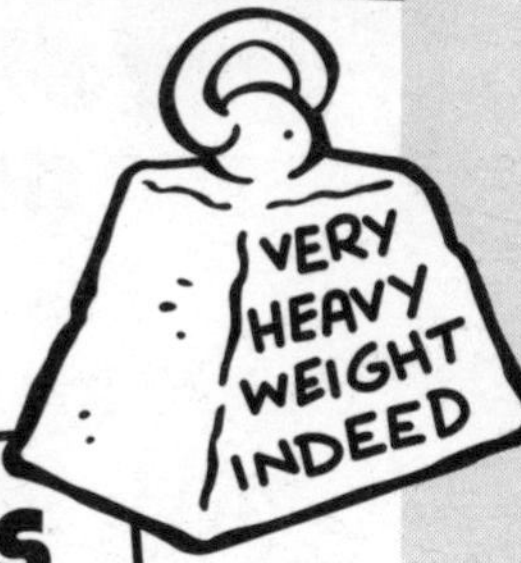
VERY
HEAVY
WEIGHT
INDEED

WHAT DO CHICKENS DO AT THE GYM?

THEY WORK ON THEIR PECKS!

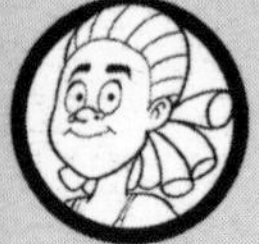

WHAT DO YOU CALL SOMEONE WHO LOVES TO WORK OUT?

JIM!

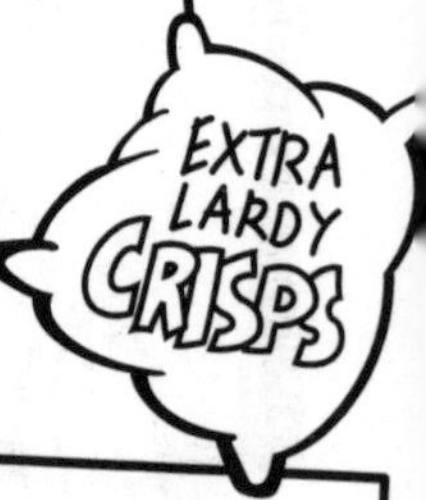
EXTRA LARDY
CRISPS

THE NEW MACHINE AT THE GYM DOES EVERYTHING!

CRISPS, CHOCOLATE, FIZZY DRINKS . . .

WHY DID THE WEIGHTLIFTER GO TO THERAPY?

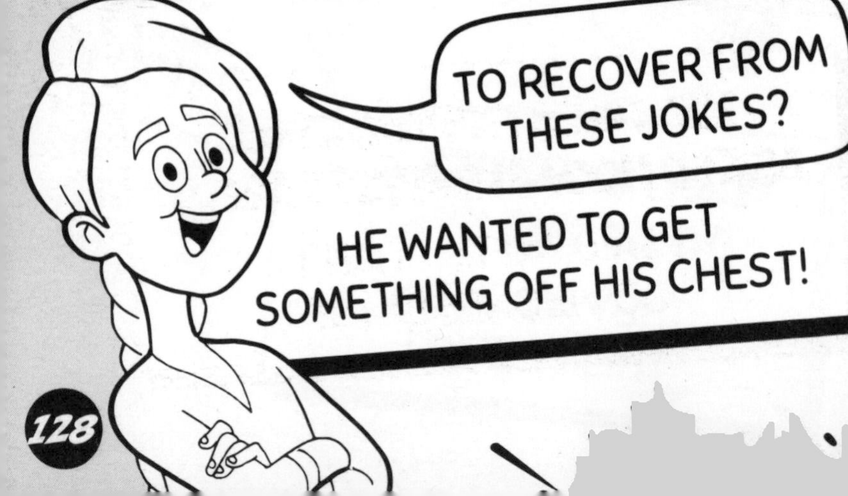
TO RECOVER FROM THESE JOKES?

HE WANTED TO GET SOMETHING OFF HIS CHEST!

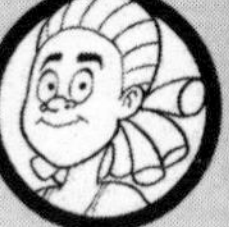

DID YOU HEAR ABOUT THE BANANA GYMNAST?

SHE WAS GREAT AT THE SPLITS!

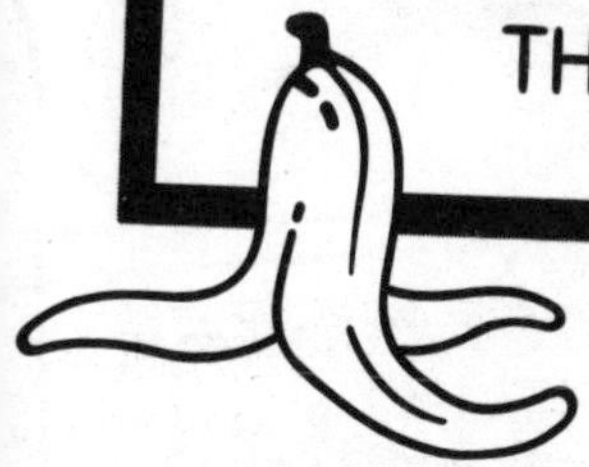

WHY SHOULDN'T YOU DO STAND-UP IN A GYM?

OR HERE!

IT'S A VERY TOUGH CROWD!

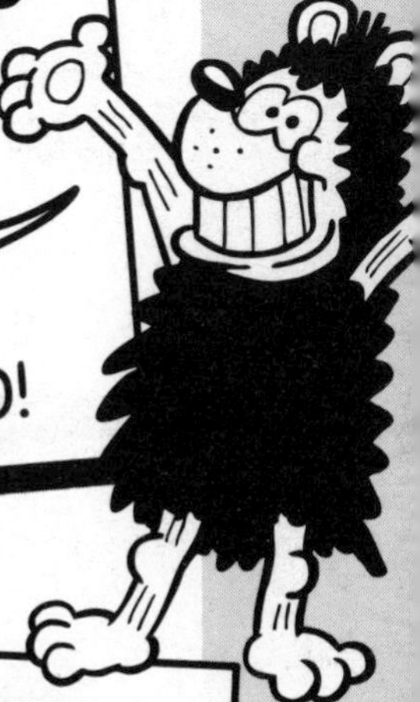

MY YOGA INSTRUCTOR ASKED HOW FLEXIBLE I AM...

I SAID, 'WELL, I CAN'T DO WEDNESDAYS!'

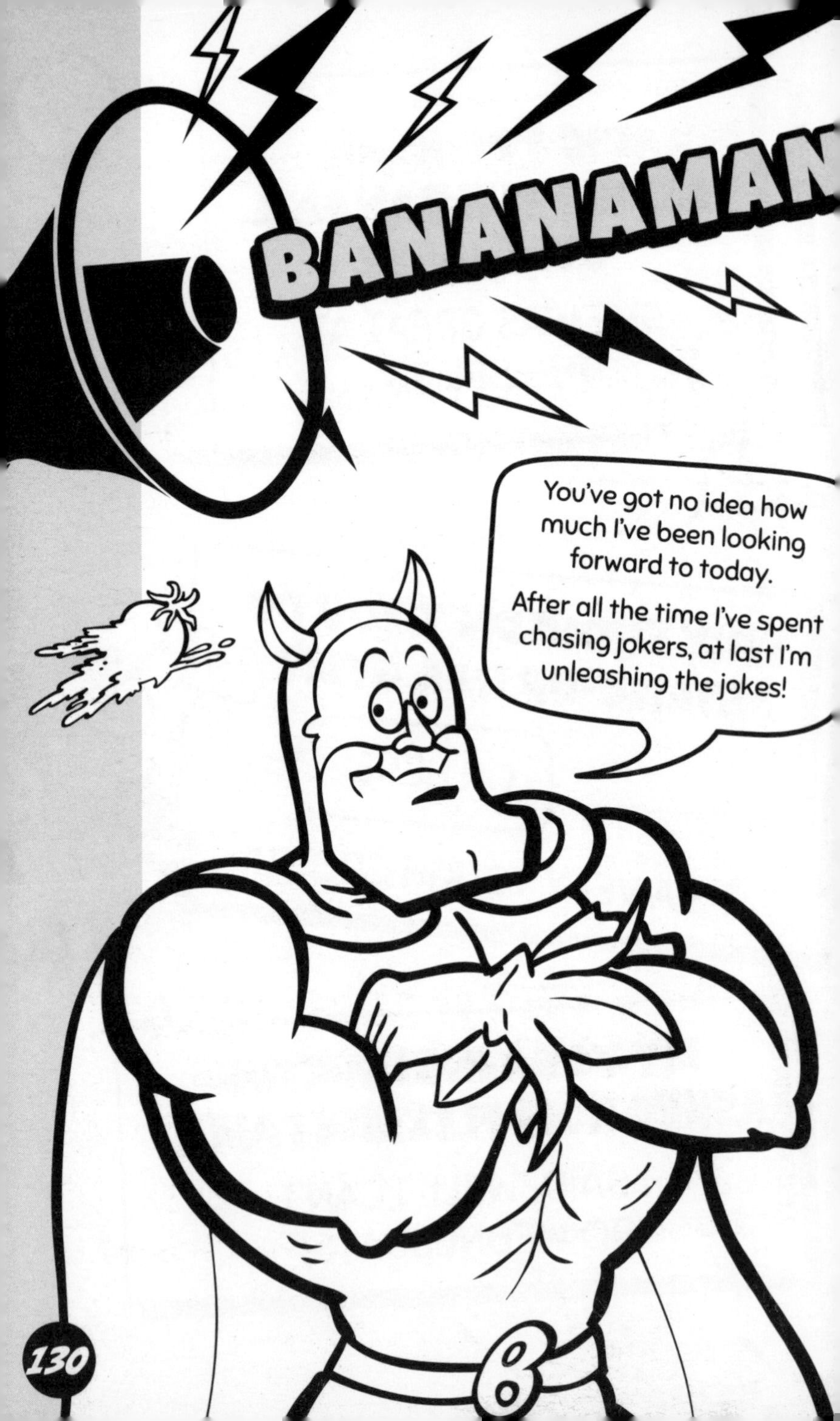

BANANAMAN
You've got no idea how much I've been looking forward to today.
After all the time I've spent chasing jokers, at last I'm unleashing the jokes!

WHAT'S THE DIFFERENCE BETWEEN SUPERMAN AND A FLY?

SUPERMAN CAN FLY BUT A FLY CAN'T SUPERMAN!

WHAT DOES TONY STARK COOK WITH?

PEPPER'S POTS!

WOULDN'T IT BE AMAZING IF SILVER SURFER AND IRON MAN TEAMED UP?

YEAH, THEY WOULD BE ALLOYS!

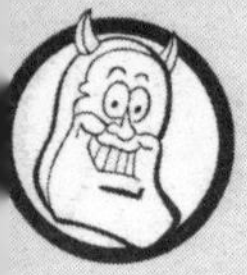

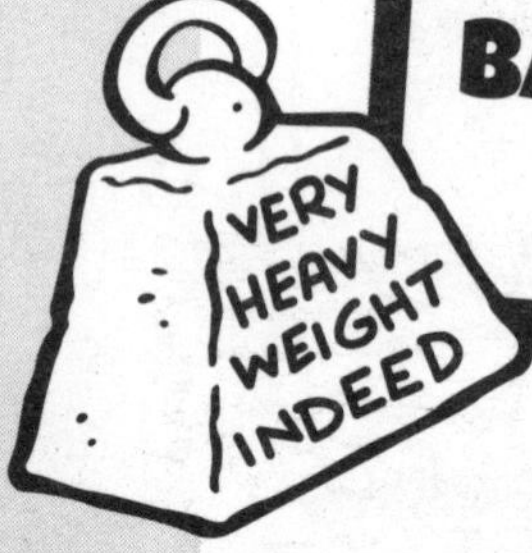
VERY
HEAVY
WEIGHT
INDEED

WHAT DO YOU GET WHEN YOU CROSS BATMAN WITH A TREE?

SPRUCE WAYNE!

WHAT'S BATMAN'S FAVOURITE PART OF A JOKE?

THE PUNCHLINE!

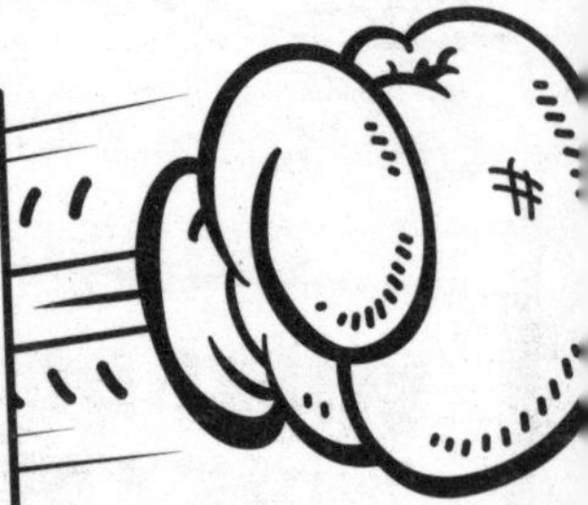

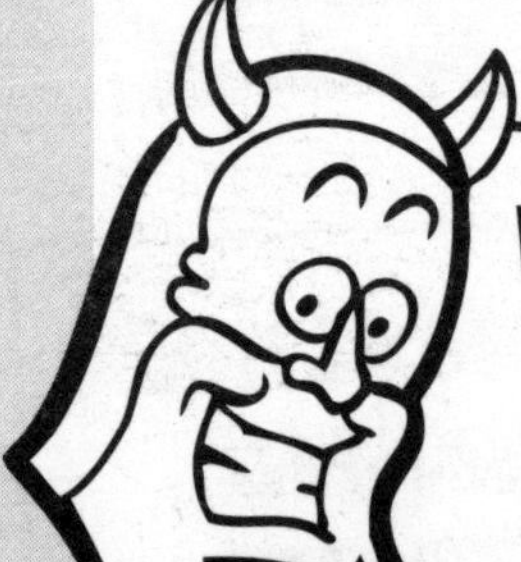

WHO'S THE OLDEST SUPERHERO?

NANA-NANA-NANA-NANA-BATMAN!

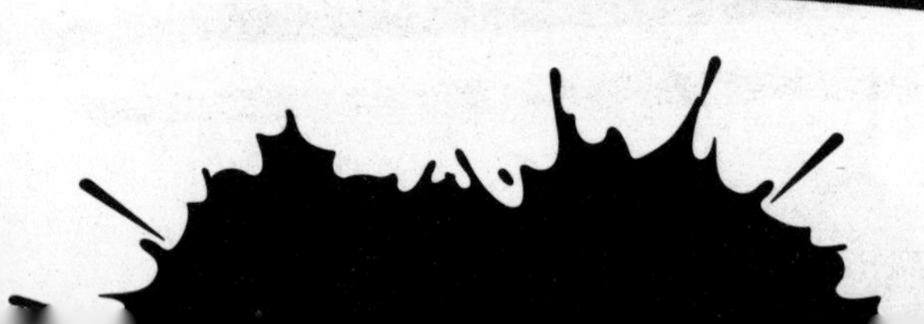

WHAT DO SUPERHEROES PUT IN THEIR DRINKS?

JUST-ICE!

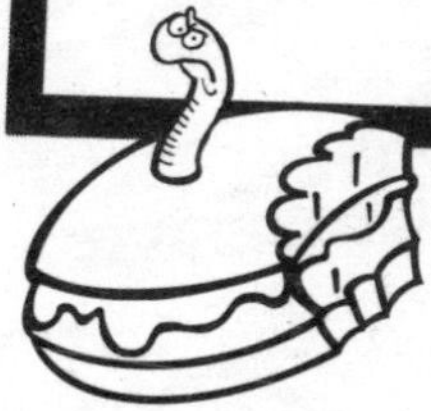

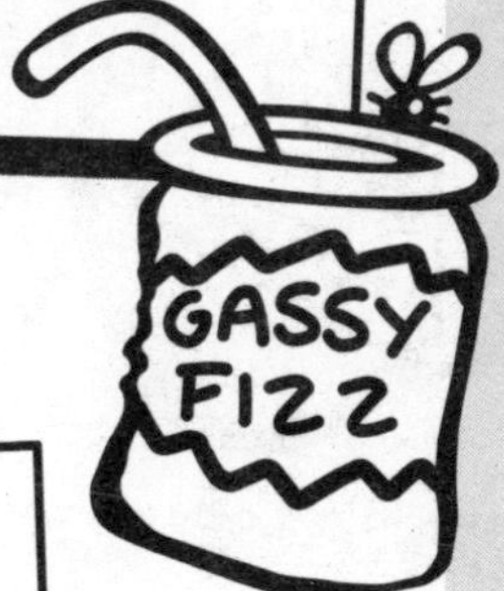
GASSY
FIZZ

WHERE DO SUPERHEROES GO ON HOLIDAY?

CAPE TOWN!

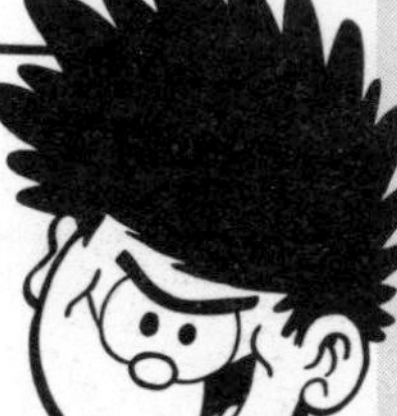

KNOCK KNOCK

WHO'S THERE?

DOCTOR.

DOCTOR WHO?

NO. DOCTOR STRANGE.

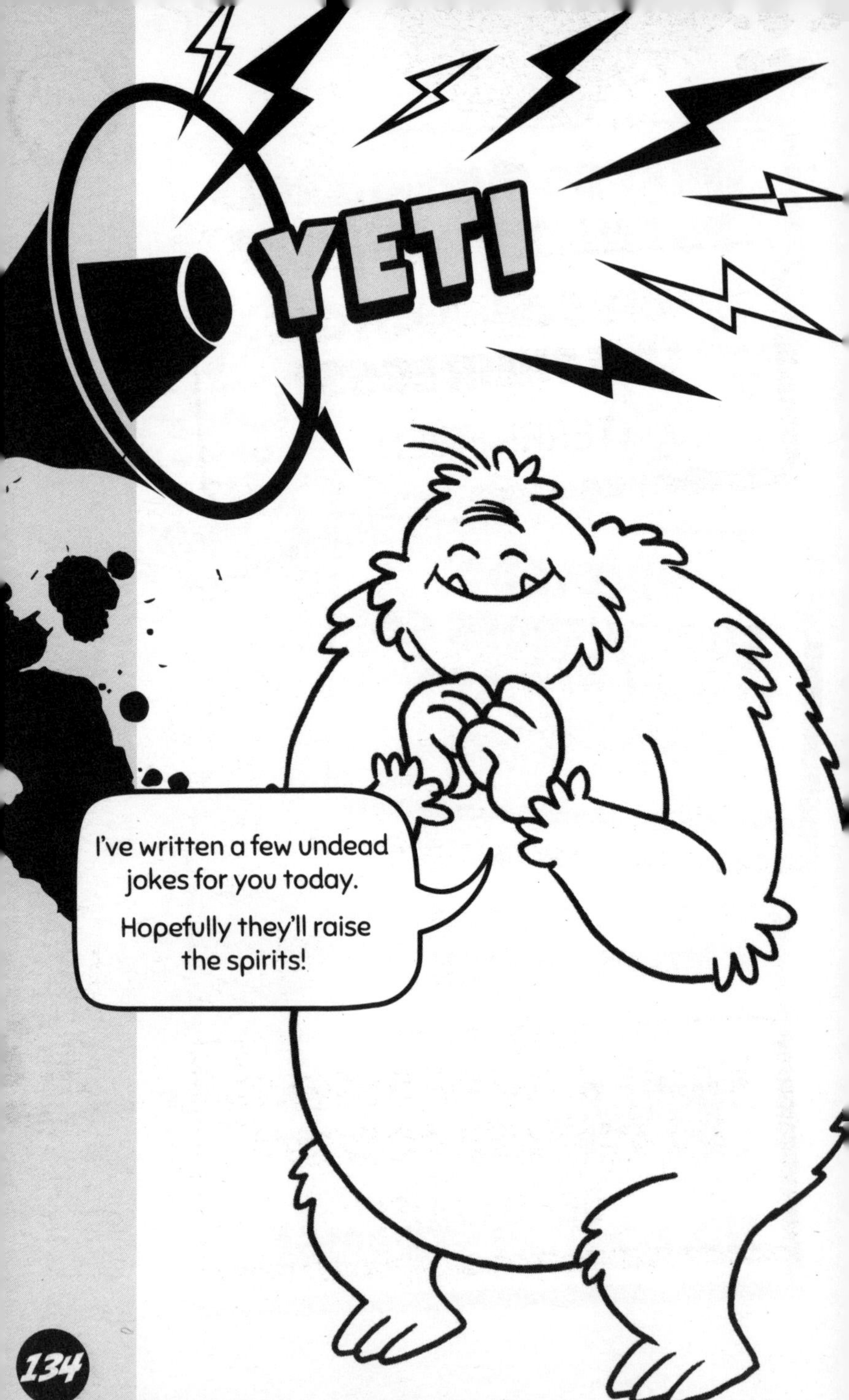
YETI
I've written a few undead jokes for you today.
Hopefully they'll raise the spirits!

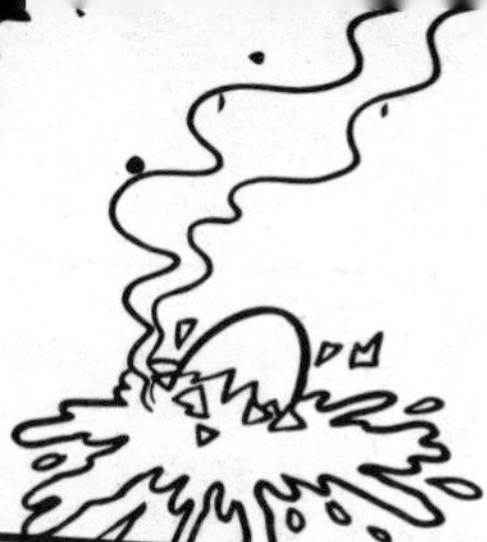

HOW DO MONSTERS LIKE THEIR EGGS?

TERRI-FRIED!

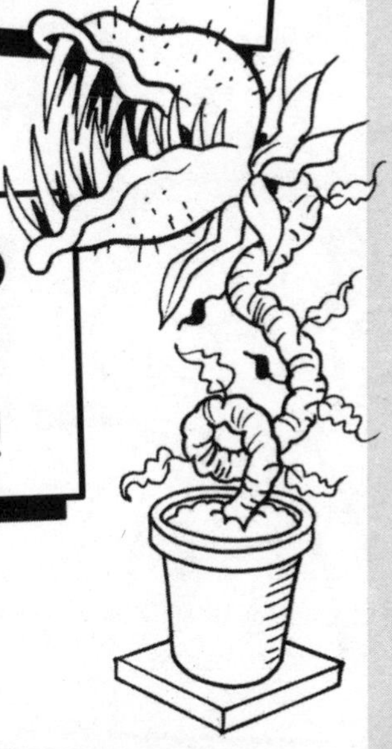

WHAT GAME DO GHOSTS PLAY?

HIDE AND SHRIEK!

WHAT KIND OF STREETS DO ZOMBIES PREFER?

DEAD ENDS!

WHAT DO LITTLE ZOMBIES CALL THEIR PARENTS?

MUMMY AND DEAD-Y!

WHAT DO YOU CALL A BEAST WITH GOOD HEARING?

EERIE!

ON WHAT DAY DO MONSTERS EAT PEOPLE?

CHEWSDAY!

WHAT DID THE BEAST EAT AFTER IT HAD ITS TEETH TAKEN OUT?

THE DENTIST!

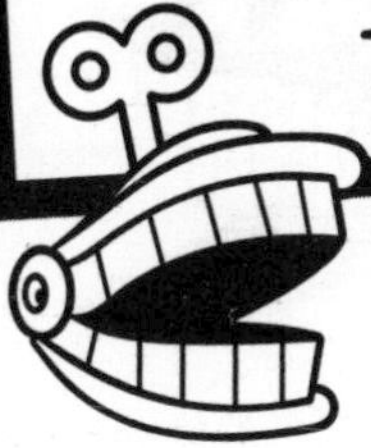

WHAT MONSTER FITS ON THE END OF YOUR FINGER?

THE BOGEYMAN!

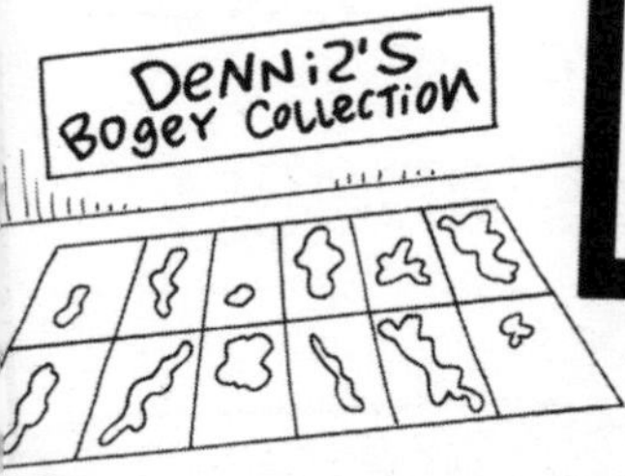
DENNIZ'S
Bogey Collection

WE ALL KNOW ALBERT EINSTEIN WAS A GENIUS . . .

BUT HIS BROTHER FRANK WAS A MONSTER!

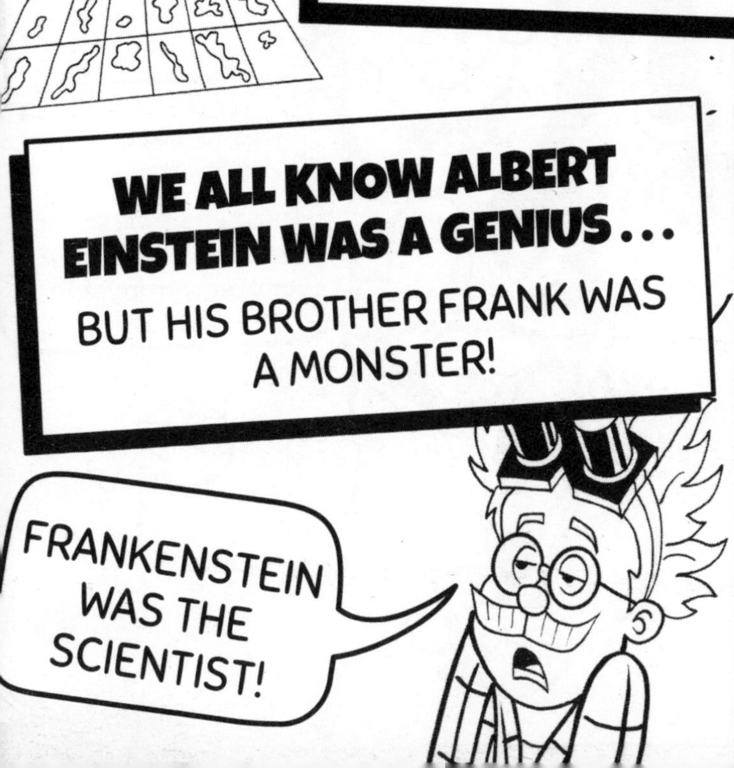
FRANKENSTEIN WAS THE SCIENTIST!

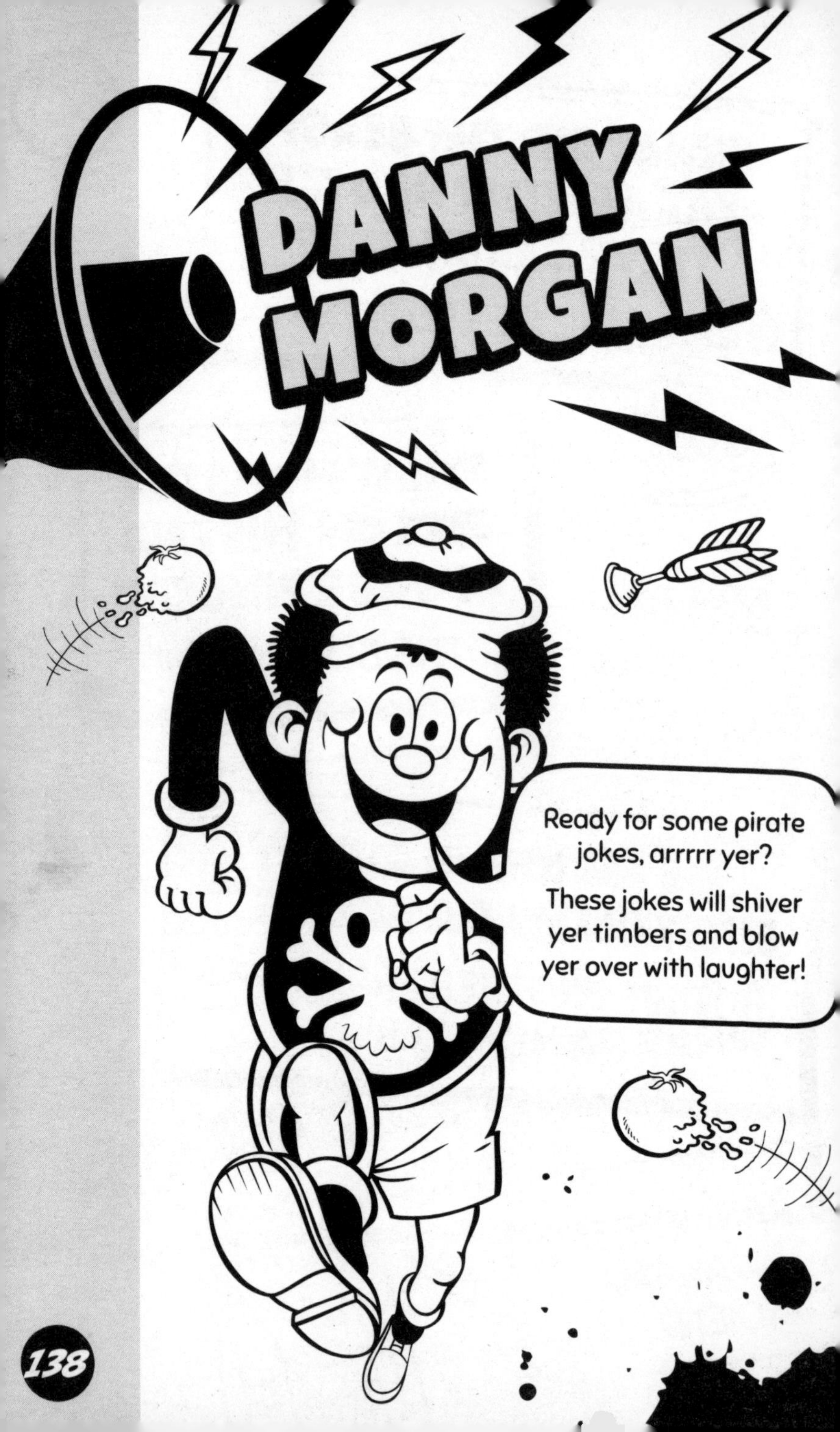
DANNY MORGAN
Ready for some pirate jokes, arrrrr yer?
These jokes will shiver yer timbers and blow yer over with laughter!

WHAT'S A PIRATE'S FAVOURITE VEGETABLE?

ARRRRRRTICHOKES!

WHAT'S A PIRATE'S FAVOURITE LETTER?

YE MAY THINK IT WOULD BE 'R' BUT A PIRATE'S FIRST LOVE IS THE 'C'!

WHAT DO TECH-OBSESSED PIRATES WEAR?

AN iPATCH!

WHAT'S THE DIFFERENCE BETWEEN A PIRATE AND A BERRY FARMER?

A PIRATE BURIES HIS TREASURE BUT A BERRY FARMER TREASURES HIS BERRIES!

WHY ARE PIRATES CALLED PIRATES?

BECAUSE THEY ARRRRR!

WHAT DID THE FIRST MATE SEE DOWN THE TOILET?

 THE CAPTAIN'S LOG!

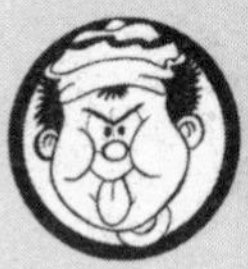

HOW DO YOU MAKE A PIRATE FEEL BETTER?

GIVE IT SOME VITAMIN-SEA!

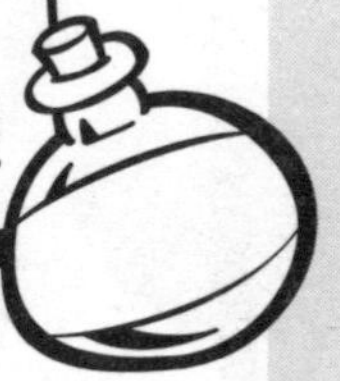

WHERE DOES A PIRATE GO WHEN IT NEEDS MONEY?

THE SAND BANK!

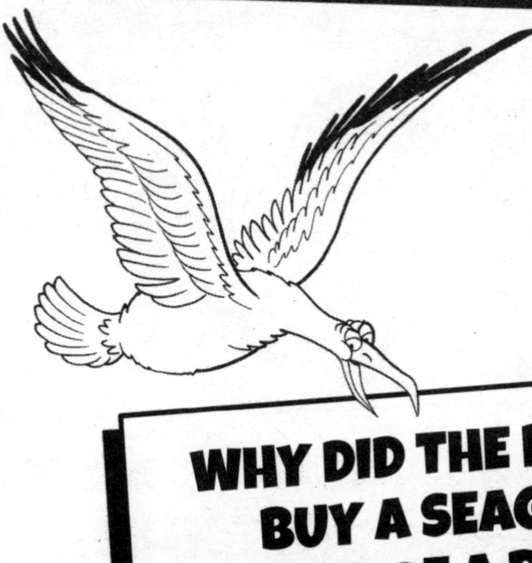

WHY DID THE PIRATE BUY A SEAGULL INSTEAD OF A PARROT?

IT WAS ON SAIL!

TOOTS & SIDNEY PYE

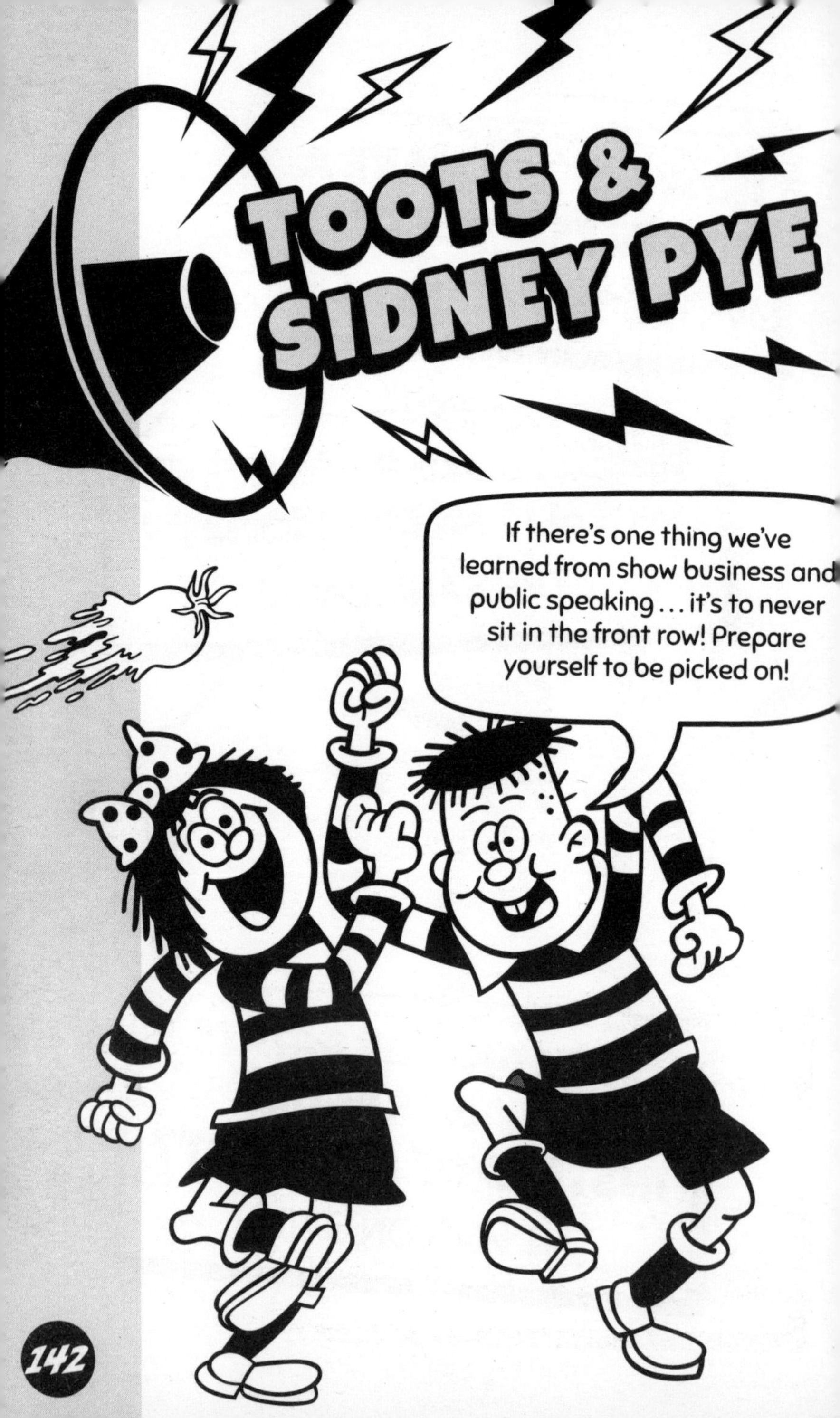
If there's one thing we've learned from show business and public speaking . . . it's to never sit in the front row! Prepare yourself to be picked on!

KNOCK, KNOCK!
WHO'S THERE?
SMELLMOP.
SMELLMOP WHO?
EW! NO THANKS.

KNOCK, KNOCK!
WHO'S THERE?
ART.
ART WHO?
R2D2!

KNOCK, KNOCK!
WHO'S THERE?
TWIT.
TWIT WHO?
HELP, ANOTHER OWL!

KNOCK, KNOCK!
WHO'S THERE?
STOPWATCH.
STOPWATCH WHO?
STOPWATCH-A DOING AND OPEN THE DOOR!

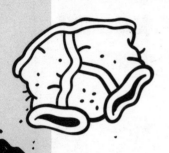

KNOCK, KNOCK!
WHO'S THERE?
ASH.
ASH WHO?
HERE'S A TISSUE!

KNOCK, KNOCK!
WHO'S THERE?
YA.
YA WHO?
WOW, WHAT A WELCOME!

KNOCK, KNOCK!
WHO'S THERE?
SNOW.
SNOW WHO?
SNOW BUSINESS LIKE SHOW BUSINESS!

KNOCK, KNOCK!
WHO'S THERE?
ORANGE.
ORANGE WHO?
ORANGE YOU SICK OF ALL THESE KNOCK KNOCK JOKES?

YES!

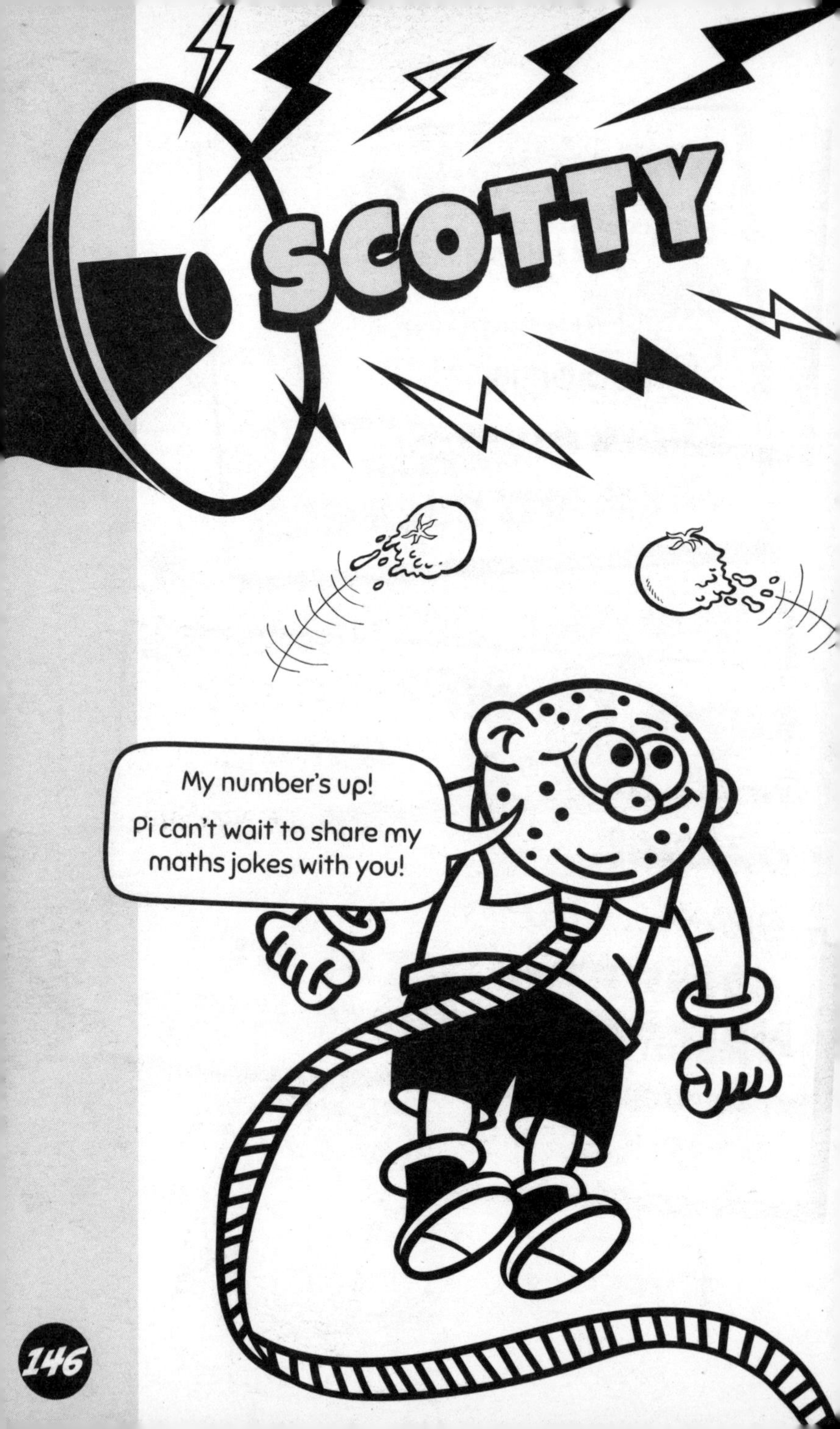
SCOTTY
My number's up!
Pi can't wait to share my maths jokes with you!

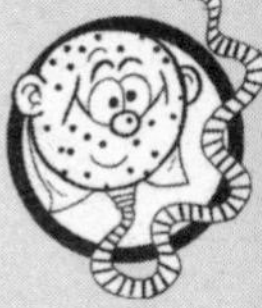

WHY WAS THE MATHS STUDENT SO BAD AT DECIMALS?

THEY COULDN'T GET THE POINT!

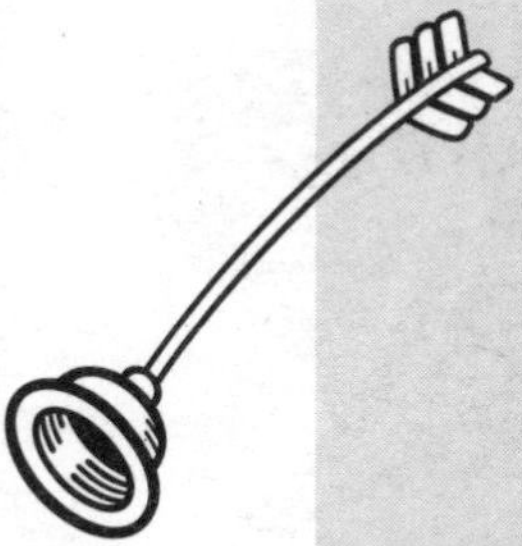

HOW DOES A MATHEMATICIAN PLOUGH HIS FIELDS?

WITH A PRO–TRACTOR!

WHY WAS THE MATHS BOOK SAD?

IT HAD TOO MANY PROBLEMS!

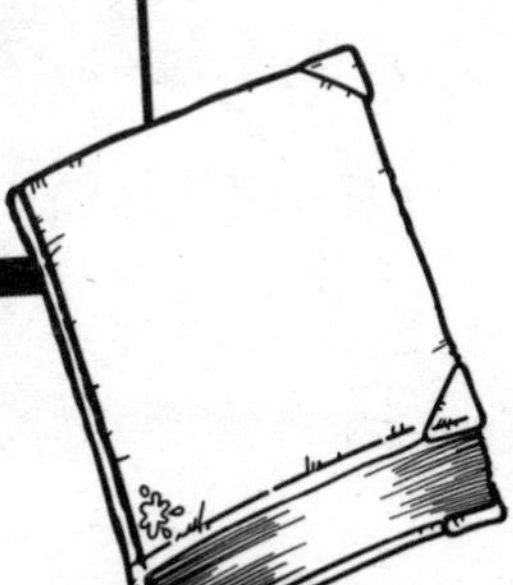

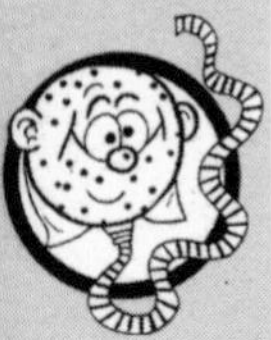

WHO INVENTED FRACTIONS?

THE DEVIL?

HENRY THE $^{1}/_{8}$!

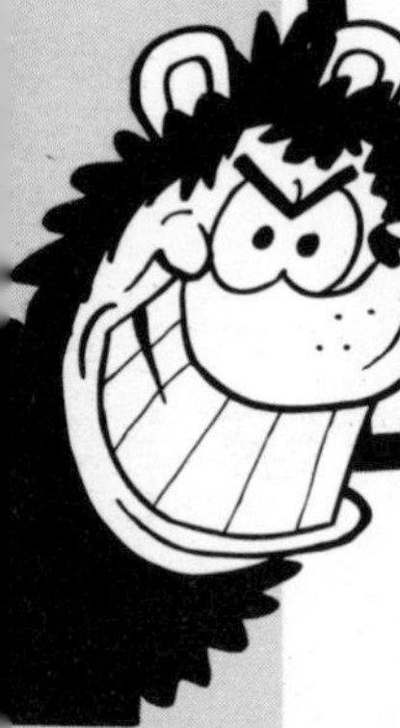

HOW DO YOU MAKE SEVEN AN EVEN NUMBER?

TAKE AWAY THE 'S'!

DID YOU HEAR ABOUT THE MATHEMATICIAN WHO'S AFRAID OF NEGATIVE NUMBERS?

HE WILL STOP AT NOTHING TO AVOID THEM!

WHICH MONSTER IS THE BEST AT MATHS?

COUNT DRACULA!

MY IDEA FOR A CHARACTER CALLED 3.14 FACE WAS REJECTED BY BEANO...

THEY SAID THEY ALREADY HAVE A 'PIE' FACE!

YOU KNOW WHAT'S ODD?

THAT YOU'RE STILL ON STAGE?

EVERY OTHER NUMBER!

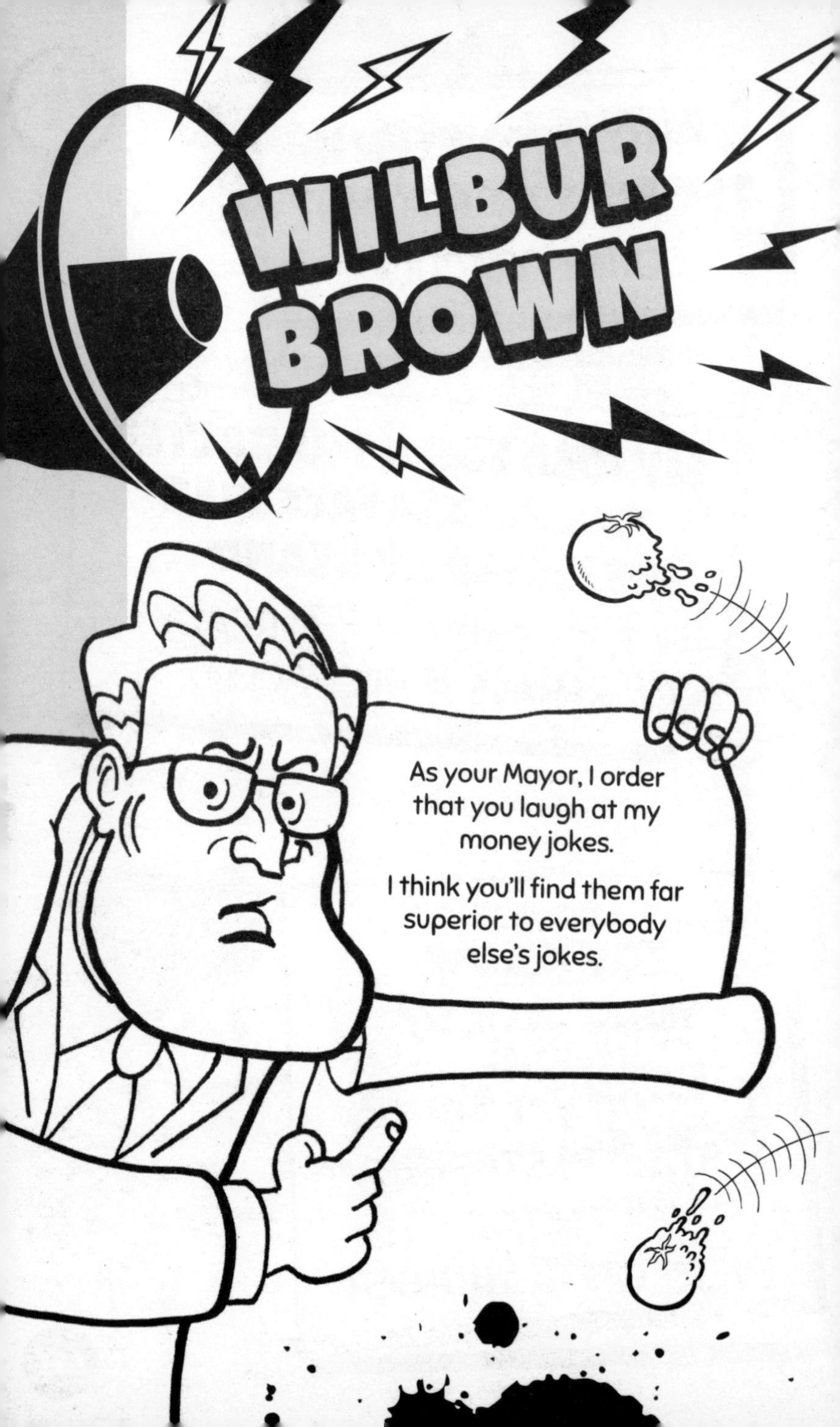
WILBUR BROWN
As your Mayor, I order that you laugh at my money jokes.
I think you'll find them far superior to everybody else's jokes.

WHY IS MONEY ALSO CALLED DOUGH?

BECAUSE EVERY PERSON KNEADS IT.

DID YOU HEAR ABOUT AN ATM THAT GOT ADDICTED TO MONEY?

IT'S SUFFERING FROM WITHDRAWALS.

WHY CAN'T YOU BORROW MONEY FROM A LEPRECHAUN?

THEY'RE ALWAYS A LITTLE SHORT!

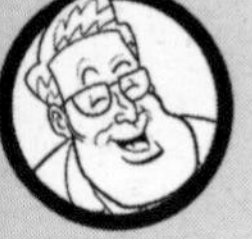

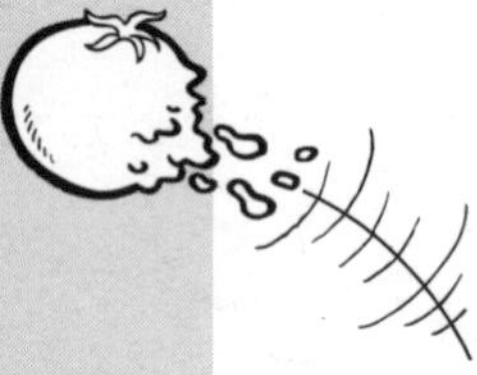

KNOCK, KNOCK!

WHO'S THERE?

CASH.

CASH WHO?

NO THANKS, I DON'T LIKE NUTS.

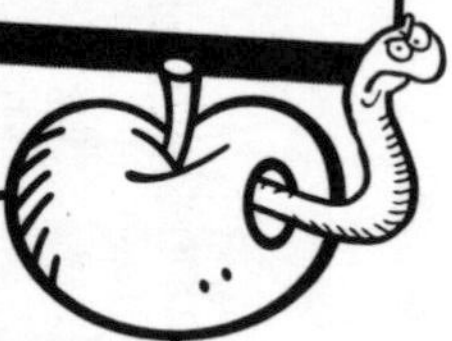

HOW DID THE DINOSAUR PAY HIS BILL AT THE RESTAURANT?

WITH TYRANNOSAURUS CHEQUES!

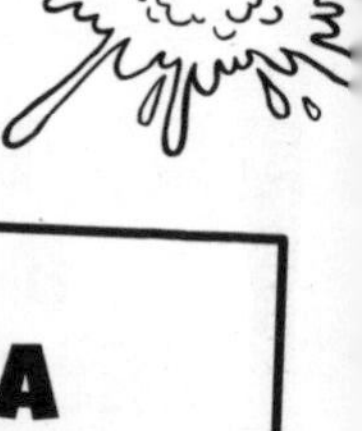

WHAT NOISE DOES A CHICKEN MAKE IN A BANK?

BUCK BUCK BUCK!

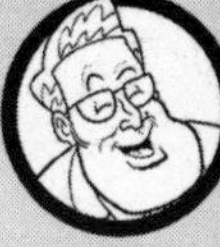

WHY DIDN'T THE COWS PAY THEIR BILLS?

BECAUSE THE FARMERS MILKED THEM DRY.

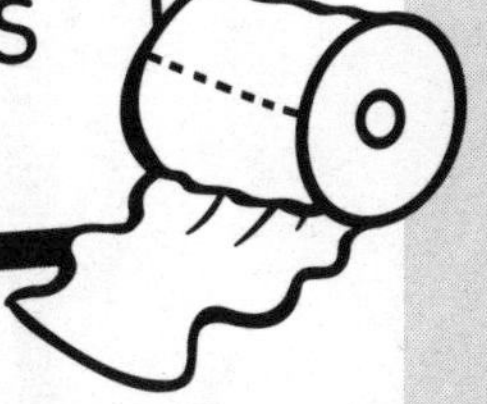

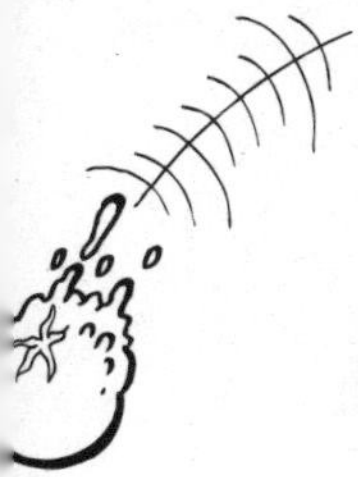

WHERE WILL YOU ALWAYS FIND MONEY?

IN A DICTIONARY.

WHY DID THE WOMAN PUT HER MONEY IN HER FREEZER?

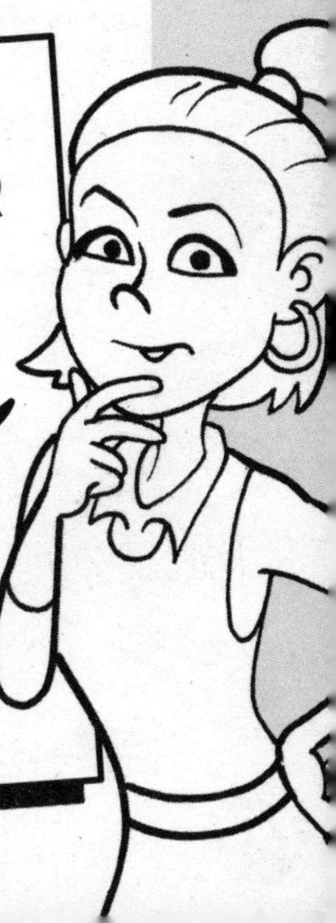
TO HIDE IT FROM YOU?

BECAUSE SHE WANTED SOME COLD HARD CASH.

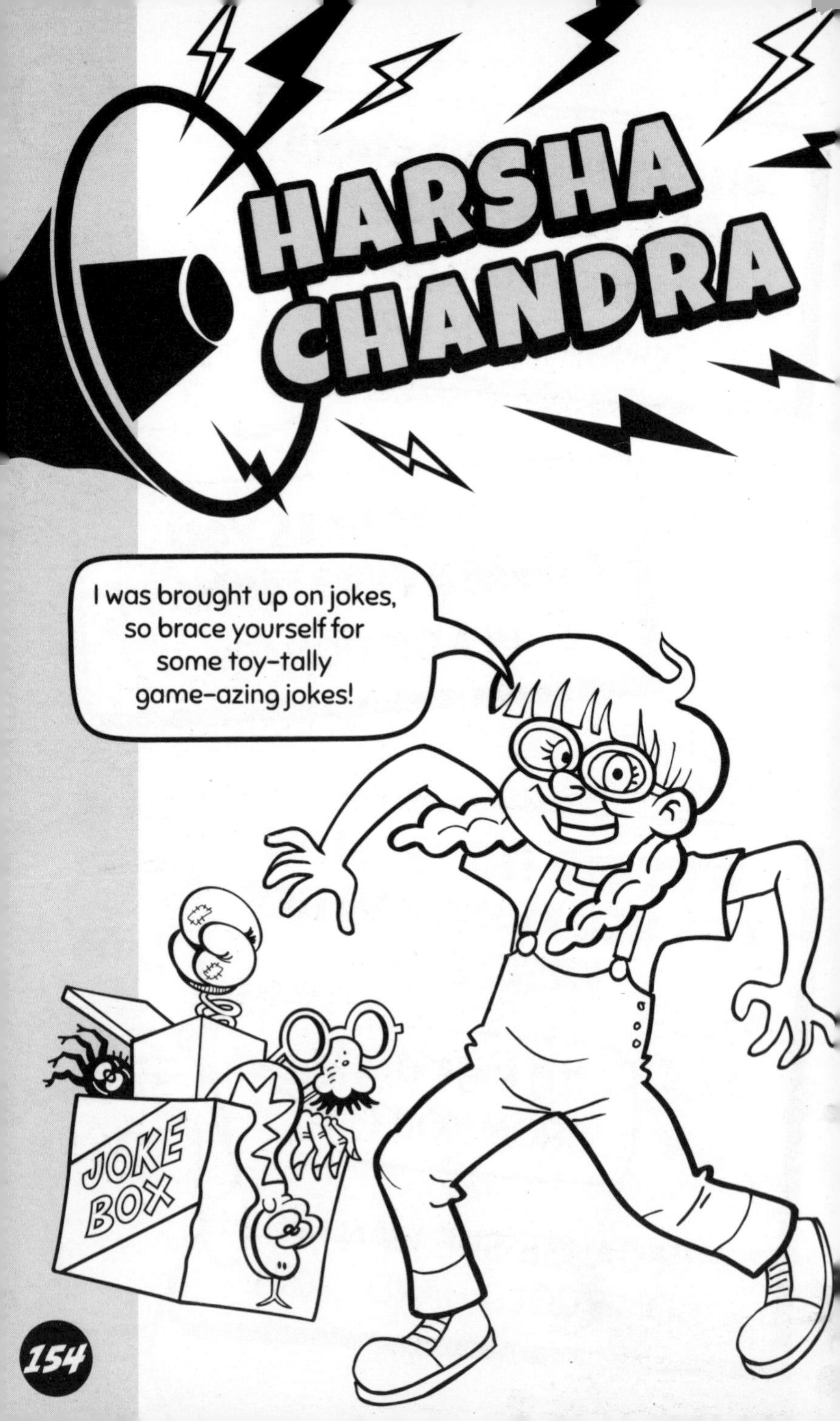
HARSHA CHANDRA
I was brought up on jokes, so brace yourself for some toy-tally game-azing jokes!
JOKE BOX

DID YOU HEAR ABOUT THE MAN WHO ATE A TOY HORSE?

HIS CONDITION IS STABLE!

WHY DO CUDDLY BEARS NEVER EAT?

BECAUSE THEY'RE STUFFED!

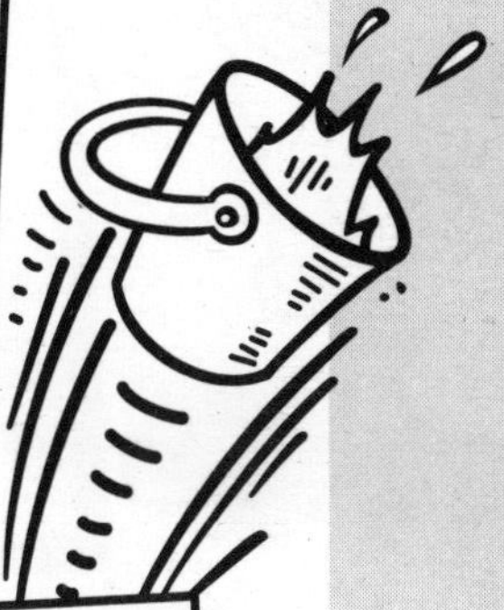

THESE TOY HELICOPTERS ARE VERY POPULAR . . .

THEY'RE FLYING OFF THE SHELVES!

WHY CAN'T TOYS MADE FROM PAPER MOVE?

BECAUSE THEY'RE STATIONERY!

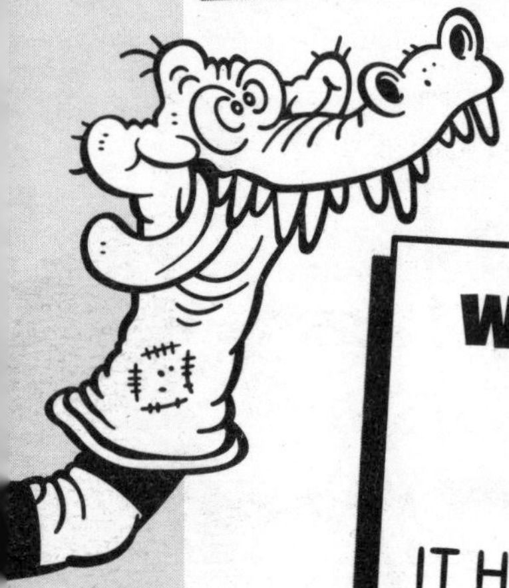

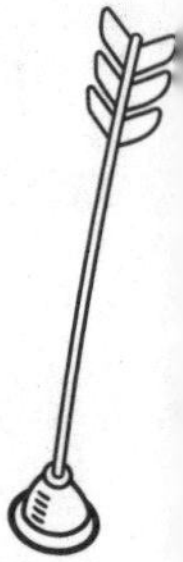

WHAT'S IT LIKE BEING A PROFESSIONAL YO-YO PLAYER?

IT HAS ITS UPS AND DOWNS!

WHY IS IT SO DIFFICULT TO SELL A TOY ZEBRA?

YOU CAN'T FIND THE BARCODE!

HOW DO YOU START A CUDDLY TOY RACE?

READY, TEDDY, GO!

WHERE DO SHOPS KEEP THEIR ARNOLD SCHWARZENEGGER TOYS?

AISLE B, BACK!

HOW DO YOU GET PIKACHU ON A BUS?

YOU POKE HIM ON!

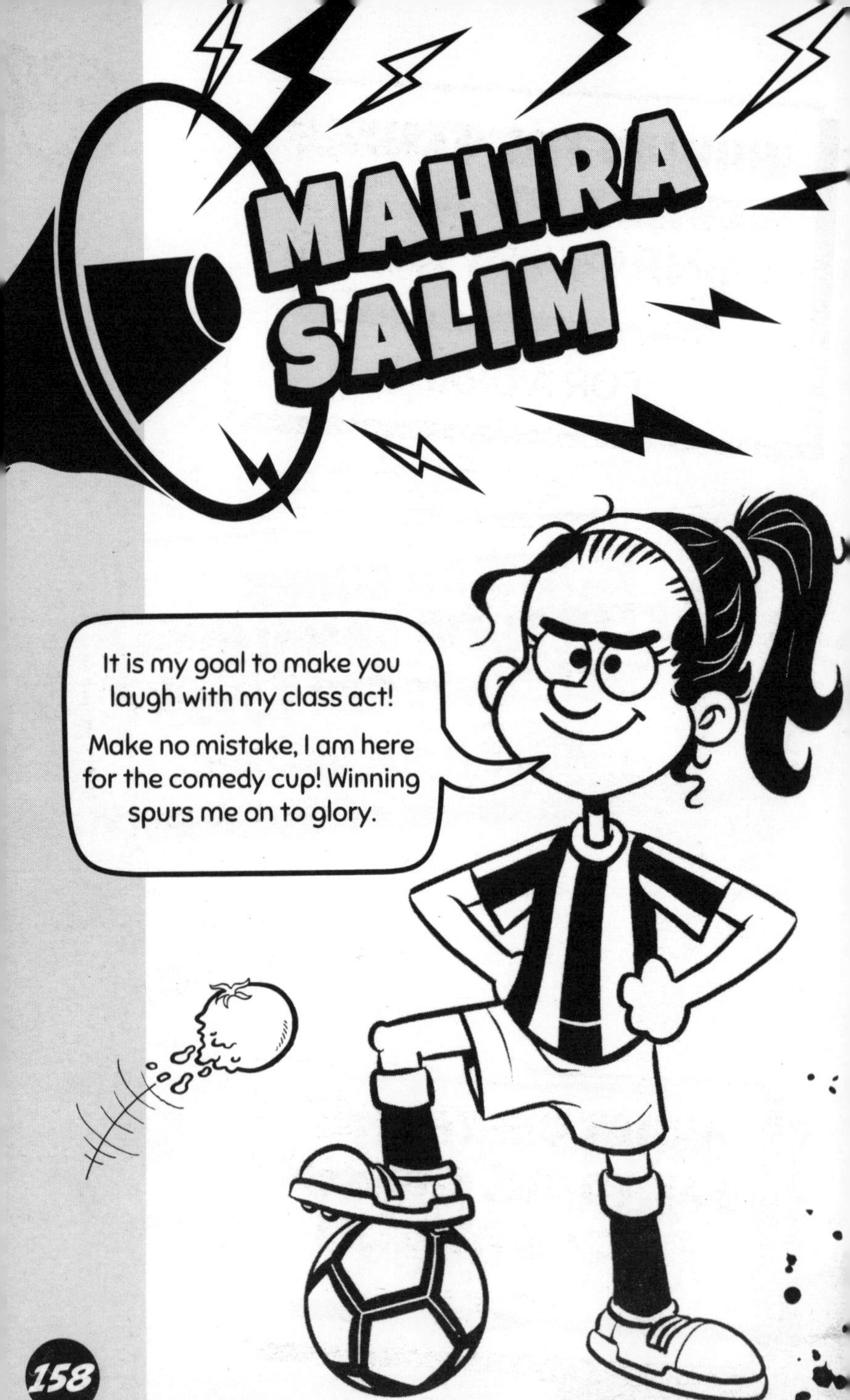
MAHIRA SALIM
It is my goal to make you laugh with my class act!
Make no mistake, I am here for the comedy cup! Winning spurs me on to glory.

WHY DID THE MANAGER BRING A PENCIL AND PAPER TO THE MATCH?

THEY WERE HOPING FOR A DRAW!

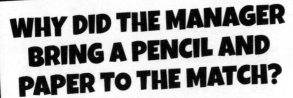

WHICH POSITION DOES A GHOST ALWAYS PLAY?

THE GHOUL–KEEPER!

WHAT DID THE REF SAY TO THE CHICKEN PITCH-INVADER?

FOWL!

WHAT DID THE MANAGER DO WHEN THE PITCH WAS FLOODED?

HE SENT ON HIS SUBS!

DID YOU HEAR ABOUT THE DOG THAT PLAYED FOR A SUNDAY LEAGUE TEAM?

THEY WERE ALWAYS FOULING IN THE PARK!

GNASHER!

WHICH FOOTBALL TEAM DO COWBOYS SUPPORT?

SPURS!

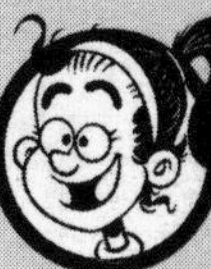

WHAT'S THE DIFFERENCE BETWEEN BEANOTOWN UTD AND A TEA BAG?

THE TEA BAG STAYS IN THE CUP LONGER!

WHAT DO YOU CALL SOMEONE WHO STANDS IN THE GOAL AND STOPS THE BALL?

ANNETTE!

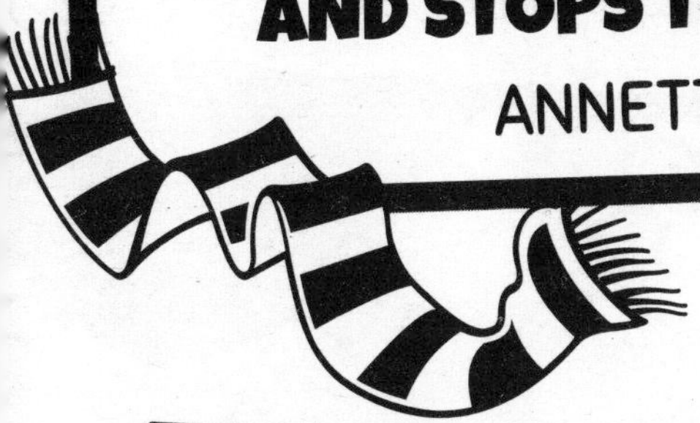

WHAT BOAT HOLDS EXACTLY 20 FOOTBALL TEAMS?

THE PREMIER-SHIP!

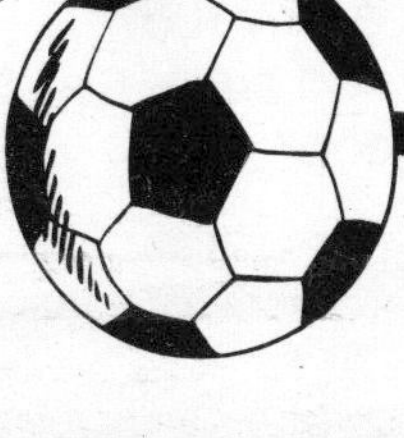

STANDING UP!

Jokes have been around since the dawn of mankind, when the world's original joker let rip the fart that caused the first known case of hysterical laughter. It was the birth of a new form of entertainment! Anyone can tell a joke, but it takes practice to make people laugh.

Stand-up comedy is exactly that: someone standing up and being funny to try to make an audience laugh.

Stand-up sounds cool, and it is – stand-up comedians can sell out stadium tours and are some of the biggest stars in entertainment. But, even if you don't become a world-famous zillionaire comedy star, there's a good chance you're going to have to stand up and speak to an audience at some point in your life, so this is a great way to build confidence with friends.

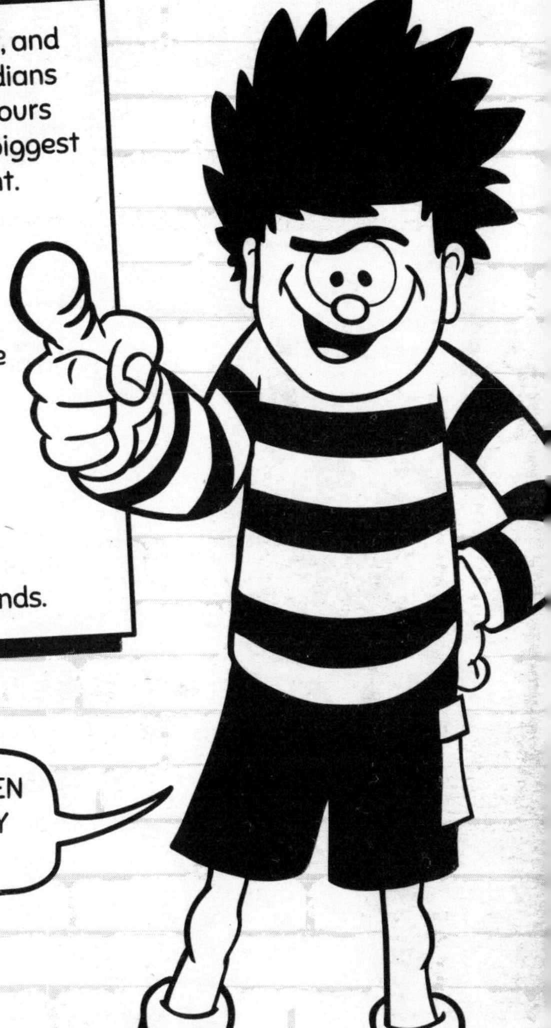
THESE TIPS HAVE BEEN TRIED AND TESTED BY DENNIS & CO.

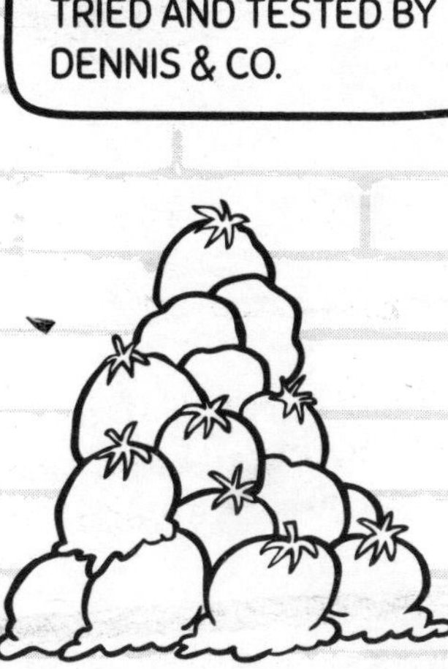

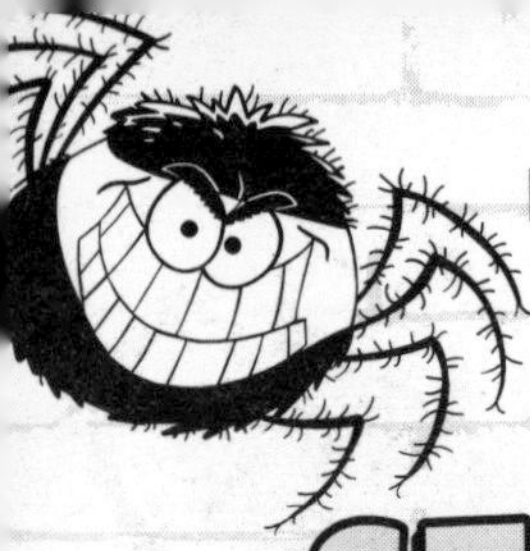

BASH STREET COMEDY CLUB:

TOP TEN STAND-UP TIPS

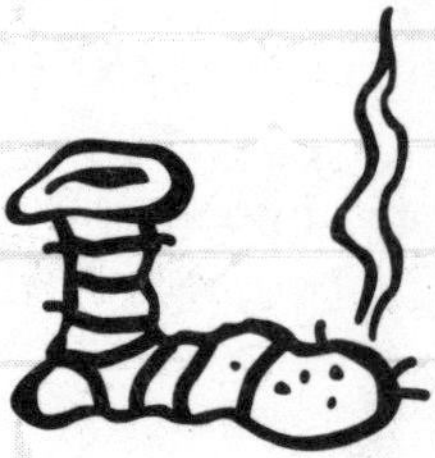

1. Aim to create a set of jokes (your material). **PUT YOUR BEST JOKE FIRST!**

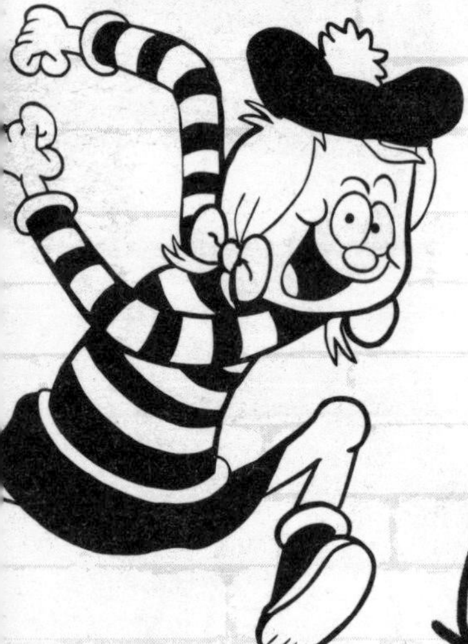

2. The best jokes are based on **EVERYDAY STUFF**. That's because more people can relate to the subject. School is a good subject to entertain friends because it's something you all have in common!

3. Take note of the **SILLY SIDE OF LIFE**. People laugh at things that make no sense and ideas that don't usually go together.

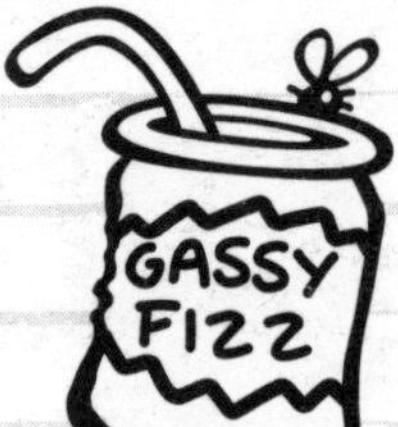
GASSY
FIZZ

4.

The **SET-UP** is the first part of the joke, which hooks your audience and makes them want to discover what's coming next. Practise this part lots!

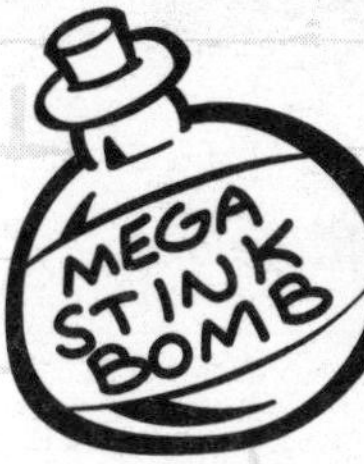
MEGA
STINK
BOMB

5.

Whatever you do, never rush. **COMIC TIMING** means choosing when to pause and what words to emphasise. It gives your audience time to catch up.

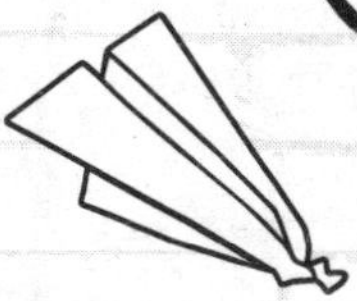

6.

The **PUNCHLINE** is the final part of a joke – what every word has been building up to. The funniest bit! Say it confidently . . . BLAM! Then lap up the laughs!

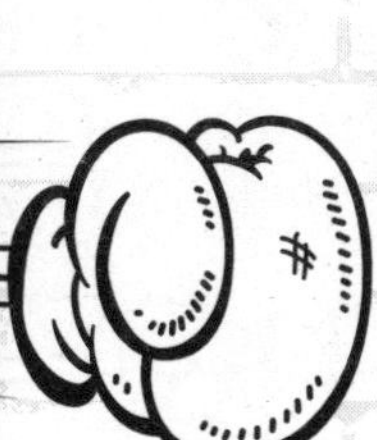

7.

Increase chuckles by **JOINING SHORTER JOKES INTO LONGER STORIES**. This works because your audience is warmed up and wants to continue laughing.

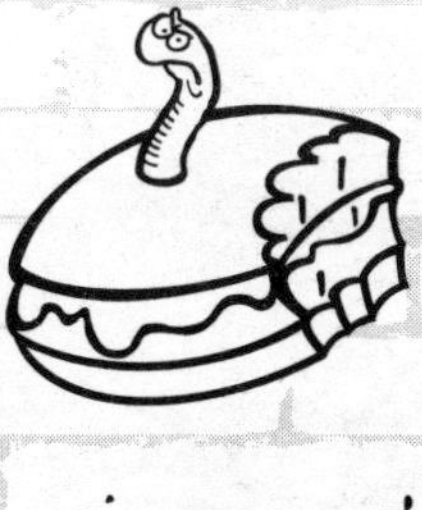

8. **EXAGGERATE!** Most jokes are entirely made up anyway, so it's not as if you're fibbing. The more ridiculous it is, the funnier the joke becomes! Watch comedy on TV or online for inspiration.

9. Why not ask your teachers to recommend their **FAVOURITE COMEDIANS**? If you're nervous to begin with, don't be worried – everyone is!

10. Team up with a trusted buddy as a **DOUBLE ACT** like Dennis and Minnie to build confidence!

There is also little difference between what kids and grown-ups find funny – when you're older, you just know more stuff to make jokes about! So ask your teacher to tell you their favourite joke.

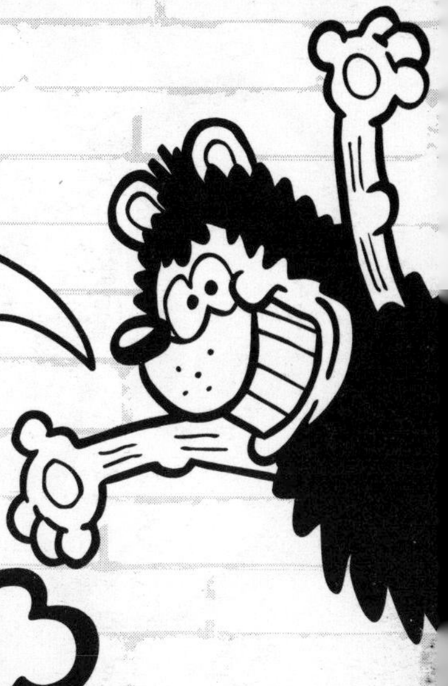

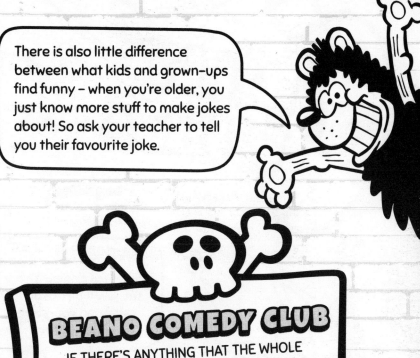

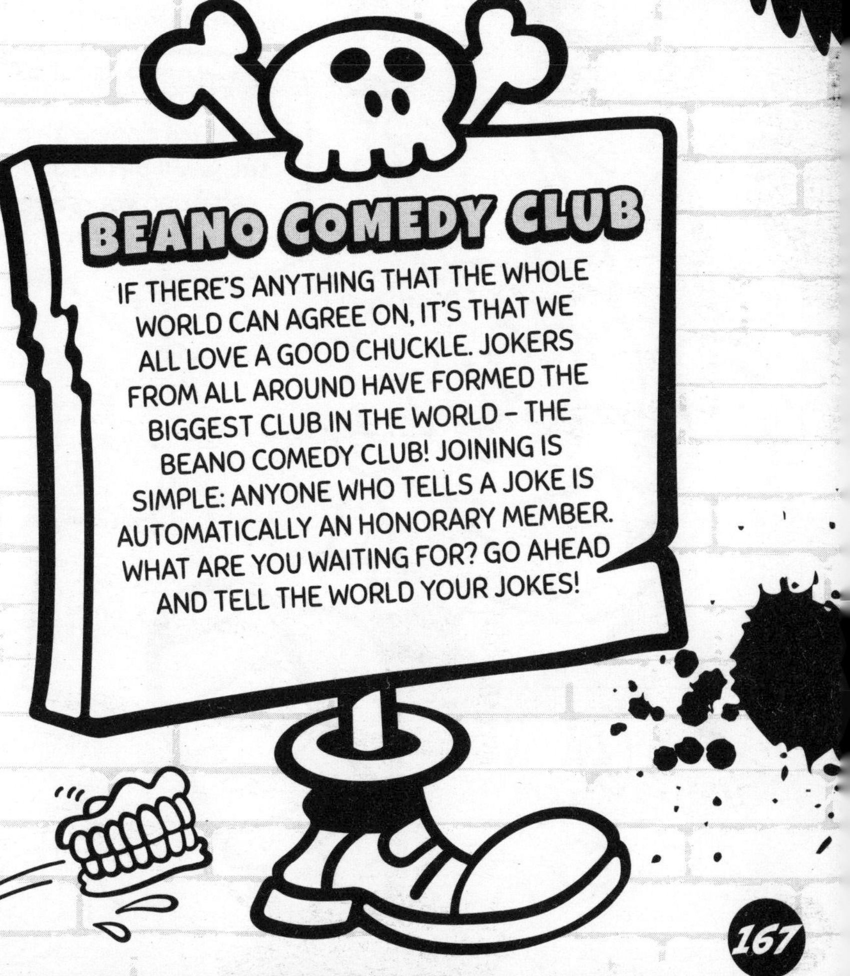
BEANO COMEDY CLUB
IF THERE'S ANYTHING THAT THE WHOLE WORLD CAN AGREE ON, IT'S THAT WE ALL LOVE A GOOD CHUCKLE. JOKERS FROM ALL AROUND HAVE FORMED THE BIGGEST CLUB IN THE WORLD – THE BEANO COMEDY CLUB! JOINING IS SIMPLE: ANYONE WHO TELLS A JOKE IS AUTOMATICALLY AN HONORARY MEMBER. WHAT ARE YOU WAITING FOR? GO AHEAD AND TELL THE WORLD YOUR JOKES!

BILLY WHIZZ

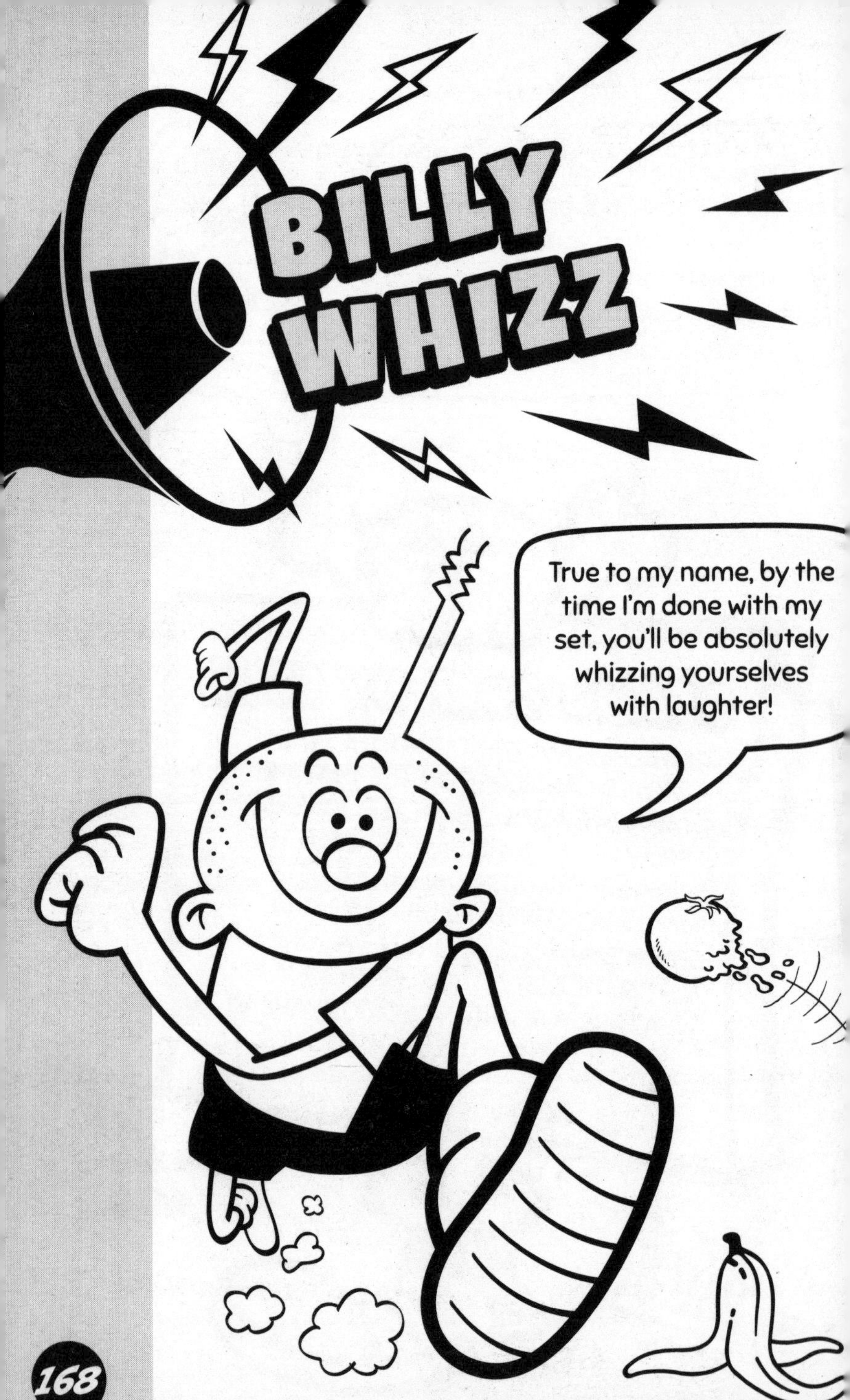
True to my name, by the time I'm done with my set, you'll be absolutely whizzing yourselves with laughter!

WHAT IS A GYMNAST'S FAVOURITE PUDDING?

JAM ROLY-POLY!

WHAT KIND OF CATS LOVE TO GO BOWLING?

ALLEY CATS!

WHICH ATHLETE IS WARMEST IN WINTER?

A LONG JUMPER!

WHAT TIME DO TENNIS PLAYERS GO TO BED?

TEN-NISH!

WHY DID THE DUCK JOIN THE BASEBALL GAME?

TO MAKE A FOWL SHOT!

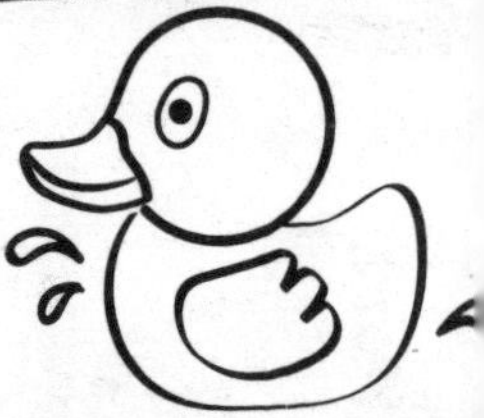

WHY DIDN'T THE HIPSTER SWIM IN THE RIVER?

IT WAS TOO MAINSTREAM!

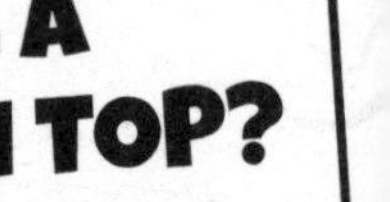

WHAT DO YOU CALL A BICYCLE WITH A BED ON TOP?

BED-RIDDEN!

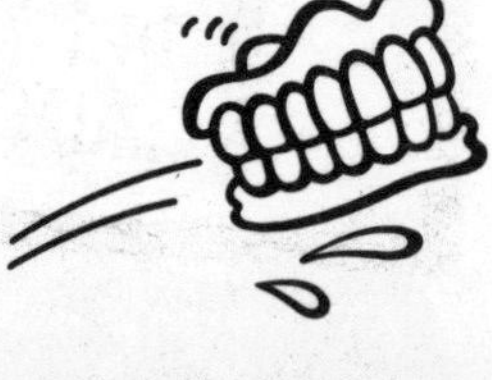

WHY WAS THE HOCKEY PLAYER TAKEN TO JAIL?

HE SHOT A GOAL!

WHY DID THE RUGBY PLAYER GO TO SEE THE VET?

HIS CALVES WERE SORE!

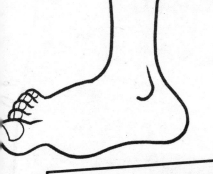

WHY DID THE LIONS LOSE THE WORLD CUP?

THEY WERE PLAYING AGAINST CHEETAHS!

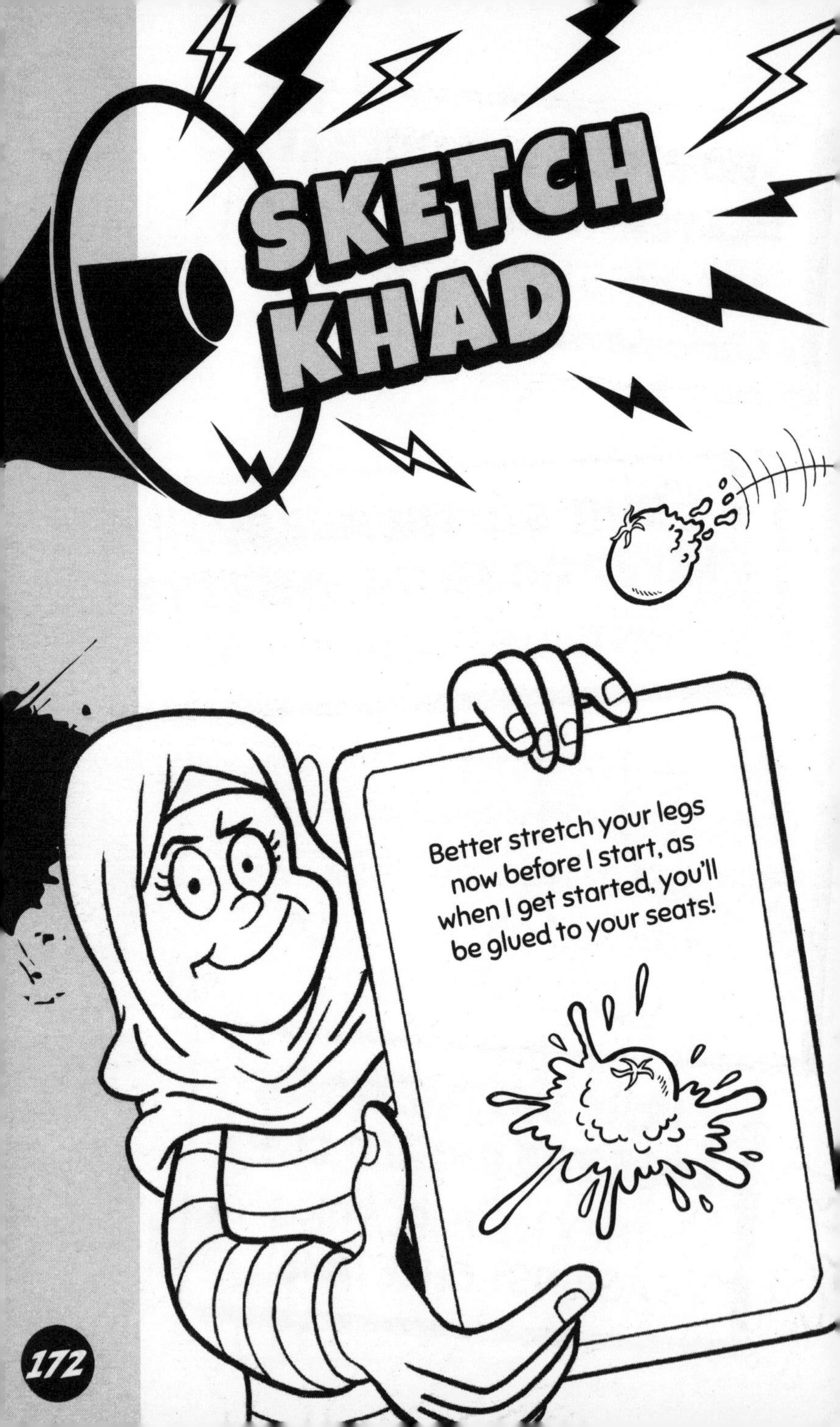
SKETCH KHAD
Better stretch your legs now before I start, as when I get started, you'll be glued to your seats!

WHY IS RAINBOW SLIME SO POPULAR?

IT COMES WITH A POT OF GOLD!

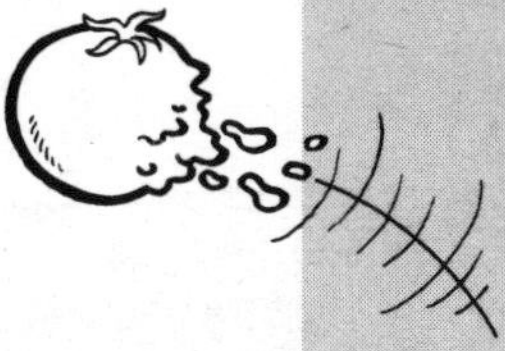

WHAT'S A MAGNET SLIME'S FAVOURITE BAND?

METALLICA!

HOW DO YOU KNOW IF TWO SLIMES ARE IN LOVE?

THEY'RE PRACTICALLY GLUED TOGETHER!

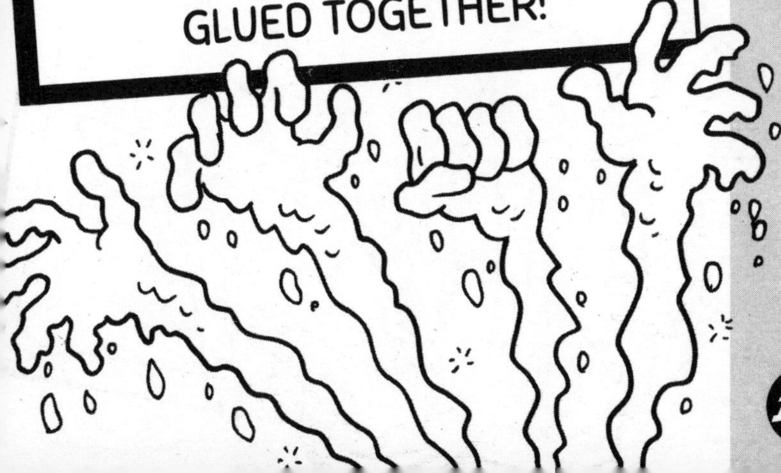

WHAT'S A SLIME'S FAVOURITE GAME?

SLIMON SAYS!

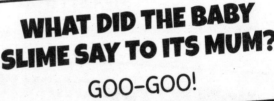

WHAT DID THE BABY SLIME SAY TO ITS MUM?

GOO-GOO!

WHAT DID THE BOSS SNAIL SAY TO THE WORKER SNAIL?

SLIME IS OF THE ESSENCE!

WHY DID THE SLIME STAY AT HOME?

TO AVOID THESE JOKES?

HE HAD NO PLACE TO GOO!

HOW DO YOU KNOW WHEN SOMEONE'S PUT TOO MUCH GLUE IN THEIR SLIME?

THEY CAN'T PUT IT DOWN!

VIKING DENNIS

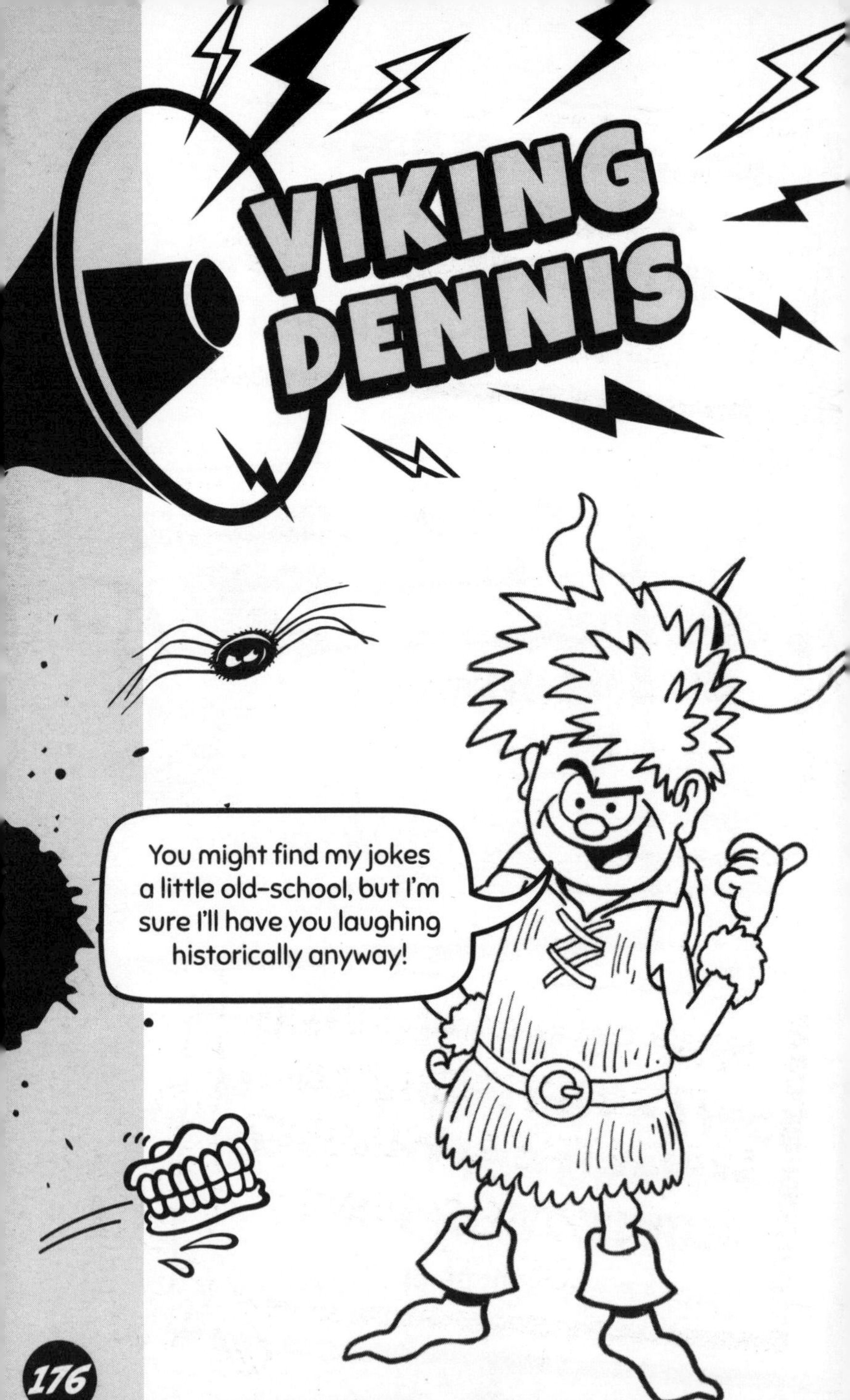
You might find my jokes a little old-school, but I'm sure I'll have you laughing historically anyway!

HOW DID VIKING SAILORS COMMUNICATE?

USING NORSE CODE!

WHY DO BOATS GO ON DATES?

THEY'RE LOOKING FOR ROW-MANCE!

WHY DO VIKINGS FIND IT SO DIFFICULT TO LEARN THE ALPHABET?

THEY KEEP GETTING LOST AT C!

WHAT DID ONE VIKING SAY TO THE OTHER WHEN THEY YELLED 'LAND AHOY!'

'ARRR, YE SHORE?'

WHAT LIES AT THE BOTTOM OF THE OCEAN AND TWITCHES?

A NERVOUS WRECK!

WHY DON'T SAILORS LIKE BUYING NEW HATS?

THEY'RE AFRAID OF CAP SIZING!

WHAT DO VIKINGS EAT FOR BREAKFAST?

B-OATMEAL!

WHAT VEGETABLES DO VIKING BOATMEN HATE?

LEEKS!

WHY DO SAILORS EAT SO MANY CARROTS?

IT HELPS THEM SEA BETTER!

MRS BINDING

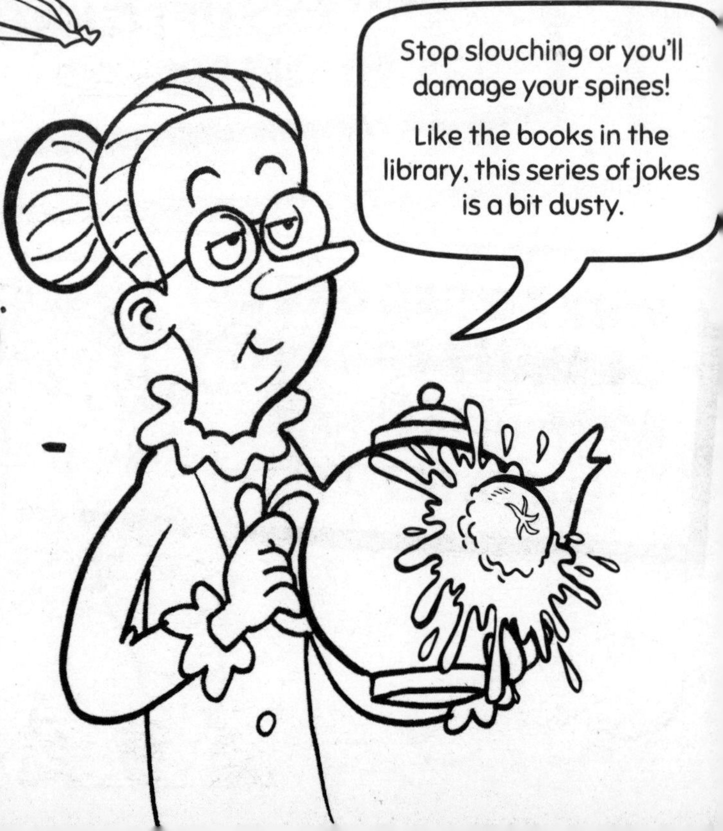
Stop slouching or you'll damage your spines!
Like the books in the library, this series of jokes is a bit dusty.

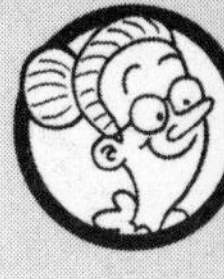

I WENT TO THE LIBRARY TO GET A MEDICAL BOOK ON ABDOMINAL PAIN . . .

BUT SOMEONE HAD PULLED THE APPENDIX OUT!

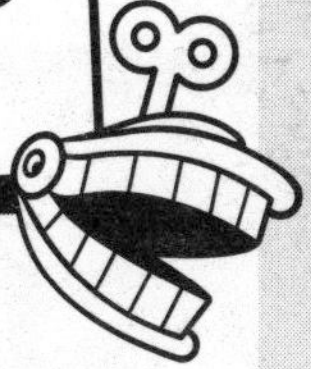

WHAT DID THE SKETCHBOOK SAY TO THE NOVEL?

I'M DRAWING A BLANK!

I HAD PLANS TO READ A BOOK ABOUT SINKHOLES . . .

BUT THEY FELL THROUGH!

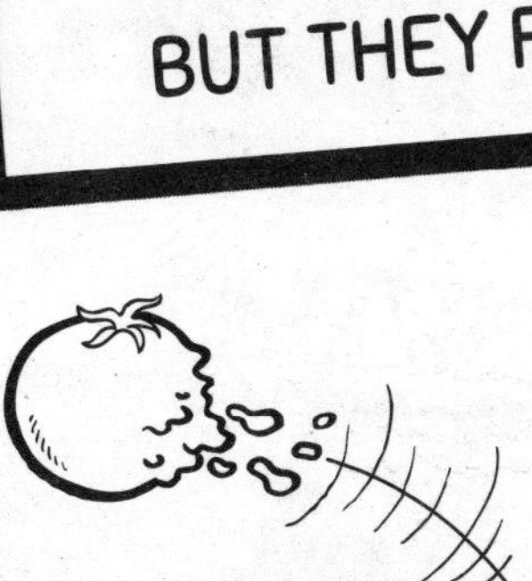

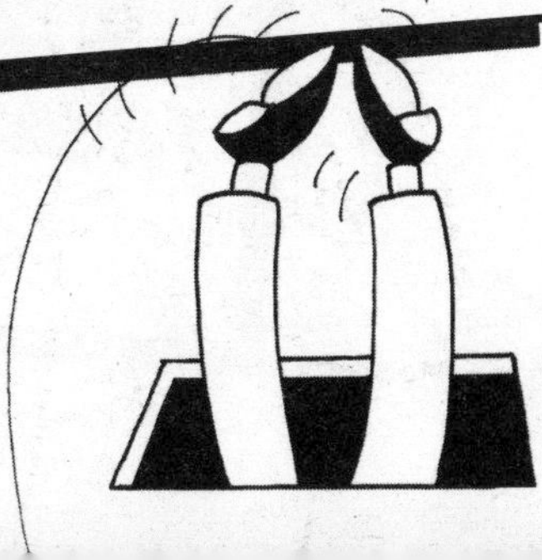

WHY COULD THE READING ADDICT NOT STOP READING?

THEY HAD NO SHELF CONTROL!

WHAT DOES A LIBRARIAN TAKE FISHING?

BOOKWORMS!

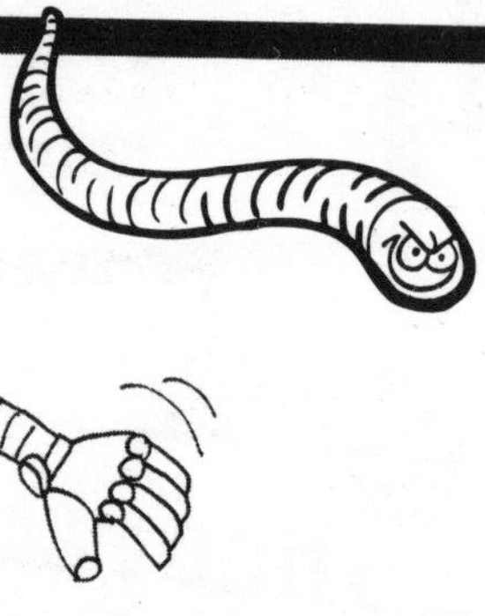

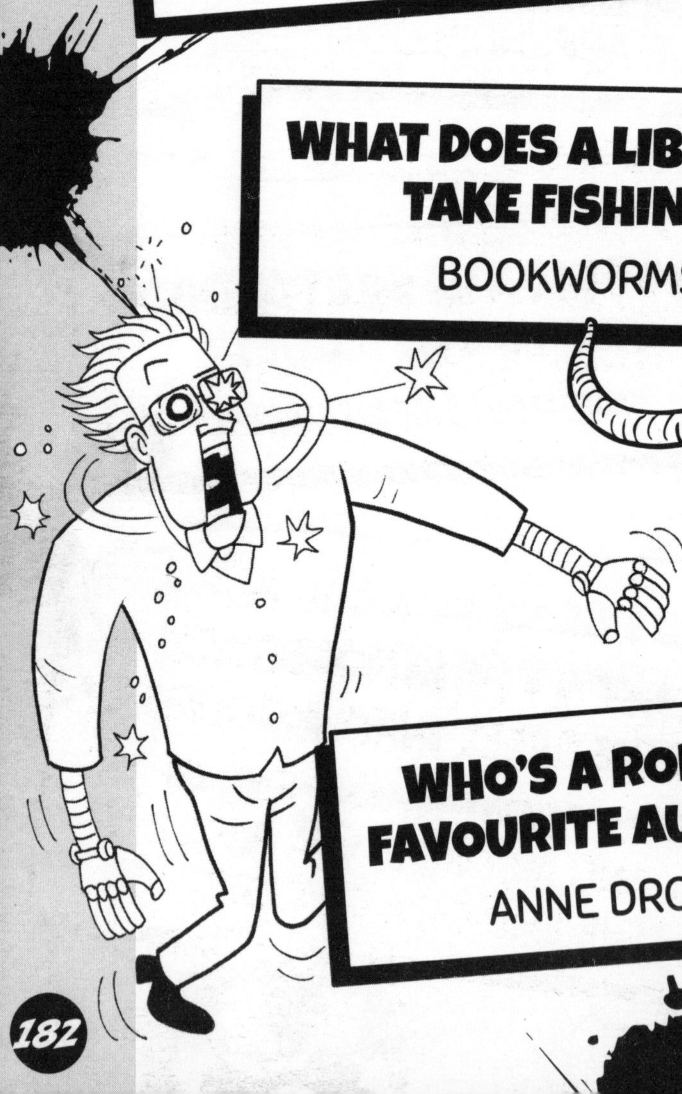

WHO'S A ROBOT'S FAVOURITE AUTHOR?

ANNE DROID!

WHY DID SHAKESPEARE WRITE WITH INK?

HE COULDN'T DECIDE WHAT PENCIL TO USE ... 2B OR NOT 2B!

WHICH BUILDING IN BEANOTOWN IS THE TALLEST?

THE LIBRARY ... IT HAS THE MOST STORIES!

WHAT'S THE DIFFERENCE BETWEEN A CAT AND A COMMA?

A CAT HAS CLAWS AT THE END OF ITS PAWS, AND A COMMA IS A PAUSE AT THE END OF A CLAUSE!

183

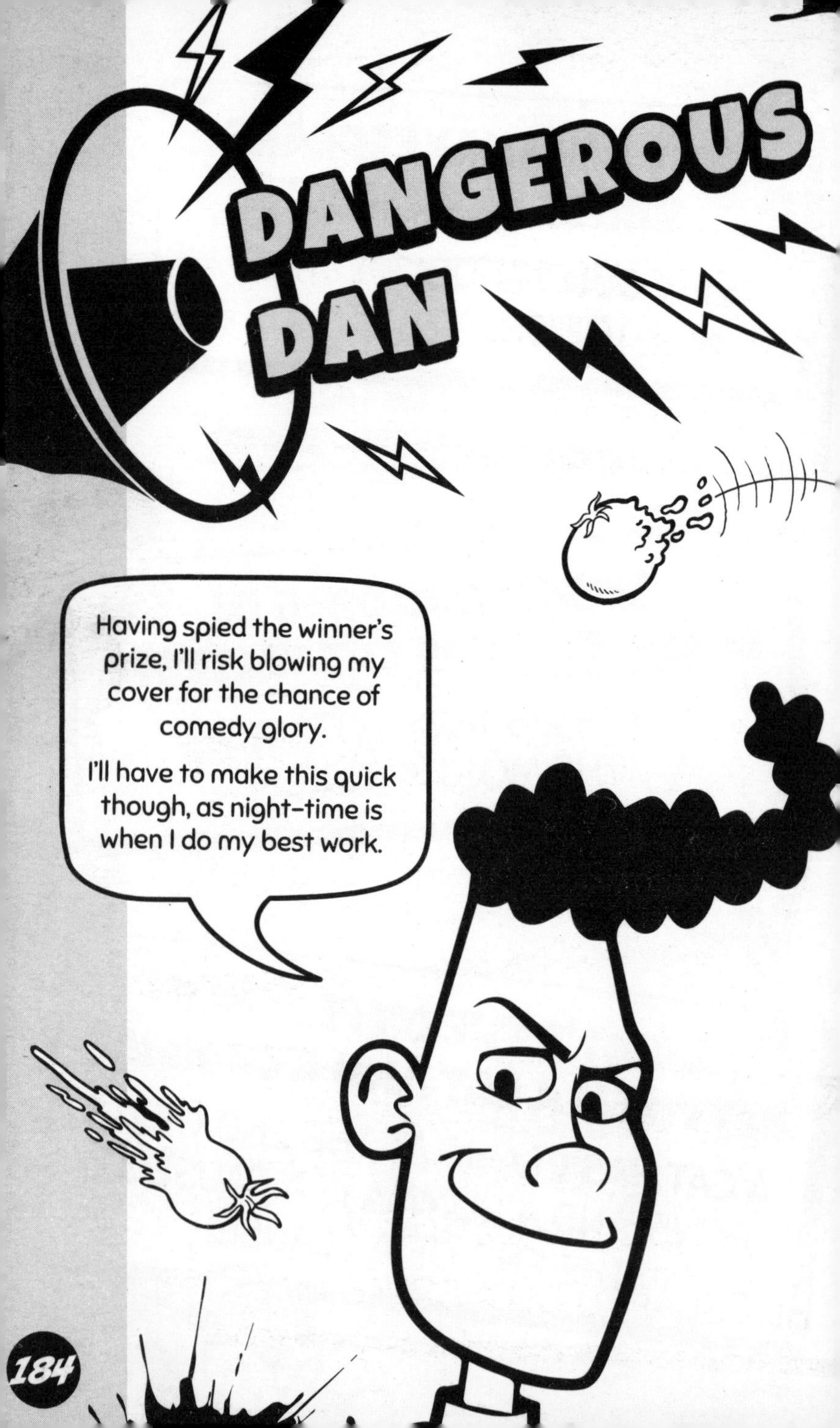
DANGEROUS DAN
Having spied the winner's prize, I'll risk blowing my cover for the chance of comedy glory.
I'll have to make this quick though, as night-time is when I do my best work.

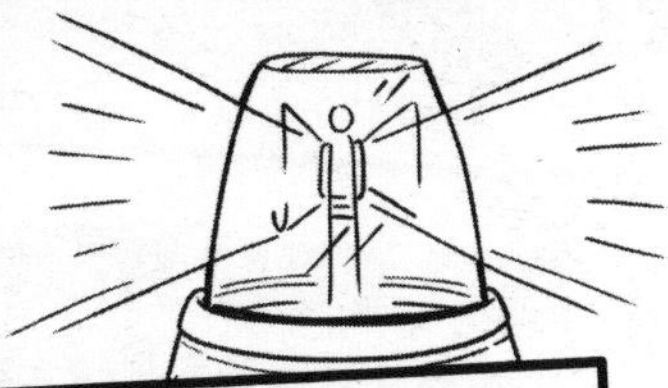

WHY DID THE ROBBER TAKE A BATH?

TO MAKE A CLEAN GETAWAY!

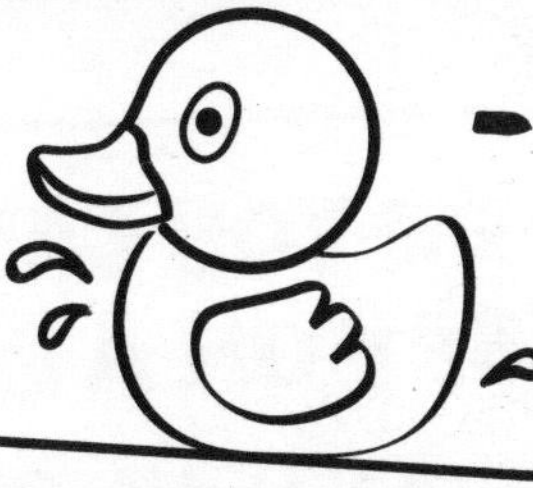

WHY DO DUCKS MAKE GOOD DETECTIVES?

THEY ALWAYS QUACK THE CASE!

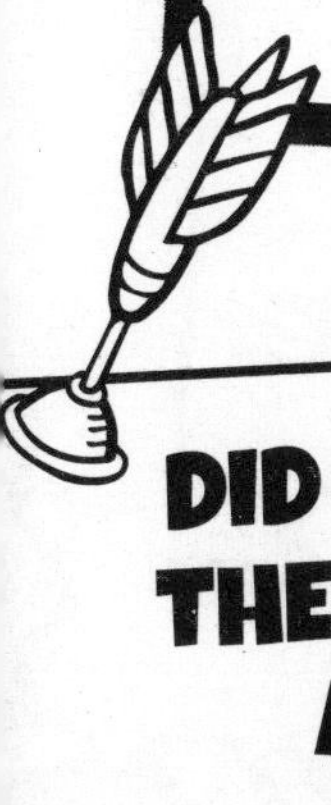

DID YOU HEAR ABOUT THE THIEF WHO STOLE A SURFBOARD?

HE ESCAPED ON A CRIME WAVE!

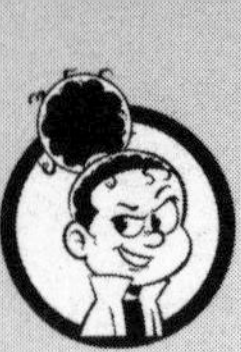

DID YOU HEAR ABOUT THE ITALIAN DOUBLE AGENT?

HE WAS AN IM-PASTA!

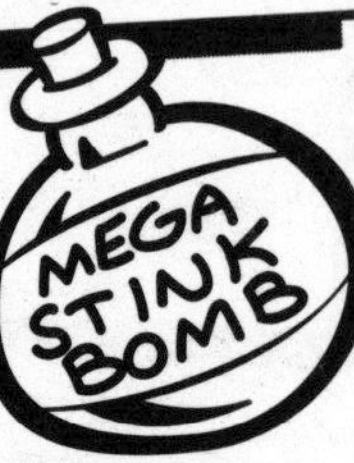
MEGA
STINK
BOMB

WHAT DO YOU CALL IT WHEN YOU SPY ON A BUTCHER?

A STEAK-OUT!

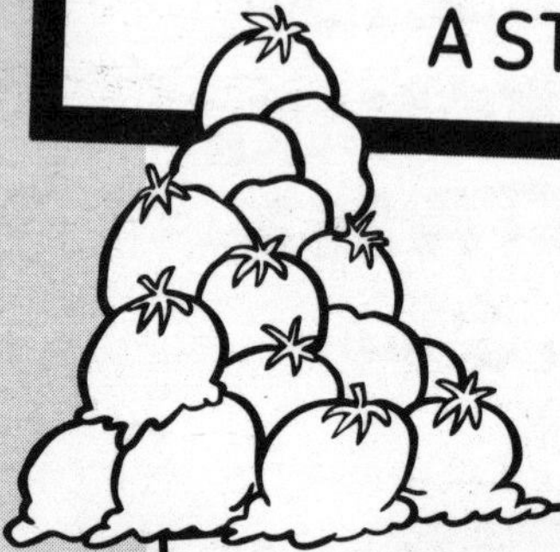

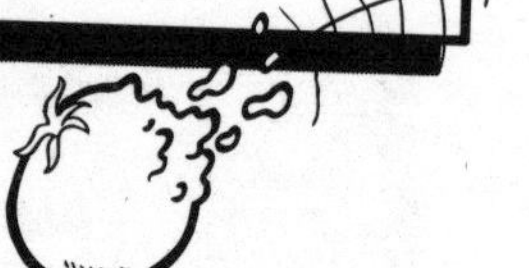

WHAT'S A SPY'S FAVOURITE FOOTWEAR?

SNEAKERS!

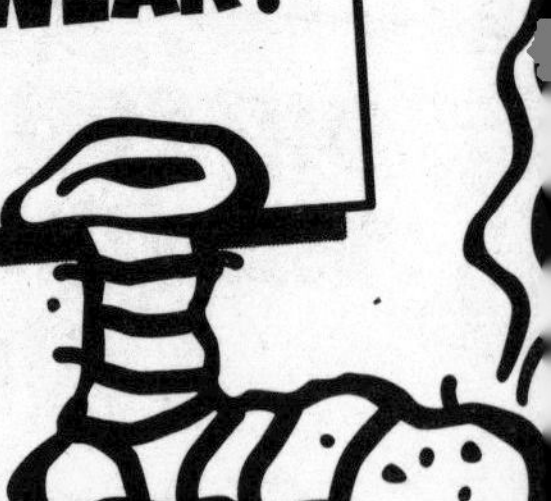

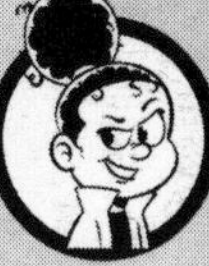

WHY DID THE SPY SPEND ALL DAY IN BED?

BECAUSE THEY WERE UNDERCOVER!

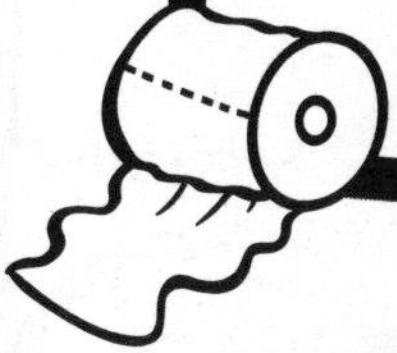

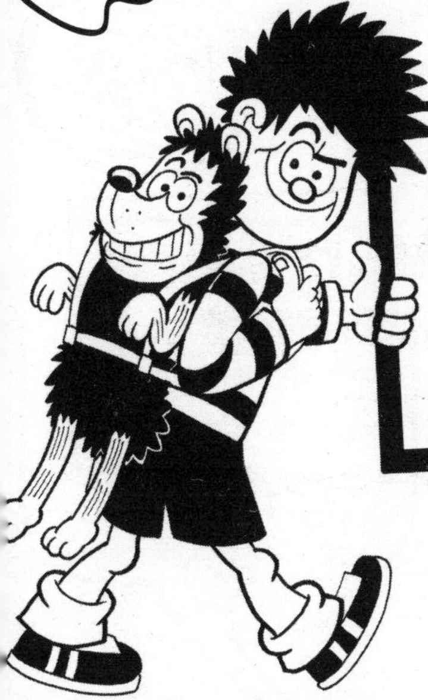

WHY DID THE SPY CROSS THE ROAD?

BECAUSE HE WAS NEVER ON YOUR SIDE.

I DON'T KNOW WHY YOU'RE WORRIED ABOUT YOUR PHONE SPYING ON YOU ...

YOUR VACUUM HAS BEEN GATHERING DIRT FOR YEARS!

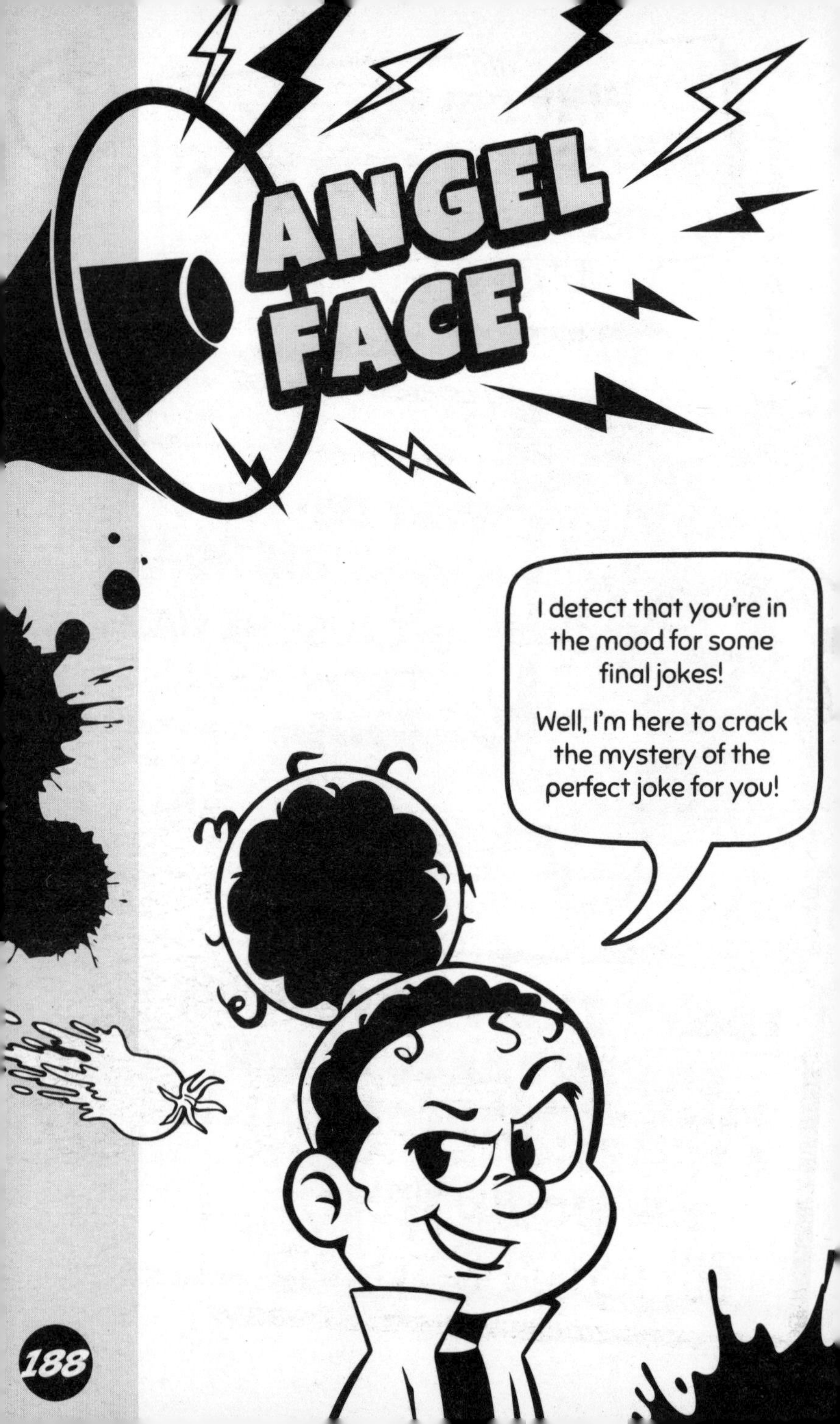
ANGEL FACE
I detect that you're in the mood for some final jokes!
Well, I'm here to crack the mystery of the perfect joke for you!

WHAT DO YOU CALL A COMEDIAN WHO CAN'T SIT DOWN?

A STAND-UP COMEDIAN!

DID YOU HEAR THE STORY ABOUT THE RABBIT'S CHILDHOOD?

IT'S A HARE-RAISING TALE!

I ENTERED TEN PUNS IN A PUN CONTEST HOPING ONE WOULD WIN ...

BUT NO PUN IN-TEN-DID!

I FARTED IN AN ELEVATOR ...

THAT'S WRONG ON SO MANY LEVELS!

WHAT WAS THE ATMOSPHERE LIKE WHEN THE PAST, PRESENT AND FUTURE WALKED INTO CLASS?

TENSE!

WHAT DO YOU CALL A COW WITH A TWITCH?

BEEF JERKY!

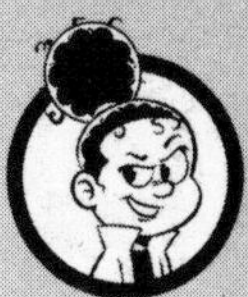

DON'T SPELL 'PART' BACKWARDS . . .

IT'S A TRAP!

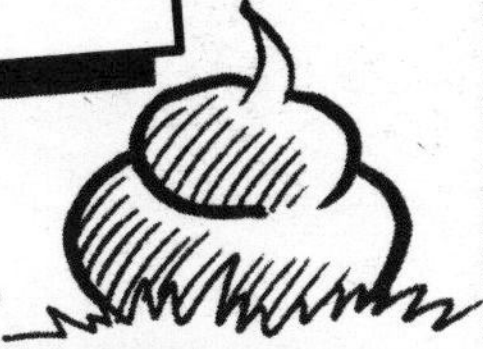

WHAT DID THE GRAPE SAY WHEN SOMEONE STOOD ON IT?

NOTHING, IT JUST LET OUT A LITTLE WINE!

PEOPLE USED TO LAUGH AT ME WHEN I WOULD SAY I WANT TO BE A COMEDIAN . . .

WELL, NOBODY'S LAUGHING NOW!

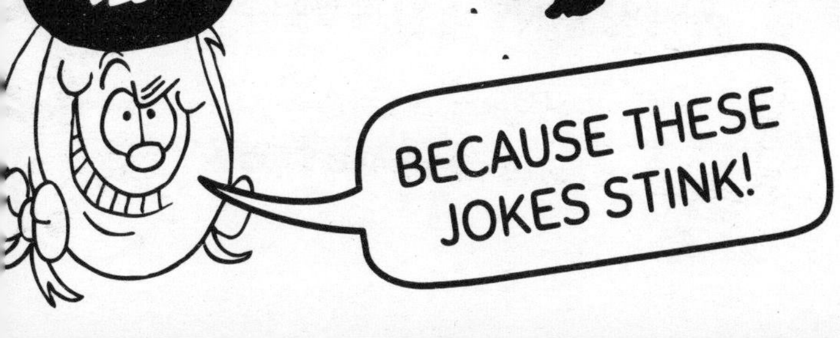
BECAUSE THESE JOKES STINK!

RATE THE ACTS

DENNIS MENACE (-------)

MINNIE THE MINX (-------)

WALTER BROWN (-------)

MISS MISTRY (-------)

CUTHBERT (-------)

PIE FACE (-------)

RALF THE JANITOR (-------)

WINSTON THE CAT (-------)

RATE THE ACTS

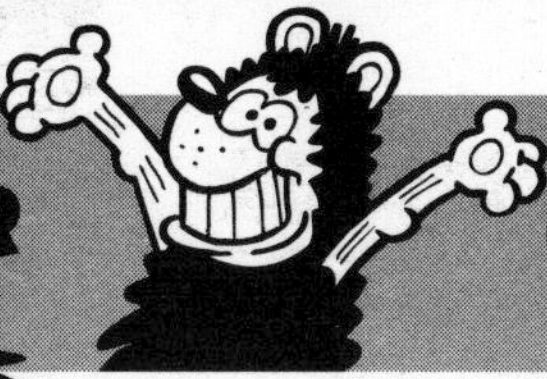

GNASHER

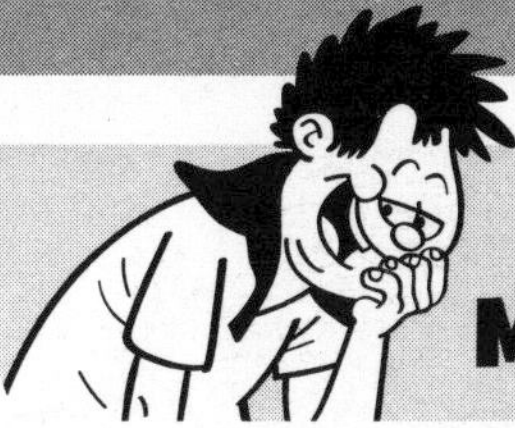

DENNIS MENACE SR.

BEA MENACE

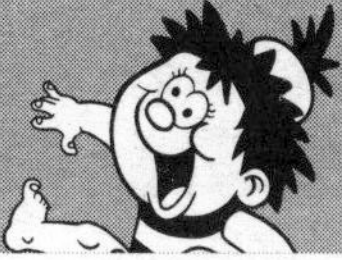

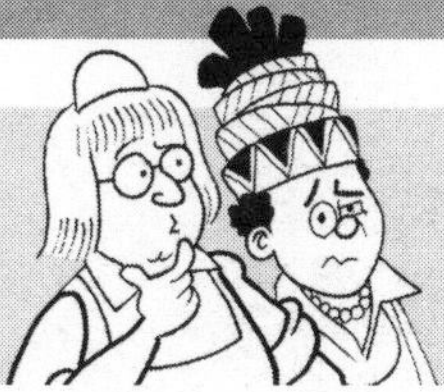

OLIVE & OLIVE

DASHER

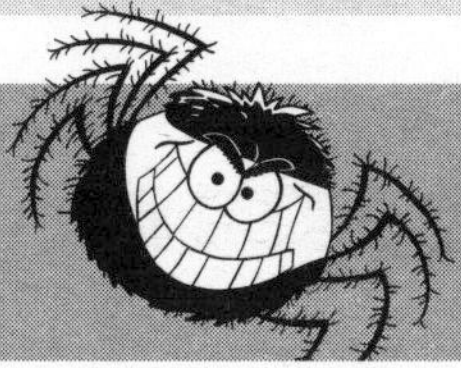

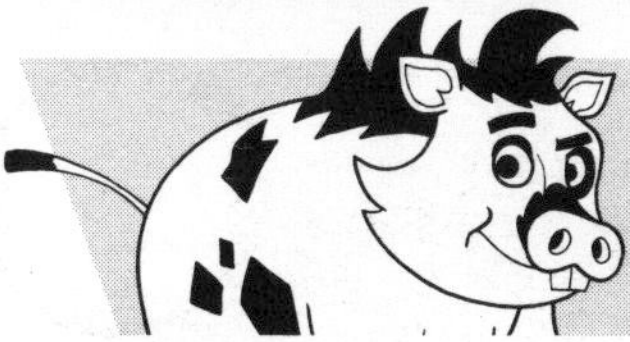

RASHER

VITO

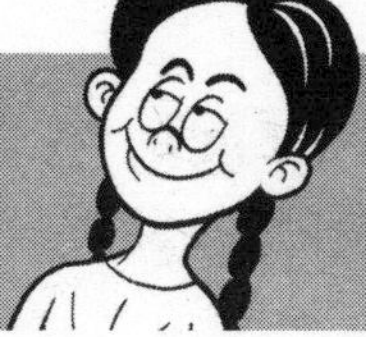

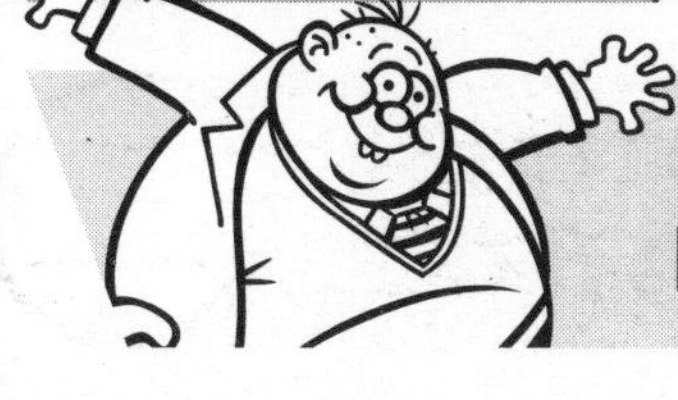

FREDDY BROWN

RATE THE ACTS

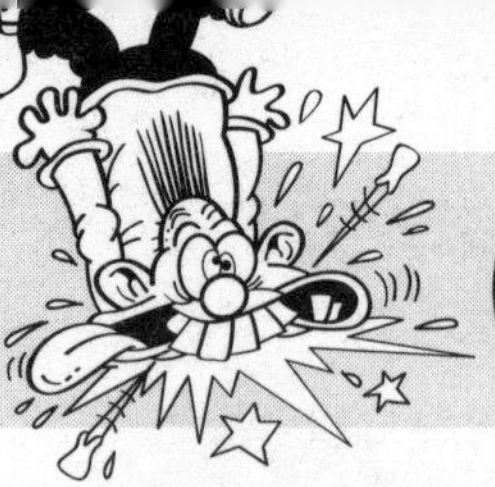

CALAMITY JAMES

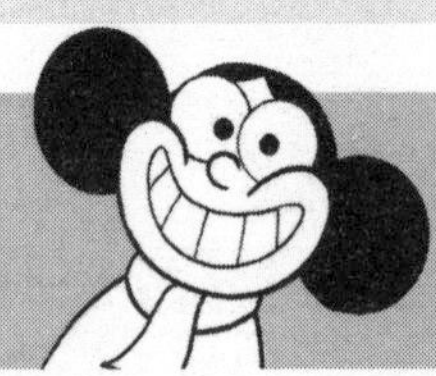

BETTY

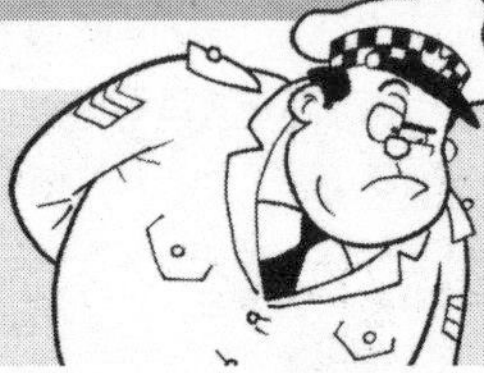

SERGEANT SLIPPER

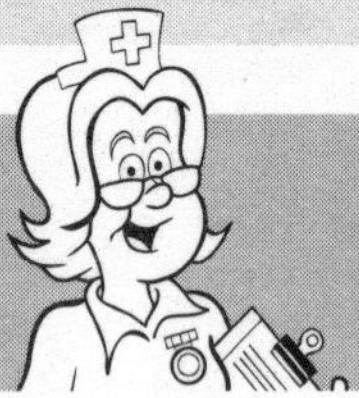

MRS SPLINT

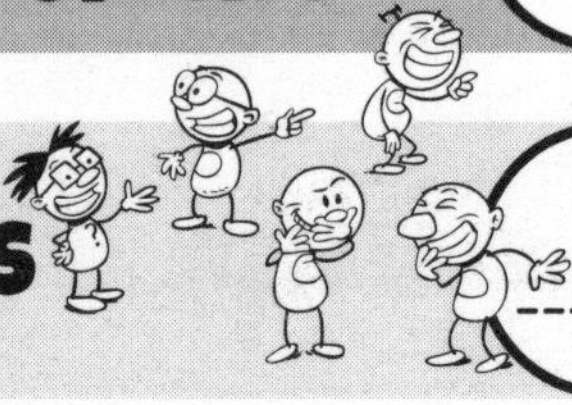

NUMSKULLS

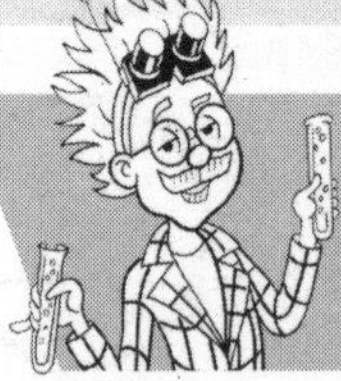

PROFESSOR VON SCREWTOP

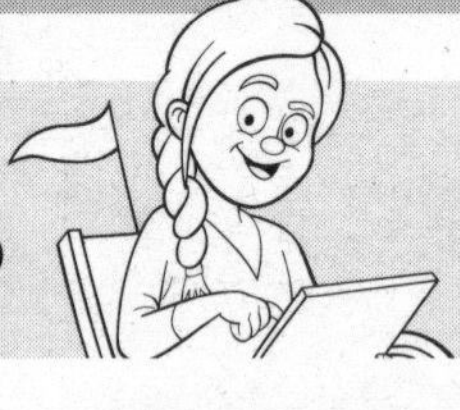

RUBI VON SCREWTOP

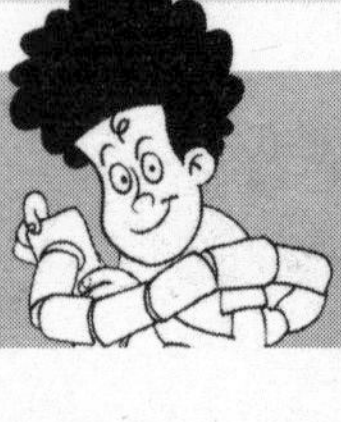

STEVIE STAR

RATE THE ACTS

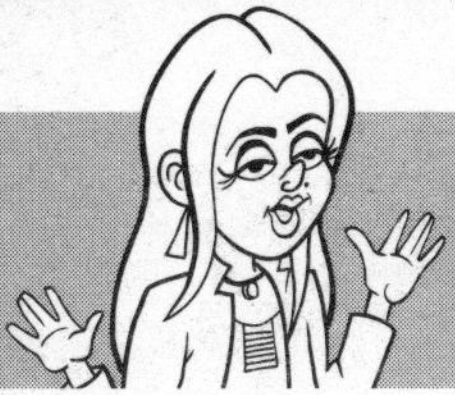

HEENA CHANDRA

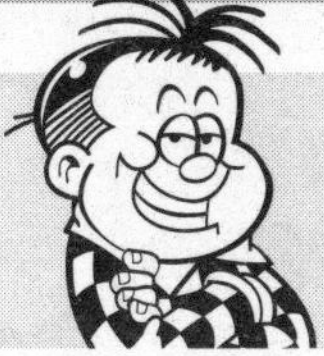

ROGER THE DODGER

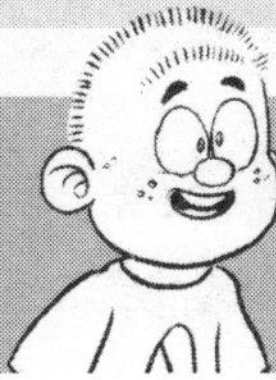

LES PRETEND

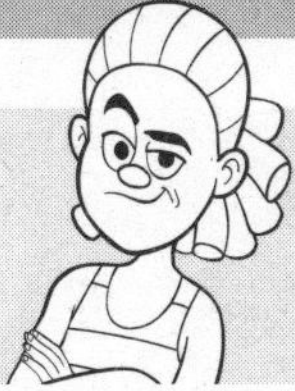

JJ

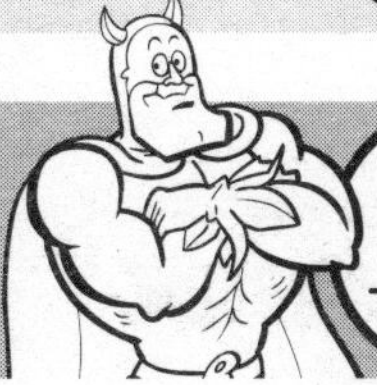

BANANAMAN

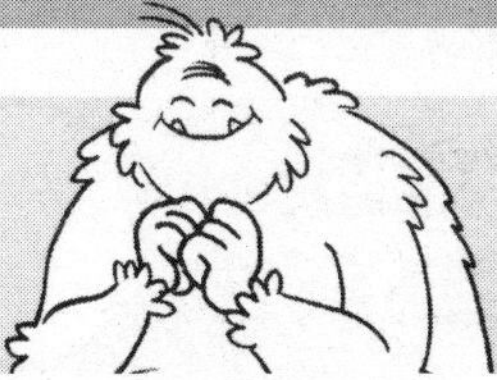

YETI

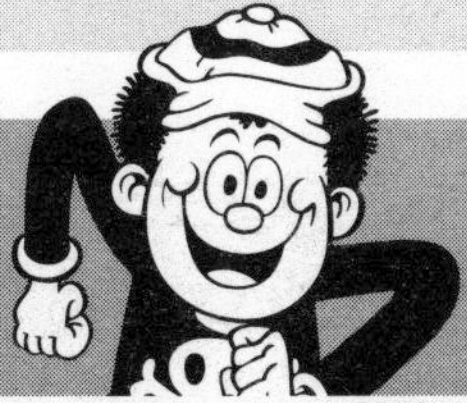

DANNY MORGAN

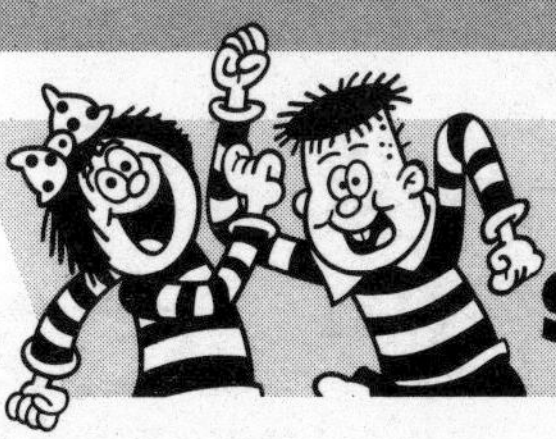

TOOTS & SIDNEY PIE

RATE THE ACTS

SCOTTY 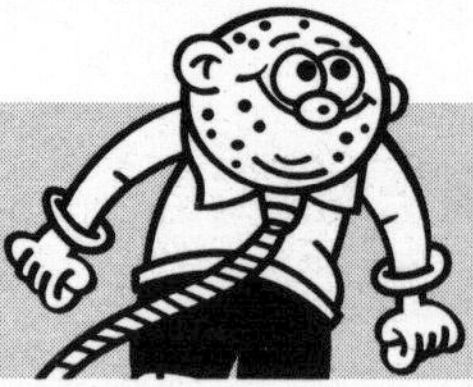 --------

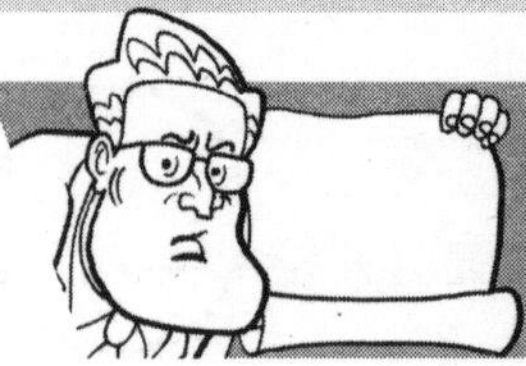 WILBUR BROWN --------

HARSHA CHANDRA 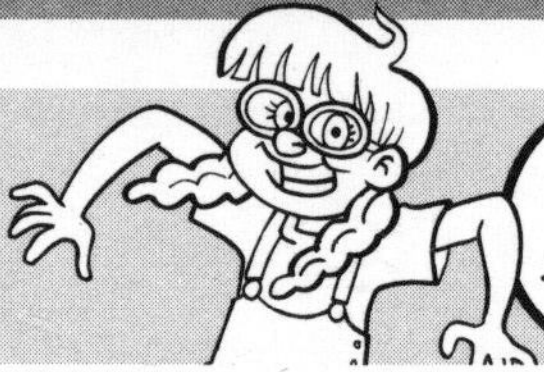 --------

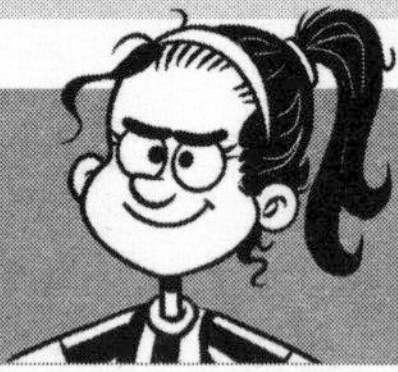 MAHIRA SALIM --------

BILLY WHIZZ 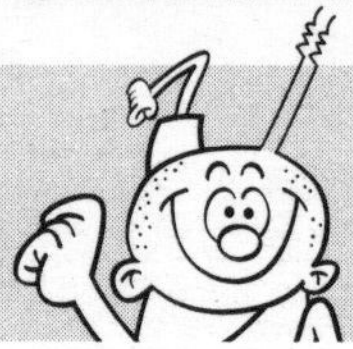 --------

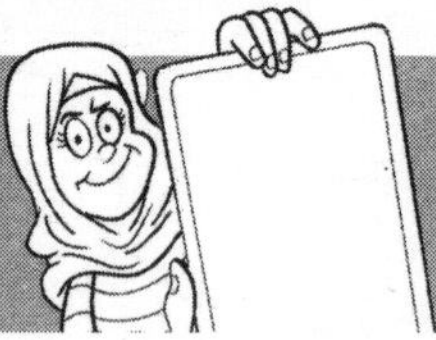 SKETCH KHAD --------

VIKING DENNIS 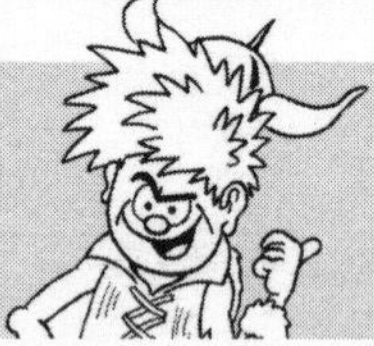 --------

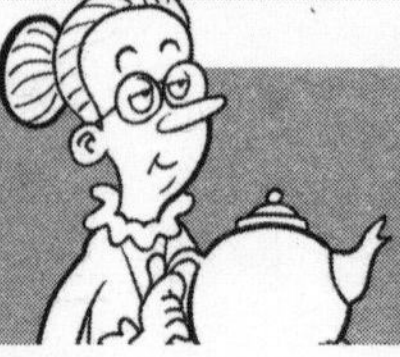 MRS BINDING --------

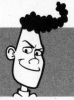

DANGEROUS DAN

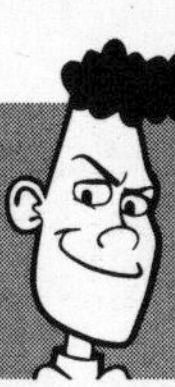

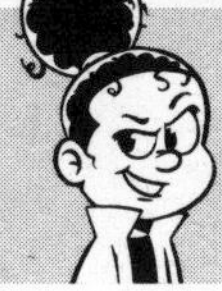

ANGEL FACE

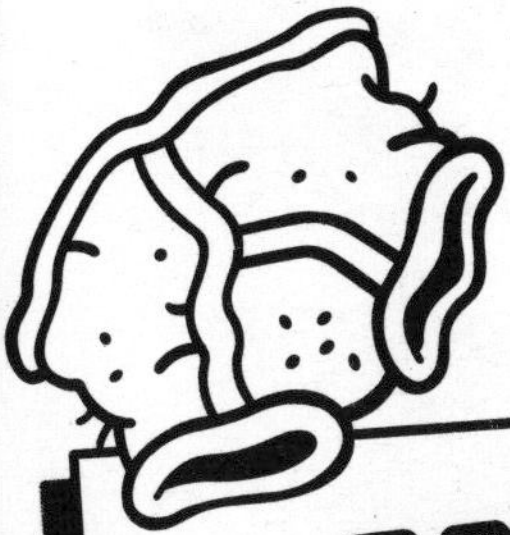

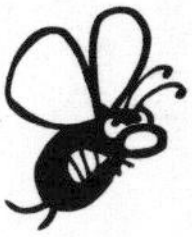

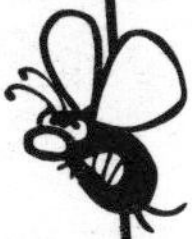

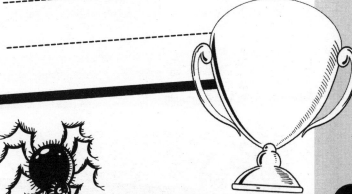

AND THE WINNER IS ...

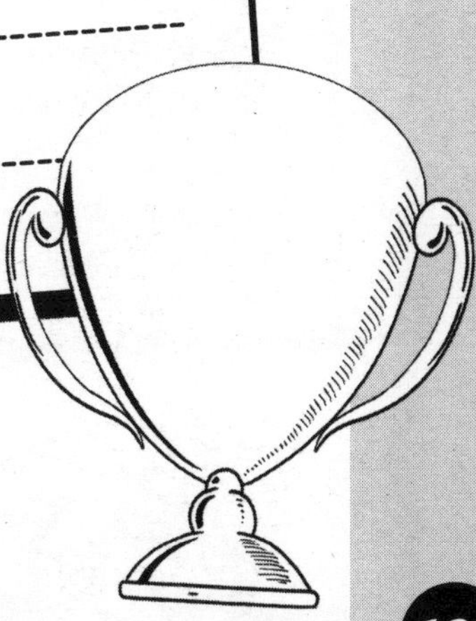

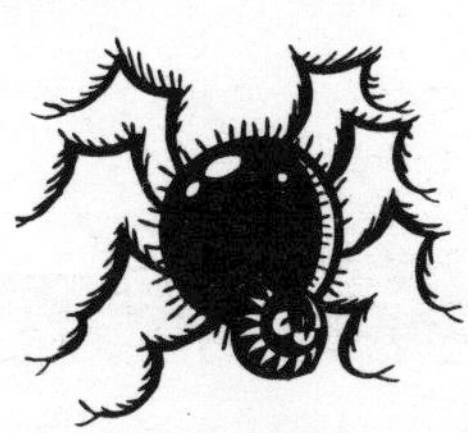

BEANO
BRITAIN'S FUNNIEST CLASS

Miss Mistry believes her class, 3C, is the funniest classroom in the country. Every year we put this to the test with Beano comic's competition to crown Britain's Funniest Class. It's like the World Cup for LOLZ!

Teachers enter their pupils' funniest jokes in for the Beano gag writers to rate.

They narrow the thousands of entries down to a shortlist of ten that are showcased on Beano.com for the public to vote for their ultimate favourite.

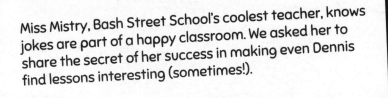

Miss Mistry, Bash Street School's coolest teacher, knows jokes are part of a happy classroom. We asked her to share the secret of her success in making even Dennis find lessons interesting (sometimes!).

Teachers like to laugh too, you know! Our favourite students are often the funny ones, so long as the jokester isn't interrupting the class. Kids who enjoy laughing are often the most confident, creative and resilient, so we should all be looking to inject some comedy into our days!

We've all heard that laughter is the best medicine. It's a largely underestimated and often overlooked force for good. I like to encourage it in my class as much as possible.

HERE ARE 2022'S HILARIOUS FINALIST JOKES!

THINK YOU CAN DO BETTER? BE SURE TO SUBMIT YOUR JOKES IN TIME FOR NEXT YEAR'S COMPETITION TO WIN COMEDY GLORY FOR YOUR WHOLE CLASS!

WHY DOES GNASHER USE SO MANY CONJUNCTIONS?

HE JUST LOVES BUTS!

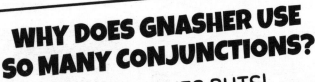

WHY IS BRUNO NEVER SURPRISED BY ANYTHING?

HE SAW IT COMING!

WHAT DO YOU CALL A MONKEY ON A ROLLERCOASTER?

A CHIMPANZEEEEEEEEEK!

WHAT DO YOU CALL AN EMERGENCY SERVICE SHEEP?

A LAMB–ULANCE DRIVER!

WHAT IS THE BEST DINOSAUR TO PLAY FOOTBALL WITH?

A TYRANNO–SCORE–US REX!

THE PACIFIC OCEAN IS ABOUT 11,000 METRES DEEP.

BUT THAT'S NOT VERY PACIFIC!

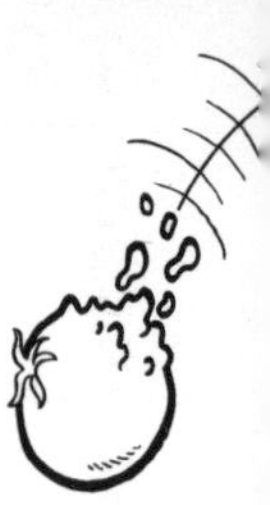

WHAT DO YOU CALL A CLASS OF CHILDREN WHO EAT POTATOES USING THEIR TOES?

THE MASH FEET KIDS!

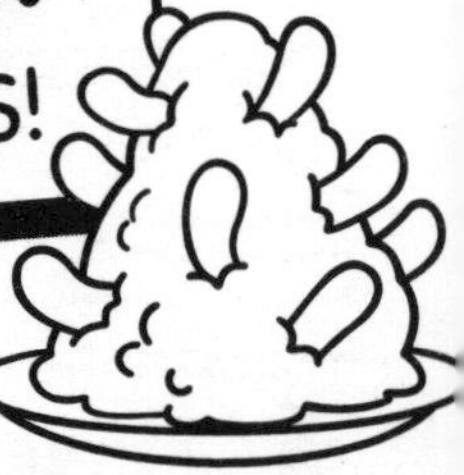

WHY DID THE BOTTOM GO TO THE DOCTOR?

BECAUSE HE HAD A FART ATTACK!

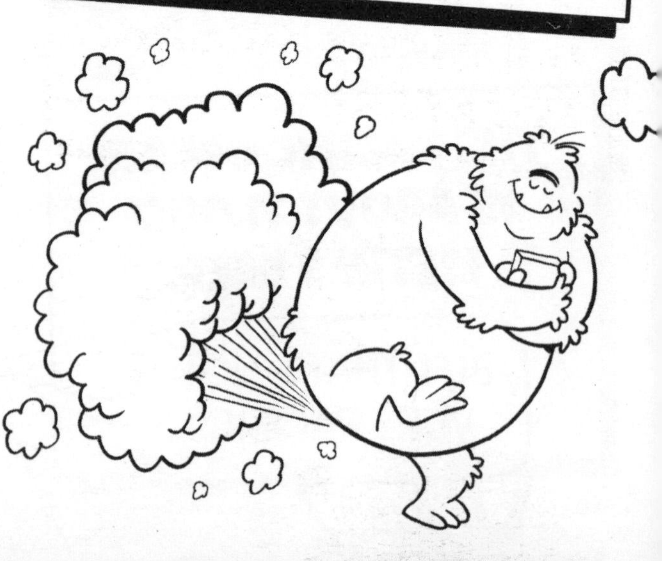

WHY DID THE WHITEBOARD HAVE NOTHING TO DO?

BECAUSE IT WAS BLANK!

DOCTOR: I'M AFRAID THAT WE NEED TO REMOVE YOUR WHOLE SPINE.

PATIENT: BUT WHY?

DOCTOR: BECAUSE IT'S REALLY HOLDING YOU BACK!

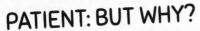

CHECK OUT SOME PAST FINALISTS' FUNNIES. WHICH ONE WOULD YOU HAVE VOTED FOR?

MORE IMPORTANTLY, DO YOU THINK YOUR CLASS IS EVEN FUNNIER? THERE'S ONLY ONE WAY TO FIND OUT. BUT DON'T FORGET TO TELL YOUR TEACHER!

WHAT DO YOU CALL A MAGIC LABRADOR?

A LABRACADABRADOR.

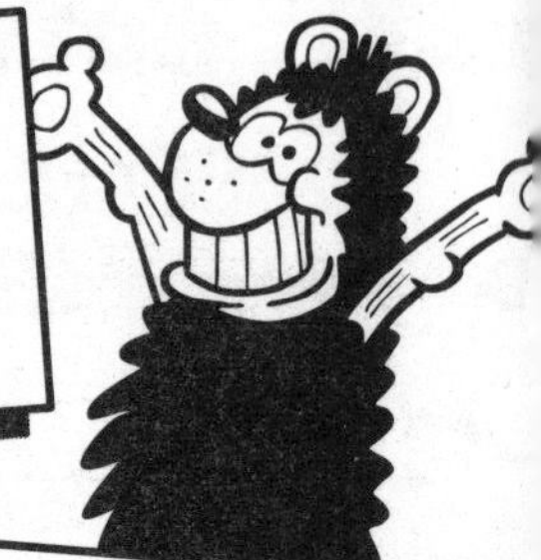

I WENT TO THE DOCTOR THIS MORNING AND SAID I HAVE A GOLF BALL STUCK UP MY BUM!

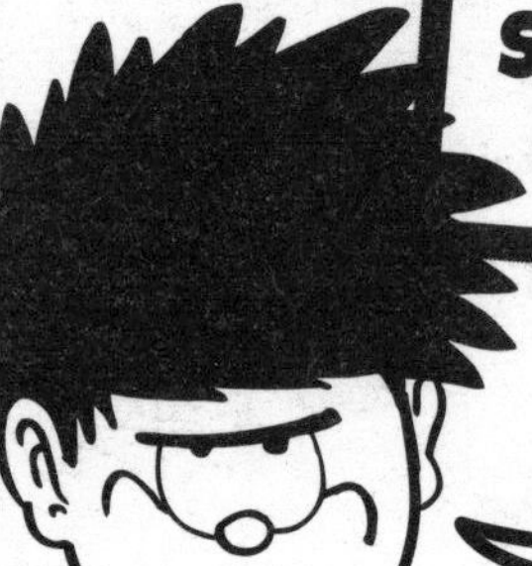
THE DOCTOR SAID, 'YES I CAN SEE, IT'S GONE UP A FAIRWAY!

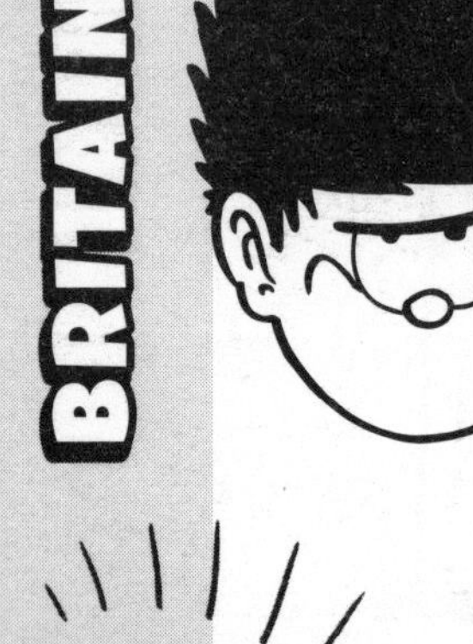

YOUTUBE, TWITTER AND FACEBOOK ARE MAKING A JOINT WEBSITE. WHAT WOULD IT BE CALLED?

YOUTWITFACE.

WHAT'S THE DIFFERENCE BETWEEN HARRY HILL AND DENNIS THE MENACE?

NOTHING, THEY BOTH HAVE GREAT GNASHERS.

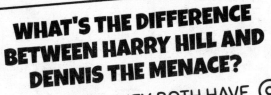

A MEXICAN MAN SAYS TO HIS FRIENDS, 'I CAN DISAPPEAR IN THREE SECONDS. UNO ... DOS ...' AND THEN HE DISAPPEARS WITHOUT A 'TRES'!

WHY DID THE CHICKEN CROSS THE ROAD?

HE FARTED, SO HE HAD TO RUN AWAY FROM THE SMELL!

WHAT IS GREEN AND NOT HEAVY?

LIGHT GREEN.

WHERE'S THE BEST PLACE TO TAKE A DOG FOR A WALK?
LEEDS!

KNOCK KNOCK.
WHO'S THERE?
JUSTIN.
JUSTIN WHO?
JUSTIN TIME TO READ BEANO!

WHAT'S THE COLDEST CHRISTMAS FOOD?
PIGS IN BLANKETS.

WHAT DID THE TEACHER SAY TO THE COMIC LOVER AS A PUNISHMENT?

THERE WILL 'BEANO' COMICS FOR YOU.

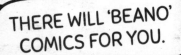

WHAT DID THE FACEMASK SAY TO THE MOUTH?

LET ME COVER FOR YOU!

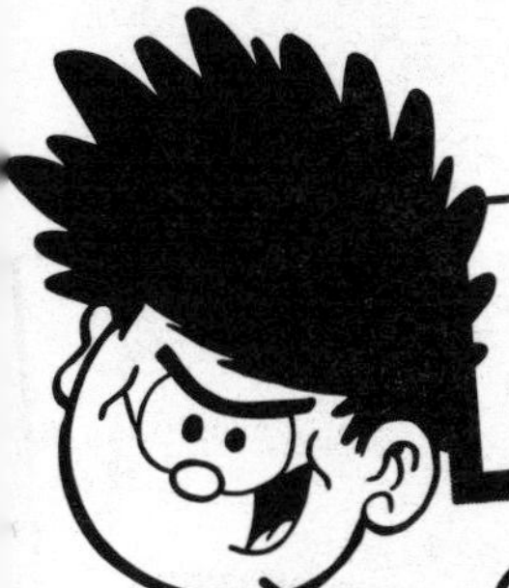

WHAT DID THE SCARY PANDA SAY?

BAM–BOOOOOOOO!

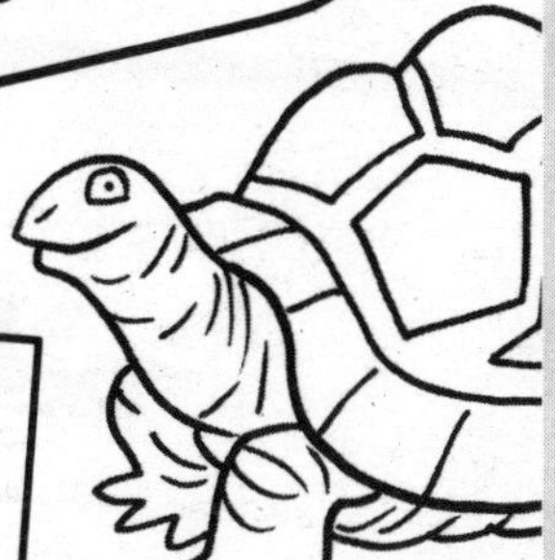

WHAT DID THE PEN SAY TO THE ROCK?

NOTHING, BECAUSE PENS CAN'T TALK.

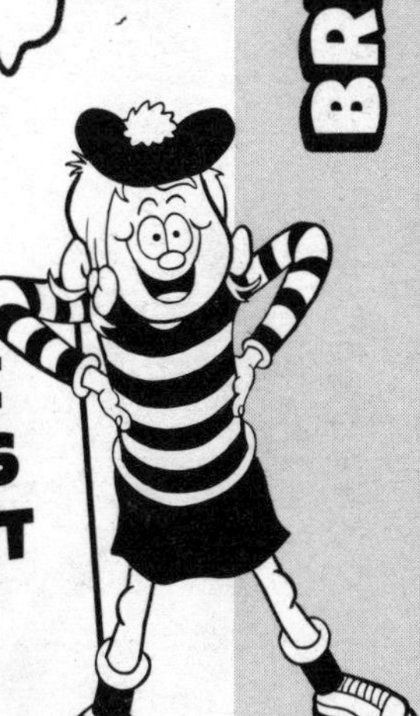

WHAT DID MINNIE CHANGE HER NAME TO WHEN RUBI'S 'GROWTH RAY' EXPERIMENT WENT WRONG?

MINNIE THE SHRINKS!

GOODBYE!

WE HOPE YOU ENJOYED BEANOTOWN'S COMEDY NIGHT, AS WE LOVED HAVING YOU HERE! REMEMBER TO KEEP JOKING AND LAUGHING!

MISS MISTRY'S TOP TIPS FOR TEACHERS, PARENTS & GUARDIANS

Our SPAG LOLZ are free-to-download packs – including cartoons, animations, comics, jokes and activity challenges – for schoolteachers and parents to use to support kids in the art of joke writing and performing.

What's more, they incorporate spelling, punctuation and grammar as part of the lesson plans, which are linked directly to the curriculum, so kids learn at the same time as having fun and building their confidence. Good luck!